W9-BIR-338

STOLEN CHINA

STOLEN
CHINA

a novel

JOHN FRASER

M&S

CANADIAN CATALOGUING IN PUBLICATION DATA

Fraser, John, 1944-
    Stolen China

ISBN 0-7710-3132-7

I. Title.

PS8561.R37S76 1996   C813'.54   C96-930897-3
PR9199.3.F73S76 1996

The publishers acknowledge the support of the Canada Council and
the Ontario Arts Council for their publishing program.

Text design by Sharmila Mohammed
Typesetting by M&S, Toronto
Printed and bound in Canada

McClelland & Stewart Inc.
The Canadian Publishers
481 University Avenue
Toronto, Ontario
M5G 2E9

1 2 3 4 5   00 99 98 97 96

For my nephews and godsons

Sandy Russell

Padraic O'Flaherty

James Chavel

Adam Bentley

Matthew Chavel

Stephen Bentley

Niall O'Dea

Huang Kai-dong

Geoffrey Heintzman

Thomas Ringer

Matthew Valpy

*Hath not the potter power over the clay,
of the same lump to make one vessel unto
honour, and another unto dishonour?*

— Romans 9:21

PART ONE

September 1979

Driver Koo was aiming for all the potholes. Halpert figured this out ten minutes after they set off from the hotel and were well into the countryside. Muttering under his breath, Interpreter Shen was criticizing *someone* for this malevolent driving, but Halpert knew enough Chinese to understand that the criticism was not directed towards Driver Koo. Both men were angry at Halpert for forcing an expedition right after the lunch hour, when nearly all of China was sensibly having a nap.

Foreigners! They are all so impetuous, thought Shen as the lumbering Shanghai sedan hit another road canker. This one was more serious than the others. The glove compartment snapped open, a clutter of papers and small engine gadgets spilled out onto Shen's lap, and a ferocious clanking of metal underneath the car brought it to a shuddering stop.

Shit, thought Halpert, still bracing himself in the back seat.

Shit, thought Interpreter Shen as he noticed the grease from a spare spark-plug casing on his second-best pair of pants. Actually, his only other pair of pants.

"Shit," swore Driver Koo out loud in his sharp regional dialect. He was determined to make this incident a major lesson for the mother of all assholes in the back seat.

Interpreter Shen, who knew less English than Halpert knew Mandarin, turned in distress to his difficult charge. "Trouble is to be about."

Trouble is to be about?

Interpreter Shen had picked up his bizarre English from Voice of America broadcasts. The VOA announcers were trained to speak at quarter-speed, lending an eerie aspect to all the world's news. Even the most electric events came across the crackling airwaves like policy announcements from funeral directors. The authorities had stopped jamming VOA broadcasts a few months after Chairman Mao's death three years earlier, and there were millions of youngish people all over China, just like Shen, who revelled in the hitherto forbidden access to the outside world. Revelled, but also nervously awaited the day when the authorities would decide that listening to VOA was evidence of a counter-revolutionary disposition. Interpreter Shen was no fool. He still kept his copy of *Quotations from Chairman Mao Tse-tung* in his jacket pocket at all times, at least during waking hours. Just to be safe.

"Look at this disaster," bellowed Koo after he got out of the car and surveyed the front chrome bumper. It had snapped off its right pinion and was dangling a few inches above the ground. "How the hell am I expected to fix this?"

He threw down his cap in dramatic, feigned anger. For several years now, the bumper had periodically fallen off, and Koo had a special cord in the trunk of the old Shanghai sedan that he used to tie it to the engine grill until he could get it bolted back on.

As his driver ranted, Halpert yawned and got out of the car to stretch. The histrionics didn't bother him. He'd been in China long enough to understand that Interpreter Shen's distress simply demonstrated that Driver Koo stood very high in the hierarchy of the Kung-hsien County Party Office. Certainly higher than Shen. He *had* to stand higher, Halpert figured, because he would know too much. Koo was master of the only automobile in Kung-hsien village – a vehicle owned by the state, assigned to the Kung-hsien office, but operated exclusively by Koo. As the only one who knew how to drive, Koo would be privy to all the gossip and schemes of the local Communist Party cadres when he chauffeured them around. *Undoubtedly dangerous*, thought Halpert as he strolled over to the side of the road, bored with all the antics.

Interpreter Shen, confused and rattled by Koo's hostility to a foreigner they had both been told to treat with watchful courtesy, nervously fingered his Little Red Book as he followed Halpert. Shen didn't know what was worse: the foreigner's impulsiveness or Koo's spluttering.

"Big trouble," said Interpreter Shen. "Our car is to be very old. Mr. Koo says big trouble. Sorry, sorry. The situation is very poor in Kung-hsien."

"No trouble," said Halpert in Chinese. If Shen wasn't going to spare him his English, Halpert didn't see why he had to spare Shen his fractured Mandarin. "We rest here a short while."

That was Halpert's little joke, which referred back to the ridiculous scene earlier at the hotel when he had insisted that they scrap the largely ritualistic nap-time and go out directly after lunch to the Long March Agricultural Commune on the outskirts of Kung-hsien. Halpert had dined with Interpreter Shen at the special foreigners' table, while Koo — conforming to Western notions of status — sat at a lowly staff table next to the kitchen.

It is all so tedious, thought Halpert. Every time he asked to do something different from a schedule that had never been discussed with him, Shen the Suppliant went off meekly to Koo the Implacable for protracted, difficult negotiations.

That was Absurdity Number One. Absurdity Number Two was the ridiculous sign on the table that read, in Chinese: Foreign Friends Only. Halpert was pretty sure he was the first foreigner to set foot inside Kung-hsien since a missionary doctor was kicked out in 1950, shortly after the Communists took over the country. When Shen importantly announced that he was from the "Foreign Affairs Bureau of the Kung-hsien County Party Office," Halpert had quietly chuckled. *Nearly three decades without even a hint of a foreigner within three hundred miles, yet still there's an office for receiving foreigners and an official to man it.* He also thought of the notorious sign in the pre-revolutionary Shanghai park that read: No Dogs or Chinese. It had been a famous propaganda tool of the Communists. The sign was still all over China, only it had been updated to read: Foreign Friends Only.

Now Halpert put his hand lightly on Shen's shoulder to calm him down. "We'll let the driver figure this out. Somehow I think he knows a solution."

He did, of course, but it wasn't going to be revealed just yet. Koo was disinclined even to touch the bumper. Instead, he busied himself with rearranging the tangled pile of clutter in the trunk. Halpert noticed, with irritation, that Koo was looking at his watch every couple of minutes.

Koo was also picking up an audience. A passing cyclist stopped and dismounted, and some young men loitering outside the compound wall of a nearby farming commune sauntered over to take a closer look. The Shanghai sedan was well known around Kung-hsien County, and its fortunes were a legitimate source of curiosity. Koo kept up the pretence of anger for a few more minutes, but – in truth – he loved onlookers because they reinforced the pleasant notion of his own importance. He also realized an audience was useful in his overall strategy of delay, a strategy that was getting increasingly obvious to everyone.

When Halpert stirred impatiently from his squatting position at the side of the road and started walking towards the car, Driver Koo smiled and turned to the cyclist. "Ah," he said expansively, "our foreign friend is coming."

The word "foreign" hung in the air, frozen in its implications of danger and excitement and novelty and rare opportunity. The cyclist and the young men looked up from the contents of Koo's trunk to Halpert's tall, angular frame. *So that's a foreigner!* The peasant youths' jaws hung open, taut on their faces: they couldn't make their mouths talk or their feet move. The cyclist was more sophisticated: he fell over his bicycle.

Shit, thought Halpert, *they're going to be all over me in a moment.* Having worked in China for almost four years, he was no longer amused when he was gawked at or had his skin pinched to see if it was real. He turned on his heel and walked the other way.

That's when he first noticed the massive stone lion's head sticking through the dense, almost fully ripened field of corn. And beyond the lion, there was a huge hewn horse. Two horses in fact, facing each other and separated by about fifteen feet. Farther on, twin warriors stood at lonely attention, on guard over the wide field. And beyond them there were more figures, until the horizon concealed whatever lay ahead.

The wind rippled through the corn stocks, rustling up excited chatter that seemed to come from across the centuries. This was the precise spot Halpert's friend, Gordon Wrye, had told him to look for: the sacred pathway leading to the shrouded tombs of the Sung dynasty emperors of China. There had been no account of them since 1949, and among those foreign scholars who catalogued the patrimony of China, it had long been assumed everything to do with the Sung tombs had been destroyed during the Cultural Revolution.

This time it was Halpert's jaw that hung open.

&

The tourists on the bus had neatly arranged themselves, without any direction, into racial and then national groupings. Eleven Japanese had managed, as if by magic, to grab all the front seats, and four English couples were sitting across from each other two-thirds of the way back. Various other Western Europeans were fore and aft of Albion, and only the Americans, thirteen in all, tried to mix. One young American woman thought of sitting by the lone Japanese who had not been able to pair up, but it was just a momentary thought. The Japanese woman looked straight ahead and gave no hint that she would move her bag from the spare seat, so the American moved on.

At the front of the bus, the driver and the guide looked anxiously out the window at the couple bickering a few feet away.

"Desmond," said the woman, who wore a broad-rimmed straw hat to ward off the glare of the late-summer sun that, at this early hour, had hardly begun to show its true force, "I don't see why I must go on this ridiculous tour if you're not coming."

"My dear," said the man with irritated control, "we've gone over this before. I simply don't know when these wretched blighters will want to see me, and it will be easier if I'm not worrying about you. Now, on you get and have a nice time."

He leaned forward to peck her cheek, but she lowered her head and his puckered lips collided with the brim of her hat. She drew in a deep breath and moved slowly towards the door of the bus. Just before boarding, she turned to say, "This is the last time you are going to dispatch me anywhere," but he had already begun to walk away. The words stayed in her mouth as the Honourable Mrs. Desmond Finch-Noyes climbed aboard and sat down on the first available seat. It was next to the single Japanese lady, as it turned out, and with various tiny gestures of annoyance both women managed to register their mutual distaste.

The bus rumbled out of the front parking lot of the Chin Chiang Hotel and, honking its horn every two seconds, eased into the traffic. The honking was exclusively for the reassurance of the driver and had no discernible effect on the unending stream of cyclists who barrelled along, seemingly oblivious to everything except the noses in front of their faces and the road below. The official guide of the Chinese Travel Service picked up the portable microphone and addressed the tourists. "Good morning. Welcome you the good foreign friends to Tsingtao City. This is most beautiful city in China, so lovely on the sea. The Chinese people like to come to Tsingtao for rest and creation. . . ."

There were some muted titters at the back of the bus at the charming prospect of relaxed, copulating couples. "This day," continued the guide, "before we to visit the tomb of our great revolutionary writer Lu Hsün, we to visit Ku Yong Antique Store on Suilichang Street."

The hint of an Oxbridge accent in his ungrammatical but carefully articulated English exposed the guide's slavish adherence to BBC Radio English broadcasts rather than to those of VOA. There was snobbery here. BBC English was a decided cut above VOA English, and this fact was not missed by even the most obtuse foreigner, who tended to be more respectful of BBC Chinese, regardless of syntax.

"Suilichang Street is a very famous street for good stores," he said. "This is the street of clothings and very beautiful gifts, and we must to take a little rest at Ku Yong Antique Store before our long trip to the tomb. If you like to buy things, there are many nice objects to buy at the Ku Yong Antique Store. If you not wanting to buy old things, that's fine. There are also many new objects at this store. My colleagues there are very happy to meeting you and . . ."

Four minutes after leaving the hotel and while Mrs. Finch-Noyes was still fussing with the contents of her large carpetbag purse, the bus came to an abrupt halt and was immediately surrounded by gawking Chinese children and teenagers. Older people kept to the periphery of this swarm, but they gawked, too.

"Ah, so quickly," said the guide with impressive-sounding surprise. "We are already to the Ku Yong Antique Store. We get out now and have a little rest. It is now half past nine and we cannot stay any longer than eleven o'clock – "

There was a groan from the back of the bus. A voice protested, "Surely to God we're not staying here for an hour and a half."

The guide smiled warmly. "I'm sorry," he said politely. "We must to spend no more time than this for visit to Ku Yong Antique Store. Our plan is for the keeping."

Mrs. Finch-Noyes reached back into her bag for the small jar of smelling salts she had picked up in Hong Kong on the way into China. The bus door had opened and the pungent odours from outside – a mélange of sandalwood, jasmine, and cesspool – had rushed in to supplant the stale interior air. She had disliked the smell of China from the first moment she had encountered it, and nothing had happened subsequently to mitigate the wisdom of her nose.

More to the immediate point, no one was going to make her budge from her seat after she had stood up to let the Japanese woman out. Behind Mrs. Finch-Noyes, there was more groaning from various Caucasians who had just realized that all eleven Japanese tourists had decamped together and were already in the store.

"Look, Eddie," said a middle-aged American woman as she scanned the store's small window display. "They've got some of those wonderful little porcelain bottles for sale. I'd love to get one for mother."

"Let's go," said Eddie with a sigh. "We've got lots of time to make a choice."

From the bus, Mrs. Finch-Noyes surveyed the American couple with almost as much distaste as she did the Chinese urchins surrounding them. Everything about this trip was a disaster as far as she was concerned. She hadn't wanted to come. She knew conditions throughout the country were primitive. She knew she would be left alone for long hours while Desmond was off doing whatever he thought he had to do with those interchangeable and uniformly obsequious officials who seemed to crowd their lives at every waking minute.

The truth was she hadn't even liked Hong Kong, where at least amenities were available. The reason for this was simple. She didn't like

Chinese people. She didn't like the way they looked, the way they talked, the way they ambled on the streets, the way they ate, the way they spat, the way they dressed, the way they blew their noses, the way they served you in a store or a restaurant, the way they rode bicycles, the way they clustered in groups, and most of all she didn't like the way they smelled. And there was one undeniable fact that impinged directly on every malevolent perception she had made about the Chinese: there were so very many of them.

But Desmond had insisted she come, and she was a woman who knew her duty. China was at long last opening up to trade, he had pronounced, and a famous company like Finch's, which dealt with antique Chinese porcelains and bronzes – with famous showcase premises in Hong Kong, New York, London, and the most recent one in Dubai – could not possibly afford to miss out on all the crucial new connections that had to be made. So she smiled the little smile she always drew upon her face when she knew something was expected of her and kept all her dark thoughts to herself. She had, after all, married into a legendary trading family and had a direct stake in its fortunes. Mrs. Finch-Noyes was not a fool.

By the time most of the Japanese returned to the bus with their purchases, the American couple finally made it through the impromptu welcoming committee of neighbourhood kids and into the sweltering dead heat of the store. When Eddie made inquiries about the porcelain snuff bottles, he was told that they had all been purchased by the "Japanese friends."

"That's ridiculous," he shouted to the impassive salesclerk as his wife, looking downcast, tugged at his sleeve to try and control his anger. "Don't you have any backup? What kind of a business is this? Who won the goddamned war anyway?"

This time, she really jerked at his sleeve. On the bus, Mrs. Finch-Noyes reached for her smelling salts again. To her nose the Japanese lady didn't smell any better than the Chinese.

∾

About fifteen minutes after Prisoner Lin was lifted into the back of the truck by two burly members of the Public Security Bureau, his left eye opened a little, but the blinding summer light made him close it again. The fact that it had opened even a little was a surprise. After the beating he had been subjected to an hour earlier when they had first come for him, his hands had been tied behind his back, so he was not able to pick away at the encrusted blood and dirt all over his face.

He understood the beating about as much as why he had been put on the truck. He tried opening his left eye again and this time he could make out the white jackets of several PSB guards. They were sharing a joke. He had been placed at the front of the truck's wagon, just behind the driver's cab, and he became dimly aware that there were two others beside him, stuck in the same jam. Hanging from their necks were cardboard placards bearing their names in brush characters, over which had been painted a large red X. Slowly, he realized that a similar sign hung from his own neck.

The PSB guards grabbed the wooden planks on the side of the truck's wagon to brace themselves for the start of the trip, and the truck crept out of the Ningpo Prison compound, preceded by two PSB automobiles and a small van with loudspeakers on top. Behind the truck, more vehicles followed in stately procession. There were hundreds of people outside the gates. The loudspeakers blared out heated rhetoric, but the man only understood small snatches – "resolute response" and "criminal elements" and "counter-revolutionaries."

He shut his eye again. But not for long. The truck halted briefly, and there was a terrific roar from the people in the streets. The left eye opened and he saw a PSB guard grab one of his neighbours by the hair and haul him to the side of the truck. Again, the truck started moving. Almost absentmindedly, the man prepared for the same treatment. When it came a few minutes later at a turn in the road, he hardly knew what was happening. In his mind, he was already dead and these final rituals were merely details. He closed his left eye for good.

Later, after he had been taken out of the truck and moved along and made to kneel and heard the explosion of gunfire close beside him and then heard nothing and was nothing, the PSB guard who had executed him leaned down to pick up the shell beside his body. His left eye was wide open.

"Here's the shell, comrade," the guard said to his officer.

"Ah, that's for our young grave-robber, is it not?" said the officer.

"Yes, comrade. Prisoner Lin."

"Yes, well, we'll send another one to his parents for payment. This one has been requested by the Cultural Relics Bureau. Most unusual."

∽

Ambassador Messier was going down the alphabetical list with a pencil, making small checks beside each name. When the lead point arrived at "Wrye, Gordon," it broke, and the ambassador threw the pencil down on the desk in anger.

"Alison," he barked into his intercom, "can you come here? Right now please."

When his secretary sauntered in a few minutes later, she could see that he was fuming, and this happened so rarely it almost made her laugh.

"How the hell did this idiot Wrye's name get on the list? I won't have him at the residence."

"He was on Mr. Halpert's list. You asked him who he wanted to invite to his farewell dinner and this was one of the eight names he submitted."

"I didn't know they were still friends. That certainly explains a lot."

"Oh yes," said the secretary almost merrily. "Still very good friends. I believe whenever Mr. Wrye comes up from Nanking, he stays with Mr. Halpert in San Li Tun. I think they're very close friends."

"No wonder Halpert's wife left him," said the ambassador with a grunt. He had cultivated his clipped speech during a one-year stint at the London School of Economics. The plummy mid-Atlantic accent even contained a slight lisp that he had picked up from his favourite professor there. "This doesn't change anything. I won't have him at the residence, Alison. He insulted several guests the last time he came and was particularly rude to Mrs. Messier. I won't put up with his antics anymore, farewell dinner or not."

"I expect it will be all right, Ambassador." Alison's voice was soothing and reassuring. "I happen to know Mr. Wrye is in Peking now and is returning to Nanking briefly before going down to Hong Kong. He won't even be in the country on the day of the dinner, so you can invite him without any risk of his coming. And you don't have to say anything to Mr. Halpert."

"You're quite sure?"

"Oh yes, *quite* sure."

She was absolutely sure. She'd left Gordon Wrye in her bed only two hours earlier, marvelling at his touch and zany sense of humour that had had her laughing and writhing in ecstasy at one and the same moment. She had come for the first time in nearly five months, and laughed for the first time in a year in this nasty, filthy, smelly, loveless city. Oh yes, she was absolutely sure. At three that morning, after revels enough for most couples, he had washed every part of her as she lay in her bathtub, floating in a world of pleasure she had almost forgotten. She came in the tub, too. And laughed again when her thrashing ceased, and he said he was relieved she had survived the spin cycle.

∾

Thrilled with her indecision, Sui-san stood in front of the closet full of Western-style dresses and silk blouses and pleated skirts, wondering what to try on next. She very much liked what she had on now. It was simple and hung a little loosely from her small frame. The foreigner's wife was obviously bigger than she was, but not so much bigger that she couldn't see some of the shape of her own self, something she had only seen fleetingly in all of her twenty-two years.

She had gone with Gordon before to a foreigner's apartment. Several times, in fact: twice in Nanking and once before in Peking. But she had never been in one this long, and never alone. Gordon had snuck her into the San Li Tun compound around ten that Thursday morning and told her he would be back in four or five hours. He was in charge of his friend's apartment, she was assured, and it was absolutely safe. The friend, an American journalist working for a Toronto newspaper, was away from Peking and knew she would be there with him. The Chinese staff would not show up until the following Monday morning.

It seemed to her that, like all foreigners, Gordon was amazingly self-assured. Nothing ever frightened him. This was not the case with most

Chinese, and for the first couple of hours, Sui-san had been immobilized by fear. Mindful of the consequences of being caught in a foreigner's apartment, she sat on a corner of the sofa in the living room, where the curtains were drawn, and hardly dared to move a hand.

Eventually, boredom and curiosity got the better of her. As her confidence returned, she started snooping, hesitantly at first, but by the time she opened the door to Halpert's bedroom she had forgotten all about consequences and was in a frenzy to satiate . . . *exactly what?* She hardly knew. When so much that has been forbidden for so long is suddenly revealed and offered up, motivation is hard to analyse.

Halpert's wife had stormed out of their home and his life five months earlier, and in her haste she left behind many of her clothes. Out of pique, he had simply declined to pack them up and send them back. So they remained in her closet, and it was thanks to this wondrous wardrobe that Sui-san first learned that she looked heavenly in Pierre Cardin navy blue, regal in Givenchy yellow, and very sexy in a plain white cotton Fred Perry tennis shift set against her dark southern Chinese skin. On the floor beside the full-length mirror, the drab blue cotton Mao suit she had discarded lay crumpled in a little pile. It was the first time in her life she had ever treated her own clothes with such disdain.

She was fingering a Peter Maas pink silk shirt when she heard the clatter at the front door and the sound of two Chinese voices – one male, one female – down the hallway. Now all her terror returned a hundredfold as she stood half-naked before the closet-door mirror.

A few seconds later, as the voices got closer, she was able to make the only sensible move open to her and quickly stepped into the large closet, pushing herself as far behind the hanging clothes as she possibly could.

"It was a bad idea to come," said the female voice in the hallway outside the bedroom.

"Don't be stupid," said the male voice. "I know the guards on duty this weekend and it's not a problem. I'm just picking up the meat from the freezer. Amazing to buy meat in April and then not eat it till September! Every neighbourhood should have a freezer."

"Why didn't you let me stay outside the foreigners' building? That's what we've always done before. I'm not comfortable here, Old Hu. Hurry up."

"Stop moaning, old woman, and help me." The voice was shouting a little from the back of the apartment, the room where Halpert's newspaper bureau kept the freezer that contained far more food than the correspondent alone could eat. Old Hu was Halpert's driver, and, along with Halpert's translator and Halpert's housekeeper and Halpert's cook, he had come to look upon the handy freezer as a communal machine, with food for the taking. Old Hu's wife wasn't so sure. She'd heard that foreigners' apartments were bugged, so she talked loudly and distinctly.

"I should not be here and you should not have made me come. Let's go this minute."

From the corner of her eye, Old Hu's wife could see Halpert's bedroom all askew, with women's clothes strewn on the unmade bed and surrounding floor. It was a decadent and disgusting scene. Exactly what she had always expected to find in a foreigner's apartment.

"I'm leaving now if you don't come this moment," she threatened.

"Relax," said Old Hu as he emerged from the back room and ambled down the long hallway. "Things are not so strict anymore. We are not doing anything wrong. We are simply here for convenience. And now we have some fine pig meat when none is available in any store in Peking, and you can thank me for this."

"You'll make pig meat of both of us if you stick to this attitude. Hurry up, let's go."

The door closed and Sui-san heard Old Hu turn the lock with his key. But she did not move. And she would not move until Gordon Wrye returned half an hour later. She did not feel so brave anymore, and the strange smells of foreign things in the closet, which had seemed so alluring only minutes before, now only caused her further anxiety.

∽

"Damn the little buggers! Don't they ever shut up?"

Desmond Finch-Noyes was swearing at no one in particular, but it

15

was his pinch-faced, distraught wife – the only other person in their hotel room – who picked up the flak and took it personally. The noise bothered her, too, but she only rarely complained. It emanated from about a dozen motorized Seafleas buzzing about in the Bay of Tsingtao in front of their hotel. The stupid machines, on which young men – off-duty officers of the People's Liberation Army – rode aimlessly around the water's surface, seemed to get started around 6 a.m. and never stopped till dusk.

Desmond took a bottle of single-malt Glenlivet from the bureau drawer. *What a stupid woman I married*, he thought as he poured an inch into a tumbler. For a brief moment, he contemplated the colour and texture of the Scotch and then added another half-inch. *She's incapable of understanding the importance of this trip.*

Finch's was not merely famous. It had once been infamous – at least inside China – having been founded in 1817 on the sturdy structure of the opium trade. In short order, it had made so much money for its founder, an adventurous merchant from Norwich named James Finch, that he was able to set up his family in great state in both London and Norfolk. The original company had spawned other lucrative enter-prises, including the venerable merchant banking firm of James Finch & Sons. By the time, seventy years later, that forcing Indian opium onto China had become increasingly hazardous and less profitable, the family had married into the landed aristocracy (the de la Noyes of Suffolk) after producing two generations of the usual progeny of Empire – generals, bishops, and cabinet ministers; remittance men, writers, and other riffraff. Since then, the various branches of the Finches and Finch-Noyeses had successfully and hugely diversified their interests, especially into property holdings and specialty enterprises.

"Desmond, I'm going to take a nap." His wife glared at the half-consumed glass of Scotch with narrowed eyes. It wasn't even 11 a.m. and the frequency of his morning drinking on this trip had started to worry her. "I don't think you'll be at your best if you have too much more of that," she said as she headed towards the adjoining bedroom.

Had she remained, he would have said something cruel, but she knew this and had timed her retreat with strategic efficiency. He swallowed the remaining Scotch in one weary gulp and continued to brood over the inventory of his business life. There had been such close moments. Finch's itself, the original firm, or more properly Finch's Importables PLC, as it was now called, had also gone through many incarnations since the opium days. It was now the premier vendor of fine antique porcelains in the world. Desmond's astuteness in handling the often tricky business of acquisition had brought him wide respect and envy within his own special universe.

In reality, he had had to extend himself and learn a bit about what he was selling, although he had never quite managed to get the various Chinese dynasties straight. When he found himself having to talk up a particularly knowledgeable customer, he played the role of an upper-class twit to cover the dustier parts of his knowledge. There were some customers who found this charming.

Yet he was clever in sensible ways. He understood, for example, that his business depended upon three things: obtaining the very best specimens at the lowest possible prices, an exclusive range, and conspicuous overpricing.

And something else. For nearly a decade now, Desmond's Hong Kong buyers had been receiving consignments of ever-increasing quality and quantity from China itself, the one place where it was supposed to be officially impossible to export *anything* over a hundred years old. This was a law promulgated in 1950 by the new Chinese Communist government and enforced by a division of the Ministry of Culture known as the Cultural Relics Bureau. There were serious punishments – long prison sentences and even executions – for illegal traffickers in Chinese antiquities, and once again Finch's operations on mainland China had all officially ended.

Unofficially, though, objects had trickled out sporadically throughout the fifties and early sixties, thanks mostly to boat traffic between the old port city of Ningpo and, four hundred miles to the south, the Crown colony of Hong Kong. But it was a hazardous business, and Desmond heard travellers' tales of peasant junks being sunk by the coastal patrols of the Chinese navy – sunk along with their owners and stolen cargo. Every time, he had shaken his head in dismay at the loss of the chinaware, but he had dramatically changed his views about the consequences after an extraordinary increase in trade that occurred in early 1967 at the height of the Cultural Revolution.

Suddenly, with no warning, Hong Kong was flooded not only with brilliant examples of early Ch'ing and Ming porcelains but also with hitherto "priceless" Sung and T'ang funereal figures and receptacles. When a few Han dynasty bronzes, which weren't even supposed to exist anymore outside museums, mysteriously turned up on a street market in Hong Kong, alarm bells began ringing on several continents.

In the turmoil of the Cultural Revolution, many private mainland collections were dispersed. Some of these belonged to disgraced party officials, some to local museums whose leading personnel had been targeted for "discipline from the masses." All such confiscated antiques were supposed to be handed over to the Cultural Relics Bureau, but the volume was heavy and the confiscations were so often conducted chaotically that a number of important pieces went permanently missing and found their way out of China.

For specialty dealers like Finch's, this unexpected development — if left unchecked — spelled disaster. Far away in London, Desmond was initially inclined to dismiss the fears of his Hong Kong buyers as hysteria, but when one of them purchased a T'ang dynasty funereal musician in mint condition on the street for four hundred laughable Hong Kong dollars, he finally got the point. His London store had just sold a similar figure, with a slight but perceptible fissure on the back of the head, to the Marquess of Milford Haven. The marquess had been told its like did not exist and was charged three thousand guineas. Staring at the staggering gap between these two prices, Desmond had realized that it was time to act. Fast.

The memory of what happened next was always the most pleasant part of Desmond's reveries, and the reveries always came to him when he was most uncertain about what lay ahead. Like now, when the future of Finch's seemed hinged on negotiations with senior Chinese officials who had been avoiding him and his sour wife throughout this trip, who had left him to fester in a hideous hotel suite with worn antimacassars on the chairs and peeling, pale-green paint on the walls. He wanted to get back to his reminiscences. If the situation he was currently stuck in wasn't worth another glass of Scotch, the remembrance of past glories certainly was. Desmond reached for the bottle again and smiled as he recalled how he had kept calm while everyone else panicked.

The year 1967 had been pivotal for Finch's. The firm had to find a way to manage the crisis, or it was finished. Desmond had made one gut assumption and issued one order: the combination saved the day and the firm. He had correctly reasoned that the sudden appearance of the tomb figure was an aberration, the result of mayhem all over China. Since he couldn't do anything about the Cultural Revolution, he had decided that he had to do something about the Hong Kong market. If Finch's acted quickly and resolutely, everything might still work out.

Inside the firm, they still talk about what happened next. Desmond flew to Hong Kong to take personal charge of operations. Primed with contacts at Government House, he quickly learned that the small staff around the British governor was next to useless, so traumatized was everyone by events in China and the expected repercussions in the Crown colony. The Royal Hong Kong Constabulary was a different matter. Ostensibly controlled by the British, prominent Chinese officers – and even one or two British officers – could, with quite reasonable bribes, be convinced to patrol *especially* the markets and narrow byways of both the island of Hong Kong and the much larger New Territories on the mainland. The bribes worked their way down almost from the top, and within less than a week, and with only two unexplained deaths, the crisis was over and Desmond was launched on a new way to do business.

This was why, a decade later, he was in the city of Tsingtao, in Shantung province, preparing to meet officials from the Ministry of Culture. A new crisis was looming as China struggled to re-emerge into the world, and over the past half-year the traffic in all antiquities had virtually disappeared. This time the Royal Hong Kong Constabulary would be of little help. This time he needed Mrs. Finch-Noyes to accompany him on a supposed tourist trip that covered his efforts to see high Chinese officials. For over a week, he had been put off and forced to twiddle his thumbs in a silly seaside resort city.

There was a light rap on the door.

"Yes, come in. I'm here," bellowed Desmond.

A slight, elderly Chinese man entered. He was dressed in well-pressed slacks and a white shirt.

"Mr. Finch-Noyes," he said with impeccable BBC diction and perfect grammar. "Would it be convenient to meet the deputy vice-minister now?"

∾

Halpert could hardly contain the giddiness threatening to overwhelm him. The alleyway of stone animals and soldiers, appearing so suddenly out of the corn field just as Gordon Wrye had described it, was part of the reason – the first concrete confirmation that this queer trip was going to prove worthwhile and bring him something of a journalistic coup. But that was professional giddiness, and he had learned a long time ago how to focus this emotion. Getting a story often depended upon such control.

It was the whoop and the holler that had erupted from long-forgotten boyhood revels that so startled him. Absurdly, and in the middle of a Chinese corn field surmounted by mythological beasts carved out of huge blocks of stone well over half a millennium ago, he remembered the day after his eleventh birthday at the Bolton School in New Hampshire. That's when he had discovered, late at night, a refuge for a secret hour of unsupervised freedom from the school's dorms on the far side of the pond beyond the football fields. Each time he crept along the hallways and down the fire escape, he experienced a thrill he had forgotten until this successful escape from the irritating, arbitrary authority of Driver Koo and Interpreter Shen.

Gordon had told him to look for stubby hills – "tumuli," he had called them. These were the burial sites for the early Sung emperors and would once have been graced by giant pagodas. So when Halpert scanned the horizon and saw no hills, he was momentarily perplexed and disappointed. Then, as he kept walking along the alleyway and came upon a small dirt road leading out of the corn field, he realized some hills might actually be vast, low mounds.

He discovered just such an alteration in the landscape about two hundred feet from the last stone warrior, and he climbed up its modest incline without any effort. His reward was to see the next two mounds. The one farthest away had a superstructure of bamboo scaffolding. Squinting through the sun's haze, he could make out the tiny bodies of Chinese labourers working closely together at the base of the mound. Around the perimeter of the tumulus, and what looked like a work compound with four or five large tents, was a high chain-link fence.

God in heaven, thought Halpert, *I am going to owe Gordon yet another almighty favour for this tip*. If you can get to Kung-hsien, Wrye had told him, a team from the Cultural Relics Bureau was about to enter a Sung tomb that had never been robbed. The contents should be spectacular, or so he had been told by an excellent source.

Deciding to approach the worksite as if he was out for a country ramble and had merely stumbled across it, Halpert strolled on. This was only about the umpteen-hundredth tip Wrye had given Halpert throughout the years of his posting, some of which had resulted in front-page stories in newspapers around the world. As far as Halpert was concerned, Gordon alone had justified the whole risky business of quitting the Washington *Post* and taking the Peking correspondent's job with a Canadian newspaper.

When he reached the bottom of the second tumulus, he started walking counter-clockwise around the fenced-in third, away from what he assumed was the main activity to the west. *Gently goes it*, he thought. That was the way he generally went through life, except when he made his big decision to leave *The Post*. His friends had thought him mad to leave such a prominent newspaper and move to another country to work for a backwater publication few had heard of, but it turned out to be the most successful professional gamble Halpert had ever taken.

He had arrived in Peking in late 1975 when the whole of Communist China seemed ready to implode – and then explode – in the waning days of Chairman Mao. There had been street demonstrations and open dissidence after the death of Premier Chou En-lai, and then there had been the catastrophic earthquake in Tientsin in which hundreds of thousands of people lost their lives. Shortly afterwards, Mao finally died, and within days his widow and her cronies – the ubiquitous Gang of Four – were under arrest, a political earthquake presaging both the opening of China to the outside world and a border war with its former ally, Vietnam. Halpert's posting had been a very successful gamble indeed, and most of his dispatches had been syndicated and carried in newspapers around the world, including *The Post*, the sweetest vindication of all.

These big political stories always wrote themselves, and all Halpert had to do was be on top of them. What gave his writing such distinction, though, was his personal journalism, the smaller stories of everyday Chinese life, or curiosity items like the history of Chinese porcelains, stories which stood out far ahead of his colleagues' efforts. The major dispatches kept his name on the front pages above the fold, but the human-interest and historical features cemented Halpert's reputation as a compassionate and discerning journalist.

A few months earlier when it had come time to capitalize on all this, he managed to gather a book contract, the promise of a lucrative lecture tour, and wonderful job offers from four prestigious news organizations in the United States, without even sending out a formal inquiry letter. Much of his early career in journalism had been a struggle, but now opportunities came running to him.

In Halpert's mind, most of this success was owed to Gordon Wrye, his closest friend and his eyes and ears to the real China, the China that lay beyond the diplomatic compounds and the propaganda circles of the Communist government. It was Gordon who first taught him how to get around China without trepidation. "Just go where you want to go until there's a bayonet aimed at your ribs, and then smile and look stupid," Gordon had said. "Naive assertiveness will get you ninety per cent of what you need, and the other ten per cent you can surmise." This was what he was doing now as he approached the back of the work area. There didn't seem to be a bayonet in sight.

He was already mentally structuring his story when he heard the first shouts. Inevitably, there would be shouting. Any foreigner in such a remote setting would be a surprise, and he knew he wouldn't get much information from the people at the tomb site. What he needed was a simple confirmation of the nature of the work, and then he could sketch in some colourful details about the site, tease readers with the unofficial information he had already obtained from Gordon, and throw in a sprinkling of Sung dynasty history. As newspaper stories go, this one would be easy.

When he raised his small pocket camera and took a photograph, the shouting turned into a chorus of outrage. A dozen men came running towards him waving their hands as they barked in Chinese, "No pictures, no pictures." They grabbed both his arms and ran him at the double to the encampment. He thought he heard someone say something about being under arrest, but that instant his hair was yanked from behind and his head pulled backwards. There was a lightning punch to his solar plexus – he couldn't see who did it – and he sagged to the ground clutching his stomach and gasping for air. He lay there for several minutes until two men picked him up and dragged him into one of the tents.

For the first time since Halpert had come to China, he felt real fear. He glanced up quickly and saw Driver Koo smirking behind a half-dozen workers. Koo must have tailed his stroll down the ancient alleyway. The leader of the group started shouting at him, and for a moment Halpert was surprised at how easy he was to understand. With a shock, he realized the man was speaking excellent English.

"You are trespassing on the People's property. You have taken pictures without permission. You are a piece of shit. You are trying to harm our country, and you will not leave here until you have written down on paper that you understand the terrible mistakes you have made. Maybe they were more than mistakes. Maybe they were crimes. It is for you to decide. Only you know what your mission here is."

He was shoved back to the ground, and paper and pen were dropped beside him. Halpert looked at them and back up at the circle of faces. Someone spat at him and then everyone seemed to be spitting. When he tried to wipe away the cascading spittle from his brow, he was kicked in the arm.

"It's not for a foreigner to wipe away the honest spit of the People," said the leader. "All that is permitted for you to do is write what your plan was and to apologize to the Chinese people."

For over a minute he was too stunned even to pick up the paper. This situation was altogether new. It was one thing to subject Chinese citizens to these little *rigueurs de régime*, but Halpert could recall no foreigner in his time being treated in this fashion. His sense of irony was returning. This could be part of a story. *Hell*, he thought, *anything that happens in China these days can be turned into a story.*

As he went through the motions of writing the self-criticism, he even felt a bit like a Chinese. True, he was simply a foreigner who would soon be free of these goons' clutches, but he still found to write an account of himself unnerving. Feeling detached from what was happening, he amused himself by writing some sarcastic lines about helping "the great Chinese people" with their ambitious new plans for international tourism by reporting the discovery of ancient stone figures in a field of corn.

For this little effort, he was required to rewrite the entire text — minus this droll observation and any other notion that he was a friend of the Chinese people. When he finished the second draft, he felt a frisson of anxiety about whether the rewritten text would be satisfactory. Apparently it was and, after another lecture on his arrogance and irresponsibility, he was released into the smug care of Driver Koo.

Interpreter Shen was nowhere to be found.

∾

The deputy vice-minister of culture stood up when Desmond, still dazed from the abrupt downing of his third morning libation, was ushered into the second room of a suite off the main lobby of the hotel.

"Mr. Finch-Noyes. How good of you to come on such short notice."

Desmond was in too much of a fog to take in the smooth English, the immaculate tailoring of the deputy vice-minister's linen suit, or the sombre expressions of the four junior officials surrounding their beaming superior.

"Short notice," spluttered Desmond, "well, yes . . . yes . . ."

Gratefully, he collapsed into the proffered armchair. One of the juniors poured some tea and set the cup on a small table by Desmond's elbow.

"Shall we get right to it?" said the deputy vice-minister as he riffled through a thick file of papers. The deputy vice-minister was not drinking tea.

To Desmond's consternation, his host reverted to rapid-fire Chinese, and another junior began translating over the rat-a-tat-tat delivery in a high, piercing tenor voice. *What in God's name is going on?* thought Desmond as it dawned on him that he was being read some sort of bill of indictment against Finch's. The firm, the deputy vice-minister stated, stood convicted of corrupting Chinese citizens with bribes to obtain stolen historical goods, goods that were then smuggled out of the country for sale abroad. This activity had been going on for many years and was causing continual anguish to the Chinese people.

While Desmond was still gasping for air, the deputy vice-minister ordered one of the junior officials to give him what looked for all the world like an empty cartridge shell.

"We've just received it, Mr. Finch-Noyes," said the deputy vice-minister, speaking English this time. "The People's security forces have had to execute one of your operatives in Ningpo, and we thought you would appreciate this little souvenir. It is what is left of the bullet used to enforce the People's justice."

Desmond looked down in horror at the cartridge in the palm of his hand. Its weight seemed disproportionately onerous, and he felt sure it was burning a hole in his flesh. He dropped it. A junior official picked it up and placed it beside Desmond's tea cup.

"Such heavy costs for a poor country," continued the deputy vice-minister. "The investigation into your company's illegal activities was long and arduous. The trial of your operative was expensive. Before you corrupted him, he was a good worker who supported his family honestly, and now this family has been left as a burden to the state."

Desmond was shocked. The alcoholic haze had evaporated and he could feel the fear oozing out of his pores.

"With all due respect, sir, I don't know what you are talking about. My company is an old and very well-regarded firm. We have never dealt in illegality and never would. I am quite astonished at what you say."

"Come, come, Mr. Finch-Noyes," said the deputy vice-minister in a friendlier voice. "I'm not saying that we can't find a solution to this problem, but please don't tell us that the very same family that began its business in my country by undermining the moral fibre of the Chinese people through the opium trade is unaware of the continuing inappropriateness of its trading practice."

"My dear sir, the opium trade ended over a century ago. Surely you can't – "

"No, no," said the deputy vice-minister, smiling benignly and leaning forward in his seat for the first time, "I'm not suggesting your company is still selling opium. I am saying that historically your company has had difficulty in dealing legally and properly with any Chinese government. What I am also suggesting is that we begin the process of changing this unfortunate pattern. If you have the Chinese people's best interests in consideration, this should not be a problem."

"It won't be a problem at all, I can certainly assure you," said Desmond eagerly. Too eagerly, in fact. He was grasping as firmly as he could at the straw of the discussion's improving tone – as he was meant to do.

"It seems to me," continued the deputy vice-minister, "in this new era unfolding, that an enterprise that has had such a long association with China, if it mended its ways, could do very well. If such an enterprise ceased its illegal operations and entered into an understanding with the appropriate department and the appropriate officials, then it might find its legal operations running securely and profitably."

Desmond was beginning to catch on. There were matters undertaken by his Hong Kong office that he officially didn't know about, but, then again, he had made a particular point of not wanting to know. He understood a wink as well as the next man. Now he was anxious to distance himself from this unpleasantness and eagerly embraced the deputy vice-minister's insinuation.

"Are you saying, sir, that it might be possible for Finch's to deal directly with the Chinese government for the purchase of definitive antique porcelains? Because if you are saying that, I can assure you we will do everything possible to ensure such an arrangement works well."

"What I am saying, Mr. Finch-Noyes, is that in China, appropriateness is everything. My country is speeding towards modernization after the terrible years in which the Gang of Four wrecked the economy.

Every ministry, every department of government, every individual entrusted to represent the interests of the Chinese people must work resolutely on this challenge of modernization. We in the cultural ministry are working on several fronts. China is a very old country, and we must ensure that our people and the people of the world understand our unique contributions to history and culture. At the same time, even our ancient culture must be harnessed to serve the modernization program. That is where an organization like yours, if it allies itself with our goals, might find it useful to assist the Chinese people. Foreign capital is very important to China at the moment. At the ministry, we are exploring many ways of obtaining foreign capital in fair exchange. I have officials here who can explain to you the details, but can I now assume you understand what I am saying?"

"Oh yes, quite, quite," said Desmond, who was beginning to feel the familiar and always intoxicating sensation of greed.

"I am so pleased," said the deputy vice-minister. "I look forward to a long and prosperous association between the Chinese people and your famous company. Once you have cleared up the outstanding problem of the illegal activities, I see nothing to stop a bright future."

"I don't understand," said Desmond, whose mind once again had been whipped around ninety degrees.

"Our costs, Mr. Finch-Noyes, our costs. Your company has cost the Chinese government a considerable sum to set things straight so that we could meet today on correct terms. An official from my office will be pleased to explain exactly what those costs have been, and he will also be pleased to hear from you any solution you may propose. It has been very agreeable to meet you in Tsingtao, Mr. Finch-Noyes, and I hope the rest of your stay in China will be pleasant."

2

Lady Morton, the wife of the British ambassador, inspected her dining room with a practised, patient eye.

"You've done a splendid job, Mr. Chou," she said to the Chinese server who had set the table. Actually, she didn't say this to Chou, but to the embassy's Number Two interpreter, a Chinese national, who walked a deferential three steps behind her. Chou himself stood to one side humbly awaiting the verdict. "Absolutely splendid. Everything looks wonderful. You've spaced it all correctly and the napkins are folded just beautifully. I think, though, that if you don't mind terribly we will put the glasses on the same side as the knives. I know it seems silly, but that's the way we do it."

Number Two Interpreter turned to Chou and grunted, "The glasses are on the wrong side. Move them."

As Chou hustled the wine and water glasses to their correct positions, Lady Morton and the interpreter went over details she wanted the kitchen staff to understand. She was going to be on her own tonight because the ambassador had come down with another of his Friday evening tension migraines and was lying prone in a darkened bedroom.

Half turning back as she headed to the living room to prepare for her guests, she sent a departing accolade wafting across the scented clouds of Chanel No. 5 her every move around the table had created. "Perfect again. Thank you so very much, dear Mr. Chou."

Number Two Interpreter, following behind, also made a half-turn and translated, "Go back to the kitchen."

There was a suspicion in Lady Morton's mind that if the dinner party had been more important politically, her husband might have been able to postpone his migraine until its usual arrival just before they got to bed at the end of the working week. But since it was a gathering of odd socks in honour of Lady Morton's old school friend, Deborah Finch-Noyes, and her pompous husband, Desmond, the ambassador had succumbed shortly after 5 p.m. The headache would not depart until he arose Monday morning, ablaze with energy to save the world through clever Telexes, adroit staff meetings, and a dozen useful *tête-à-têtes* with senior Chinese officials or foreign colleagues of equivalent rank.

On this particular occasion, Lady Morton didn't mind her spouse's absence. It would be easier without his irritating penchant for delivering the last word on any substantive discussion about the Chinese situation. To make the evening fun, she had gone wider afield than usual to find her guests: the witty young second secretary from the embassy would sparkle, she was sure; the nice little ambassador from Canada and his wife could be counted on for good company – those wonderful anecdotes he told in his quaint accent were always so endearing; Professor Jenkins and his wife (he was a professor at the London School of Economics on a three-month contract with Peking University to help restructure the economics faculty); the Finch-Noyeses, of course; and then the wild cards of the evening – Mr. Potlow, the Hong Kong financier, and his half-Chinese daughter, Julie.

Desmond Finch-Noyes had asked Lady Morton to invite Potlow and offspring, but when this information had been passed along to the ambassador, Morton had felt the first twinge of the migraine. He did not like Anglo Hong Kong merchants. They tended to think they knew it all. They also tended to lecture people, even people like the British ambassador, who actually did know it all.

But Lady Morton wasn't in any way perturbed about the prospect of

Mr. Potlow's presence. With ten at the table, no one could ruin a dinner party, and she was so looking forward to getting to know the charming new second secretary better. What she didn't know was that there was already complex texture to this little plan, for the ambassador had bedded the second secretary for the first time a week earlier and marked him for future approbation – diplomatic and otherwise.

If she was a bit dim about the bisexuality of her husband, Lady Morton was nevertheless a whiz about the sociology of dinner parties. She was sure her soirée, despite the inevitable occasional hiccup, would go swimmingly, and as the guests gathered in the embassy residence, there was nothing said or done to disabuse her plucky certitude.

That night at dinner, the second secretary obligingly took on the roles of acolyte and co-host and did both so sweetly that she made a mental note to trumpet him a little to her husband. The surprise of the evening was not Mr. Potlow *et fille*, who for the most part seemed well trained, but Professor Jenkins, who turned out to have a lot to say about the emerging new China. After they were all seated at the dinner table, Desmond Finch-Noyes started the discussion by asking Jenkins what he made of the remarkable directions the Chinese economy appeared to be taking.

"My impression is that they want to try things in a different way," said Desmond, who was still recovering from his meeting with the deputy vice-minister of culture in Tsingtao.

"Well," said the professor, "I can't quite believe I am able to say this, but it is my growing conviction that everything is up for grabs. And I should underline the word *everything*. I have been overwhelmed at what has been demanded of me. They want to know all about the capitalist system. No holds barred. I have been three times to China since 1972, and if the kinds of questions I have been asked this time had been put to me even a year ago, the questioners would have been trundled off to prison."

"So you think there is strong government support for the new direction," Desmond said. "But do you think this support will last for an appreciable time? We've all seen the politics of this country change dramatically over very short periods."

It was a damn good question and acknowledged as such by Professor Jenkins. What the academic didn't realize was that just three days previously, the Honourable Desmond Finch-Noyes had written out a personal cheque for seventy-five thousand pounds sterling to "clear the decks" for a new relationship with the newer New China. He had found it a little galling to have to barter on the price of a shame he did not feel, but he did understand fully what was beckoning. At the time, however, this hadn't stopped him from a bit of patronizing sarcasm.

"And to whom precisely should I make this cheque payable?" he had asked tartly of the junior official assigned to clear up all the unfortunate misunderstandings.

"I think it will be sufficient if you make the cheque out to yourself and endorse it on the back," said the young official politely but firmly. "We count on you and your bank to ensure that there will be no problem when it is cashed."

It was never easy to earn Desmond's respect, but that junior official got it. It was also why Desmond was now hanging on to the professor's every word.

"The big danger for the Chinese government," said Professor Jenkins, warming to his thesis, "is in controlling what one can only assume will be rapidly growing demands by its people for better lives while at the same time transforming a society that has been trained for nearly three decades to expect everything from the state. We've never seen anything like this before and it's not at all clear if it can be done. There is also the high risk of escalating corruption. Traditionally, in China, corruption is tolerated up to a certain point, but unfortunately that point is always at the boil, and this obviously would mean a very great deal of serious trouble. One does not contemplate with equanimity a billion people seething in righteous anger. I don't say this is going to happen, but it remains a possibility for the future. At the moment, though, it's all very exciting. It's a rare moment of optimism for the Chinese. If everything holds together, there is a considerable potential for this country to dominate the world economy through an unending supply of extraordinarily inexpensive labour."

The second secretary, who had been listening impatiently for several minutes, burst into the conversation. "It's all a bit thick, don't you think, sir? I mean, when you consider they were all crawling over this embassy building barely ten years ago and set it afire because we were such a symbol of decadent capitalism."

Miss Potlow stirred uncomfortably in her seat. The second secretary's "they" had disturbed her, but out of sight of the other diners her father patted her on the knee, and she kept her anger to a low simmer. It was flattering, when she thought about it, as the second secretary had become oblivious to the duality of her racial background: she had clearly been promoted to the status of honorary Caucasian for the evening.

"I think," said her father, quite carefully, to the young man, "that if you do not understand the eagerness with which this regime wants to distance itself from the policies of Chairman Mao during the Cultural Revolution, you ought not to be posted here at this critical juncture. The stakes are far too important for such a supercilious reading of recent history."

The second secretary blushed to the roots of his hair, and Lady Morton was momentarily annoyed. She did not like unpleasantness of any sort at her table. She also disliked long monologues on Chinese politics.

"Deborah, my dear," she said, turning to Mrs. Finch-Noyes, "you and Desmond have been travelling all over the place and we've hardly heard a peep from you. Has it been absolutely fascinating?"

"Oh yes," came the dutiful answer, "but I shall be glad to get back to my own home. There's so much I don't understand and never will. Do you find it difficult dealing with Chinese staff, for example? I think it's wonderful how you handle everything so smoothly. Do you speak Chinese to them?"

Lady Morton chortled as Chou circled the table, pouring out a lesser Sauternes to accompany the embassy trifle. "Of course not. It would upset the Chinese interpreters too much if I spoke directly to all the staff. I use a few words of greeting to handle the higher-ups at state functions, but it doesn't do to say much more to them in their own language. I don't think they like it, really."

As Chou finished pouring the Sauternes into Julie Potlow's glass, she looked up at him and asked in pointedly audible Mandarin, "Do you enjoy working at this embassy?" Chou paid no attention whatsoever since he didn't realize he was the one being questioned – in whatever language. Since her glass had finished off the bottle, Chou retreated to the kitchen to get another. No one except the second secretary understood what Miss Potlow had asked, but as she was simply reinforcing her father's slight, he was the only person who needed to understand.

"You see," said Lady Morton, grinning kindly at Julie Potlow, "you've probably scared poor Mr. Chou half to death. Let's hope he comes back soon with some more wine. And the coffee. Is anyone ready for coffee?"

"Don't believe our gracious hostess for a moment, Miss Potlow," Ambassador Messier said as he drained his fifth glass of the dinner with a small flourish of the crystal. It was his signal to Lady Morton that he hoped there would be more. Chou had not been able to keep the ambassador's glass adequately filled throughout dinner. "I'm sure they all understand English perfectly and are reporting every word we utter back to the Public Security Bureau. Of course what the PSB is going to do with everyone's table talk is another matter altogether, but I wouldn't trust any of the local staff. You know my theory about what would happen if a serious crime ever occurred in one of the diplomatic compounds?"

Mrs. Messier sighed inwardly. She had heard the ambassador's theory before. Dozens of times. So had Lady Morton, but on this occasion she urged him on as a welcome diversion from table conversation that was showing some risk of becoming constipated or even nasty.

"Oh, Pierre, do tell everyone your theory. It's so fascinating."

"Well, I don't know if it's all that fascinating, dear lady, but I have observed over the years that when any sort of serious or quasi-serious incident happens inside the foreign compounds – vandalism, for example, or a personality dispute that turns violent – there's no official investigation, at least none that any outsider could perceive. No one from the authorities approaches anyone to get to the bottom of the matter. Heads of the affected missions are rarely consulted, formally or informally. And yet, eventually, something always happens to clear up the situation, although it's not what any of us would call justice. I'd call it burying a problem. For the Chinese side, it is not a question of guilt and innocence, but merely one of convenience. I'll give you an excellent recent example . . ."

Chou returned with a new bottle of Sauternes and went straight to Ambassador Messier's glass. In the time-honoured way of heavy drinkers, Messier waved the server away after the glass was more than two-thirds full. "Good Lord," he said to Chou, "enough is enough."

A generous sip consumed, he continued his tale. "Over in the San Li Tun compound, where many Canadian officers live with their families, there is something of a problem with our African friends. It's not talked about too much, but it exists. These are very exuberant people, but in many cases their governments are so poor that they must post their diplomats here for long periods with virtually no home leave. Tensions often arise. We live in the same building – or we did until recently – as the minister-counsellor for Mali, who had a twenty-year-old son among his large brood. This young chap did nothing all day long, so far as I was able to determine, but ogle the ladies. And he was not without success. He was a strapping fellow and there are a lot of lonely young secretaries in the compounds.

"In any event, a couple of months ago, Mrs. Messier and I were returning from a dinner party one evening and to our dismay the entire foyer to our block was completely askew – chairs broken, table overturned, papers strewn this way and that. That was bad enough, but when we got to our floor two flights up, we could see there was still an awful row going on in the Mali apartment. Two windows were broken in the corridor, with glass all over the carpet and even some blood on the sill. We could hear terrible shouting coming from the apartment. Quite threatening and horrible language really, in French and English.

"Now I ask you? What on earth do you do in Peking if you came across such a scene? And this isn't any fiction, mind you. Mrs. Messier was very upset, and I don't mind admitting that I thought it a pretty bad situation. The fight had already spilled out into the corridor and down to the foyer. Where might they go next?"

Lady Morton shook her head sympathetically, and Mrs. Messier caught the signal and widened her eyes as if to say, "Well, this is the sort of thing you have to expect in such postings." The gestures were done perfectly, but then they should have been, since they had been practised twice before at other dinner parties when Ambassador Messier had felt compelled to detail this particular adventure.

"Well," piped up Desmond Finch-Noyes, "I suppose I'd go get some of those soldier-johnnies I've seen loitering about in all the sentry boxes outside your compounds."

"That's logical, but quite wrong," said the ambassador with immense satisfaction. "Those sentries are from a special detachment of the People's Liberation Army, and their job is not to protect us but to prevent unauthorized Chinese from coming into our compounds. They are under strict orders never to enter these grounds, under any circumstance."

"But surely they'd report it to their higher-ups," said Desmond.

"Oh, they'd report it all right, but still no one would come directly to investigate or to our aid. And so far as we would know, there would be no follow-up inquiries – no matter how serious the incident."

"Is there not a special telephone number foreigners can call in an emergency?" asked Mrs. Finch-Noyes, who, for the first time during the evening, had got thoroughly caught up in the conversation.

The ambassador laughed, but not unkindly. It was the laugh of a patient teacher with an earnest – if naive – student. "There's no one to call, dear lady, and no one to go to, and no one to come, and no one to do a blessed thing. What you have to do is what Mrs. Messier and I did. We quickly went into our apartment, double-locked the door, and then I telephoned the duty officer at our own embassy to rouse some of the younger officers. They were told to come by the residence immediately and support their ambassador in the event of some possible unpleasantness.

"Then, while awaiting my protectors, I telephoned the Dutch cultural attaché, whose apartment was on the other side of the Malis, and asked if he knew what the devil was going on. They were still fighting, he said, and there had been several bad bangings against a shared wall. He supposed they might be killing each other, but what on earth could he do? He and his wife certainly weren't about to intervene in a fight between two randy black men."

"Did anyone think of trying to locate the young man's father?" asked Miss Potlow.

35

"All in due course, young lady. Look here, you have to make sure of your reserve strength before doing anything that precipitous. But you're thinking in the right direction. Since Mali is a former French colony and still heavily dependent on French aid, I called the French ambassador, and he in turn tracked down the Mali ambassador, who was dining at the Sudanese embassy. Within thirty minutes, we had half the diplomatic world of Peking in our building. It turned out to be quite a splendid evening. Mrs. Messier made pots of coffee. The French ambassador and his wife came to support us, and before we got our answers, we had five more ambassadorial couples in the living room. A great show of solidarity!"

"Weren't you concerned," asked Julie Potlow, "that in the time it took for all that diplomatic nicety, someone might have been badly hurt? With all that extra manpower, couldn't a group have gone next door to calm things down?"

Chou filled a seventh glass for the ambassador, who was on a roll. "Absolutely not, Miss . . . Miss. . . . Absolutely the wrong strategy under the circumstances. If those gorillas want to go around smashing each other, or killing each other for that matter, this is the perfect place to do it. The very last thing any other foreign national should do is get involved. Our missions here are too important to be waylaid by such tribal drum-beatings.

"So, you see what I mean? If foreigners can't intervene and the Chinese side won't, who's to stop anyone doing anything? In the end, that's all it was: a drunken fight over a girl. We were not to find out who the girl was, and the French ambassador made the minister-counsellor apologize – in writing – to myself and the Dutch cultural attaché, and as far as I could tell at the time, that was an end to it. Three weeks later, though, three Chinese sedans pulled up outside the compound. What do you think? We saw the minister-counsellor and his entire family of eight decamp and leave us forever. The women had their belongings bundled up in sheets and were carrying them on their heads. It was a colourful sight. Later, the French ambassador told me that, thanks to this and other incidents, they had been ordered back to Mali in disgrace, presumably after some sort of complaint had been made by the Chinese government. But that's pure surmise. There was also a rumour that the

Chinese agreed to pay for the return trip to Mali, but we don't know that for sure either.

"In any event, the point of this story is to tell you that if you ever wondered about finding a perfect place to murder your wife, Peking is that place – "

Lady Morton, on cue, let out another timely interjection: "Oh, Pierre, that's enough. You know we don't approve of killing wives."

"No, no, dear lady, I mean it perfectly seriously. You can literally get away with murder here. It would make a terrific mystery story, don't you think? I'm part of a luncheon group, and we often speculate who would make the most intriguing corpse and who would be the unappointed detective amongst the foreigners who solved the case. Now that the Americans are about to open up an embassy here, the favourite victim is the Vietnamese-born wife of an American diplomat – first secretary level, I should say – who is somehow mixed up in illegal drugs out of the Golden Triangle. And I am very happy to report that everyone's nomination for the successful detective is the Canadian ambassador – *moi!* So there!"

Lady Morton beamed with pleasure. All her guests, one way or another, had become enveloped in the ambassador's tale. Even snippy Miss Potlow had stopped bristling.

Chou came back to the dining room, his eyes glued on Lady Morton. After half a minute or so, she looked directly at him and, with the tiniest shake of her head, indicated that there was to be no more wine for Ambassador Messier and no more coffee for anyone else. The dinner party was over, and she was an expert at ending such events sweetly and properly. Her only remaining challenge was to keep the new second secretary *in situ* till everyone else had left and then see if he might be cajoled into a nightcap, or two. For Lady Morton, the night was still young and held promise.

∽

It took the better part of two days for Halpert to return by train from Kung-hsien to Peking. After the debacle at the tomb site, the departure had been bleak. Driver Koo had taken him, wordlessly, back to the guest house, where he was met by a new, no-nonsense interpreter. The authorities, Halpert was informed, were now "unwilling to take responsibility for him," and he was confined to his room, under guard. The next morning, shortly after dawn, he was deposited at the train station, where he was made to wait for four hours. He thought of trying to badger his way onto an airplane, but he wasn't in a good bargaining position. Besides, he loved the old Chinese steam-driven trains, and the soft-class compartments that foreigners and higher Party cadres were entitled to travel in were excellent places not just to take stock of the passing scene but also of the passages in one's own life.

Halpert had much to think about. There was the promise of his own immediate future, of course, but he repelled all this delightful speculation with the memory of the abject failure of his marriage. It was a failure he had observed disinterestedly at the time, declining all helping hands and rescue missions offered by friends and even his increasingly distraught wife.

He could pinpoint the moment when he realized he no longer wanted to rescue the relationship. Typically, by this time Gordon Wrye was mixed up in the whole business. There had been an official lunch at the Canadian ambassador's residence when Gordon was staying with the Halperts on a study furlough away from Nanking. Offering Gordon open hospitality was one of the few things Halpert was able to deliver in compensation for all the favours that came the other way.

Gordon was always very busy with a variety of projects when he came to Peking, and he never accepted Halpert's hospitality simply to escape the loneliness and squalor of provincial life. He found little to relish in the society of the foreign compounds that so many others longed for after a few months in the boondocks. Rather, Gordon found the diplomatic round in Peking laughable and never bothered to disguise his contempt for the instant China experts and other charlatans he kept encountering.

Once, famously, he had humiliated the Canadian ambassador's wife in her own home in front of three other ambassadors and their wives when she had mildly pontificated on the "charming naiveté" of a local exhibition of peasant painting. It had been put together by the Ministry of Culture to show the artistic breakthroughs amongst the masses "emboldened by the liberating winds of the Great Proletarian Cultural Revolution."

Gordon had started in on the Canadian ambassador's wife *pianissimo*, quietly reminding her that China had a continuous tradition of great art that went back at least three thousand years. By the time he had concluded his attack a few minutes later, he had indicted the poor woman for her cultural ignorance, patronizing racism, and – unforgivably as far as Ambassador Messier was concerned – her dull indifference to the suffering of the Chinese people under Maoist rule. The deadly silence around the dinner table after this little bromide had been administered was broken only when Gordon lifted his wine glass and said, "But, by all means, let us drink to the glorious victories of the Great Proletarian Cultural Revolution."

"*Ça suffit, monsieur,*" the French ambassador's wife finally said, feeling the humiliation of her hostess.

That was the moment Halpert's wife decided that she loathed Gordon Wrye. She told Halpert later the same day she particularly resented every ounce of influence Gordon wielded over him and that he was no longer welcome to stay in their apartment. That was when Halpert realized he cared more for Gordon than for his wife. This killed the marriage and cemented a friendship that was still producing dividends three weeks before Halpert's scheduled departure from the China posting.

The train slowed and made a short stop at a nondescript village. In his earliest days in China, Halpert would have had detailed maps spread out on the compartment table and be madly looking up place names and other information in *Nagel's Guide to China* and in several additional reference books. Now he simply gazed dully out the window at the crowded station platform. Some of the passengers had got off the train to inspect what food was for sale at the spartan canteen inside the station. Since so few people were scrambling to get aboard, Halpert correctly reasoned that another, more local train must be scheduled to stop at the station shortly afterwards. An autumn heatwave blanketed the sunken loess land the train was travelling through, and the lethargy it induced stilled most activity except for the tag games of the youngest children on the platform.

Near a sentry guard-house, a woman was sitting on a portable folding stool combing out the lice from her daughter's hair. The weapon was wooden and fork-shaped, and the woman went about her work with methodical passion. Each time she pulled it through the girl's hair, she looked between the tines for her prey, nabbing a louse between her thumb and index finger and squeezing it till it popped.

Along the platform wall, peasant labourers leaned upright or squatted on their haunches, their burden left to hang from bamboo shoulder-poles resting at their sides. A few of the older men played at cards, but even when they had a winning combination they dropped their aces with the lassitude of sleepwalkers. Halpert remembered Gordon once describing a heatwave in Nanking in which the thermometer seemed stuck at forty-one degrees centigrade. The heat was so enervating, he said, all you wanted to do was find a hole in the ground and curl up and die.

The train started to move.

Halpert's thoughts turned to his friendship with Gordon. He knew that after his wife left, a few of the more malicious Sunday psychologists in the small, tight world of the Peking foreign community had started talking about "an all-consuming obsession." Real psychologists would have left the relationship mostly alone, knowing that the human heart is a capacious place that can accommodate many sorts of affections and obsessions, not all of which end up between bedsheets. But then a real psychologist would have gone mad in Peking: neither the Communists nor the foreign residents appreciated disinterested analysis. And even Halpert would have admitted a professional dependency on Gordon Wrye so complex that it was unproductive to examine it closely.

Halpert's mind wandered briefly to less murky thoughts. As he was about to return to Toronto, the point was rapidly approaching where he would have to inform his Canadian editors that he wanted to take a two-year leave of absence. Something like this was expected, and both he and his editors knew that, after his leave, he would never return to *The Toronto Observer*. Still, he figured, the request was an astute, face-saving solution for both parties. He would be free to write his book and rake in some loot on the lecture circuit, and the *Observer* could still claim him as its own while "on leave." This was the least he owed the editor-in-chief, who had taken so much criticism for appointing an American citizen to this choice foreign posting.

The old steam engine chugged slowly through a landscape that switched from city to countryside, from arid scrubland to lushly cultivated fields about to be reaped of their second harvest of the year. The heat made any prolonged soul-searching depressing. Idly, Halpert thought what a perfect metaphor the compartment window of his train was for so many of the things he didn't understand about China. There it was, all in front of him: a billion actors, a thousand different sets, a visual panoply rich in exotic contrasts and ripe for speculation. And all of it just beyond reach and untouchable. All of it, in the end, unknowable. Just a constantly changing view. More than enough to write home about, more than enough with which to make a reputation. But, finally, *nothing*. He had a ticket to the movies, that was all, and now – for him – the show was about to end.

Halpert knew this line of thought would lead to depression, but west of Loyang he was of a mind to be negative, so the question of professional dependency reared itself again. The very wealth of accurate and penetrating detail and incident provided by Gordon Wrye only embellished the question of that dependency, and not for the first time, Halpert despaired over his lost edge as a reporter.

So much had simply been handed to him. There were stories he had written in which he hadn't even bothered to double-check easily obtainable historical details because they had come straight from Gordon's encyclopedic knowledge of Chinese politics and culture. He knew his fame among his readers had grown in direct proportion to the withering of his skills as a researcher.

After the train left Loyang station, he dozed off for a bit. When he awoke, the bigger – and bleaker – introspections had disappeared, and he pondered instead the more constructively disturbing escapade at the Sung tombs.

In the four years of his posting, he'd been to several archaeological digs and had made something of a name for himself as a feature writer who could make the painstaking and often tedious business of unearthing antiquities seem exciting to readers. One of his expeditions had been to the old Imperial pottery works at Ching-tê Chên, south of

Nanking. He'd gone with Gordon on that trip, but while it had been fascinating, it had also been without incident. The most fabulous site he had visited, a few months later, was in Sian, where, nearly two millennia before, an army of life-sized pottery figures had been buried along with the mortal remains of the mighty Ch'in Shih Huang Ti emperor – the unifier of the Middle Kingdom, the builder of the Great Wall, the slaughterer of scholars, the emperor with whom Chairman Mao most identified.

Both these adventures resulted in well-read but benign feature stories, untroubled by any controversy either during their reporting or afterwards. The visit to the ancient Imperial pottery works, where he and Gordon had gone on a whim, had not even been authorized, while Halpert had been completely open with the Information Department of the Foreign Ministry about his desire to see the early Northern Sung tomb sites as his last official trip in China.

He shifted in his seat, reminded of the pain from the bruises on his ribcage. He was amazed that any Chinese citizen would dare strike a foreigner. Generally, he and his small band of journalistic colleagues were treated with excruciating politeness. He had heard tales of foreigners being roughed up during the Cultural Revolution, but that was such an abnormal period it didn't really count as precedent. Only twice before in his posting had he experienced anything even approaching the degree of hysteria he had encountered in Kung-hsien, and on both occasions, although the threat of violence had been implied, none had occurred.

The first incident was a product of sheer happenstance. Out and about in the Peking suburbs on the newspaper bureau's trusty Flying Pigeon bicycle, he had stumbled across the entrance to Number Five Prison, which had a wing reserved for fallen state leaders and other Party pooh-bahs. It was rumoured that Ch'iang Ch'ing, Mao's embittered widow and chief member of the Gang of Four, was currently detained there and employed in basket-weaving and purse-making while awaiting her day in court.

Since the prison's exterior was made to look like the entrance to an ordinary factory, Halpert had unwittingly pushed past the guard-house without a second thought. He hadn't a clue it was a prison, but he did know that even the most innocuous factory in the capital region deployed guard-houses, and Gordon had taught him that many of these could be walked past for at least a few minutes of snooping without any problem. This time, though, his entrance set off the alarm, and within seconds he was surrounded by a dozen soldiers.

That turned out to be the only dangerous moment. It was followed by a brief but polite interview in a prison official's office and a phone call by the official to the Information Department to corroborate identification. Within fifteen minutes Halpert was sent on his way with profuse apologies. It helped that he hadn't taken his camera that day. He knew that an unattended foreigner with a camera sets the Chinese security system into a trajectory of high paranoia. Considering that there was nothing external of importance in the country – including a headline in *The People's Daily* – which could not be photographed by U.S. or Soviet satellites, the paranoia was a nostalgic holdover from the romantic days of Kuomintang spies, Shanghai film stars, and the world of Fu Manchu.

The second incident, on an official trip with the foreign press corps to Tibet, wasn't quite so benign, but then Halpert hadn't been quite so innocent either. On the fourth day in Lhasa, he had decided not to join the other correspondents for lunch in the communal dining hall and instead went for a ramble. He came across a great barn of a building a block or so from the Potala compound and decided to poke around. It seemed to be part of a primitive metalwork factory with exterior shelving and a few small outer buildings nestled in the shadow of the barn. It was still the eating hour and no one seemed about, so Halpert walked past the makeshift main gate and into the interior courtyard. There was still no sign of anyone.

When he reached the double door leading into the barn, Halpert pushed it only slightly, not wanting to be seen as too aggressive by anyone who might be inside. There was a creak from old hinges, and he pushed some more until light poured in through the open doorway. At first, he simply could not comprehend what lay before him, then gradually he realized he was on the threshold of a huge room everywhere tinged by the dull glint of gold.

Halpert squinted and then started making sense of what he was viewing. On one side there were hundreds, maybe thousands, of golden Buddhas: sitting and standing, glowering and smiling, peaceful and censorious, sleeping and waking, forgiving and judgemental, pacific and warlike. In just this one section of the room, it seemed, there was a Buddha for every mood known to mankind. And they formed only a part of the treasure stuffed into the vast barn. Another section was crammed with intricately carved woodwork, highlighted in gold. There were storage shelves with thousands of silver bowls and silver prayer wheels; golden altar tables were stacked on top of each other, resting against two makeshift pillars.

Halpert gazed at this spectacular cache for several minutes before it struck him that he better start making as quick an inventory as possible. He knew that the Chinese had closed down all but a handful of Tibetan temples and monasteries. This vast stockpile must consist of the articles confiscated from these former places of worship.

As he scribbled notes, he heard a shout. A Chinese man came running up, gaped at him for a second or two, and then went running off.

The jig's up, thought Halpert, who quickly tore out the page from his notebook, stuffing it down the front of his trousers and safely into the pouch of his Jockey shorts.

In Tibet things happen a bit more slowly than in China, so it was several minutes before a posse of officials descended. They were furious that he had seen what he had seen. But he was let off with a sharp reprimand in the presence of a senior official from the Information Department. Feeling fairly confident on this occasion, he was able to leave everyone with more concerns than they were able to send his way. He told the official that he would like an explanation for this storage house and that if he didn't get one, he would feel quite free to speculate on what it all meant.

The question, like all difficult ones, was taken "under advisement." Two days later, just before boarding the airplane back to Peking, the lowliest Information Department minion buttonholed Halpert at the landing field in Lhasa. He said he had been asked to inform the Canadian correspondent that the local branch of the Cultural Relics Bureau in the Tibetan capital had stored the religious objects in the barn to protect them from vandalism. Halpert was entertained by the lie, but knew that an official lie was nothing to be ignored or scorned – it carried its own story and inner meaning. He played the game.

"Now who on earth would dare to vandalize anything in a country so well protected as Tibet?" he asked.

The official had his stock answer ready. "It was during the time when the Gang of Four ran riot over China and Tibet. Taking the religious objects under protection is proof that the Chinese government has a lively concern for the Tibetan people, unlike the Dalai clique that deserted their people. . . ."

The minion was off and running. As Halpert understood the rules of the game, the moment the Gang of Four was invoked, they had reached stalemate. Occasionally, it had amused him to explore the geography of a stalemate, but this time it simply irritated him, so he thanked the official for his answer and then snubbed him.

The train gradually slowed as it went up a long incline that would take it to the crest of the Taifu ridge, beyond which, to the northeast, was the broad plain that spread all the way to Peking, to his last three weeks in China, to the end of one life and the beginning of another, to a frantic social round of farewell parties, to one final dinner with Gordon Wrye and his new Chinese girlfriend, Sui-san. Liang Sui-san.

Halpert had seen the girl just once, in Nanking, where she was a student at the city's university. Gordon introduced him to her as "my research assistant." He said it with a smile that seemed halfway between a teenager's leer and a father's doting fondness, so Halpert couldn't quite figure out the parameters of the relationship. Later he decided his initial impression was the correct one: Gordon regarded her with both unrestrained lust and avuncular pride.

She was very beautiful, probably in her early twenties, nearly ten years younger than Gordon. Her shapeless Mao suit lent her face a transcendent quality, but then Halpert had this thing about beautiful Chinese women's faces adorning the drabness of proletarian garb. He generally found the faces of Caucasian women too fleshy and poke-eyed. High cheek bones, almond-shaped eyes, flared nostrils, dark colouring: these were the features he fantasized about when he shut his eyes and made love to his wife. Each morning, when he awoke and stared into her pudgy face, the looming estrangement gathered speed.

Not that Halpert would have tried to have a Chinese girlfriend, even after his wife went back to her family in Boston. He was too careful for that and too concerned about the precariousness of his posting. He also knew the trouble – the monumental trouble – any sexual relationship he might have with a Chinese citizen would bring. Gordon didn't give this prospect a second thought, but then he wasn't a journalist, exposed to the darkest suspicions of the regime. A large part of their relationship was based on differences precisely like this.

However, at least one person at the Canadian embassy had noted that the intense friendship between Gordon Wrye and Halpert was the opposite of what one would expect considering their respective backgrounds. Alison, the secretary to the Canadian ambassador, had broached the topic one evening at her tiny apartment where she had made dinner for the two men and herself. Gordon Wrye, she said, was Canadian. Therefore, he should be cautious, a bit dull, considerate, restrained, and – above all – gentle. Halpert, on the other hand, was American, so he should be assertive, a bit obstinate, self-absorbed, unbridled, and – above all – aggressive.

"And yet, what do we have here?" asked Alison in mock amazement and quite delighted with her theme. "We have one bantam-sized Canadian prepared to smash the entire Chinese Communist Politburo with a single mighty blow, who gets around China faster than a speed-ing train – "

Halpert let out a whoop. "It's actually faster than a bullet and more powerful than a speeding train."

"Whatever," said Alison, who was not to be diverted. "And what do we have in the other corner? We have Halpert the Friendly Giant, who wouldn't hurt a flea, and worries about Washington's geopolitical swagger, and sends thank-you notes to lonely secretaries when they say hi to him on the street. Now I ask you, does any of this make sense? Were you two snatched from your cradles at birth and switched as some sort of atonement for the Autopact deal?"

After three bottles of Tsingtao beer, Alison was unstoppable. "Are you aware, Gordon, that your embassy, the dear old embassy of the Dominion of Canada, considers you more of a menace than the Public Security Bureau? The PSB understands its place in the scheme of things,

46

it knows how to take orders, it is predictable. *The* Gordon Wrye can be counted on for none of these things. *The* Gordon Wrye is a loose cannon. *The* Gordon Wrye does not know when to stop. *The* Gordon Wrye . . ."

Eventually, Halpert figured out he was an inconvenient observer to foreplay and made his goodbyes, assuring Alison that he could be as brutal and selfish as the next American.

"I'm prepared to explore that thesis another time," she said with a grin. "Tonight, we're flying domestic. See you soon."

Halpert had smiled all the way back to the compound. It was late, and in the distance he could hear the drivers from Peking's farming communes on their horse-drawn wagons bringing in the morning's produce. He thought of them as having wondrously unrestrained souls. They worked at night, when the commune managers were asleep and the city streets were deserted. As their wagons creaked slowly along the main thoroughfares towards market depots all over Peking, they sang arias from their favourite operas with such wild and glorious abandon that it sometimes made Halpert shiver. Passion, in almost any form, intrigued him, perhaps because he had spent so much of his life trying to control it in himself. By observing its various permutations, he found he could more easily resist it personally.

Gordon, he knew, was the most passionate man he would ever meet. During the earliest days of their friendship, he hadn't taken a lot of what Wrye said too seriously, at least not until Halpert mildly chided him one night for the amount of loathing he expressed for his own country.

"You're nuts," he said to Gordon. "Canada's a nice place. People leave you alone. The media isn't all puffed up like in the States. Governments come and go without all the mess we put ourselves through trying to get rid of Nixon. I don't understand your gripe."

Halpert would never forget the heat of his response, and he would never again goad him on a subject about which he was so sensitive. He could only vaguely remember the specifics of his complaints about Canada, but he was astute enough to realize that whatever they were, the dossier was up against Gordon's own view of himself in the world. It was the smallness of vision, the smallness of mind, that seemed to upset him the most about his country. He hated the "bigoted" town in Ontario where he had grown up. He hated his father's timidity and his mother's neuroses. He hated the schools he had attended. He hated the local university where he had done his undergraduate work. He hated the way his peers had sold out for bland, placid lives. He hated the length, depth, and breadth of the place that had spawned and nurtured him. Canada was a joke of a country, he said, and its pathetic yearning towards some sort of national identity had taught him to be suspicious of all inchoate sentiment that made people blind to reality.

While Gordon raved on, he twisted the silver dragon ring on the little finger of his left hand. Halpert had learned that this obsessive fidgeting with the ring was a sign that his friend was dangerously agitated. When he saw Gordon go for the ring, he knew it was time to change the topic, if he could.

China, Halpert remembered from the same rant, was everything Canada wasn't. It was, Gordon said, a great country, a land with an unparalleled history and an extraordinary people. Even if it had a government that was off the rails, China was a place worthy of dreams and ambitions. In China you could understand the true nature of hope and, at the same time, appreciate the imminence of apocalypse. China was forced to drag along its ancient history, but for the most part it embraced the complex present while looking forward with longing to the future, a future that remained impenetrable but tantalizing. Canada . . . *Canada!* . . . Canada was hardly worth a pee stop.

Halpert dozed off again, and when he awoke he realized that the train was within a few miles of Peking.

∽

At about the same early morning hour that Halpert's train was pulling into the station, Leading Comrade Fu, second-in-charge of the Foreign Ministry's Diplomatic Service Bureau, was surveying the security reports forwarded to him by the night duty officers. It was the usual compendium of predictable non-events: overly boisterous foreigners from a Danish embassy party had driven somewhat recklessly back to their own compounds; a couple of Tanzanian teenagers in Chi Chai Yuan compound had amused themselves by slashing several tires; the Belgian second secretary's wife had been taken at 3:22 a.m. to the Capital Hospital to give birth to her baby. . . .

Fu flipped through the reports casually and then came to a startled stop. A female Chinese citizen had been spotted, seemingly alone, in the San Li Tun compound apartment of a Canadian journalist. The report had come initially from the eleven-year-old granddaughter of an army officer whose apartment building was adjacent to the foreigners' compound where Correspondent Halpert lived and worked. The officer reported that his granddaughter had started watching the journalist's apartment when she noticed the curtains were drawn in the morning. The girl constantly observed the foreigners' apartments, and her grandfather had even started calling her "my little security chief." Of all the apartments under her careful scrutiny, none provided rewards to equal Halpert's. There was always something happening.

Once, eight months ago, she had even seen the foreign man and his wife have a terrible fight. It was nighttime, when they usually drew the curtains, but they hadn't this time so the lights were blazing as they never did in a Chinese apartment. The fight was memorable because, at one point, the woman had picked up the porcelain displayed on a scroll table and began smashing vases and bowls against the walls, on the floor, all over the place. The man did not try to stop her. He just walked out of the room.

This time though, the curtains had been drawn during the daytime. She had never seen this happen before, so she kept up a careful surveillance of the remaining two uncurtained windows that faced her grandfather's apartment. One gave a view of the journalist's office, and for about three minutes she saw a Chinese woman sit at the desk and inspect the things on it. Then, when her grandfather's cock crowed in his balcony cage, she saw the woman give a startled look.

After the Chinese woman ran out of the foreigner's office, the girl reported everything to her grandfather. He immediately called his superior. One of the conditions of getting the nice apartment was the responsibility of keeping an eye on foreigners. The entire building housed either army or police officials and their families. It was the family members, rather than the resident officials, who did the best spying.

Leading Comrade Fu was not startled by the story itself. Increasingly, there were reports of Chinese citizens entering foreigners' apartments, a thing that would never have happened even a year ago. Some of these visits were officially condoned, and the Chinese nationals would check in at the guard-house before entering. Others, however, snuck in, either by crouching down in the back seats of foreigners' cars, or hiding among the crush of Chinese domestic staff who poured into the compounds six mornings out of seven.

What Leading Comrade Fu found so worrying this time was that the Chinese national was not only unattended but was also in this particular journalist's apartment. Six days earlier, the very day Halpert set off for his trip to Kung-hsien, the Diplomatic Service Bureau had received a special vigilance alert from the Public Security Bureau division of the Ministry of Culture. Anything untoward that happened in Correspondent Halpert's apartment was to be reported immediately to the PSB, no matter how insignificant it might seem.

As soon as he had finished the girl's report, Leading Comrade Fu dialled his superior. Within the hour a dispatch rider from the Ministry of Culture arrived at the Diplomatic Service Bureau office to pick up the testimony so lovingly and patriotically provided by the littlest security chief.

Leading Comrade Fu did not rest easily until his superior finally called him a few hours later and said the Diplomatic Service Bureau was to get a special commendation for its security work. When he put down the phone, he contemplated the possible rewards of such highly placed approbation. Then he thought again about the subject of his report and cast a spare thought towards the unknown Chinese woman who had been spotted in Halpert's apartment.

Stupid slut, thought Leading Comrade Fu. *Her life is already finished.*

3

At the entrance to Peking's Sun-dappled Park, workmen on a scaffolding in front of a large poster were painting out an obsolete quatrain of Chairman Mao's, reproduced from the Great Helmsman's own calligraphy in four-foot characters:

> *Our friendly ties stay knotted,*
> *Entwined within a wreath,*
> *One mind, one heart, one future:*
> *As close as lips and teeth.*

Kwai Ta-ping got off his bicycle and motioned to his cycling companion to do the same.

"This is history," said Kwai eagerly. "The old fart is really dead if they're finally erasing his words. He wrote that damn thing to celebrate our eternal solidarity with Vietnam and now the People's Army marches on Hanoi. History! History!"

Kwai was flushed with enthusiasm, but his companion said nothing and was clearly uncomfortable with both the tenor and volume of his friend's observations. Quickly he looked around the park's entrance to make sure no one was observing them. It was an automatic action any ordinary Chinese citizen took at the least suspicion of trouble.

They deposited their bicycles at the park's lock-up and headed through the main gates. Kwai's mood was clearly holding, and he began to sing out loud, further perturbing his companion, who had come along with this dangerous man only because there was a slight chance of meeting a foreigner. Not any foreigner, but someone who might be able to help him study abroad.

"*The hunter's arrow twangs in the wind, but the brook pays it no regard* – " Kwai abruptly stopped singing as they saw two uniformed Public Security Bureau officers saunter across the pathway just ahead of them.

"They've ruined my beautiful song," said Kwai with dramatic disgust. "It is the Yung Lo emperor's song to his beloved and now I have to see these nose-picking motherfu – "

Kwai's friend put his arm out to gently touch his shoulder and shut off the bravado. He was getting the distinct feeling this expedition was a major mistake, and not for the first time that morning he thought of bolting.

"Where is the foreigner? Where are we supposed to meet him?"

Kwai ambled on, aware of his friend's unease but paying it no mind. As a veteran dissident, he had long ago abandoned any unnecessary caution.

"I told you," said Kwai, "he may not turn up. We have an understanding that if we are both able, we meet here at this hour. I just walk around. If he's here, we walk together. If he's not here, well . . . he's not here. Sometimes he comes and I'm not here. That's all. Let's walk around for half an hour. If we don't meet him today we can try again another day. I'm sure he'll have some good advice for you."

Partway around the path of the park's vast central flower bed, they again encountered the PSB officers, one of whom looked Kwai up and down. That was enough for Kwai's friend. As soon as they had passed by the policemen, he turned and started walking briskly back to the bicycle lock-up. He did not say goodbye nor did he look back.

Kwai Ta-ping contemplated the retreating figure with both pity and envy. Pity for the fear, of course. He had pity for most of his countrymen, so long burdened with fear they wore it like a robe, hoping against hope that the mere act of donning such crippling anxiety would be sufficient to ward off both its real or imagined consequences.

And yet Kwai knew that his friend would survive. He would bend like the bamboo tree in any storm, no matter how fierce, no matter how far the bending, even if he had to bend so low there was no space left between him and the earth. And his friend would probably get to America, because in bending there was avoidance and in avoidance there was always another day, and on that new day there was always a chance. There lay Kwai's envy: the little matter of chance. Two brutal sessions in labour-reform camps between 1966 and 1978 had ended all chance for him. When he embraced caution these days, it was only because he wanted to postpone the inevitable return to prison. These prison sentences were little deaths, but once you had learned to die, living became much easier.

He was actually being somewhat cautious these early autumn days, although his departed friend didn't notice it. There had been a recent round-up of Democracy Wall activists. Somehow he had not been included, and as he sat down for a few minutes on a park bench, he reflected on the fragmentary pleasures of the unfettered life.

There was no sign of Hai Pei-teh, the Canadian newspaper man, his friend, his source of extra cotton and cooking-oil coupons, his window on the world beyond labour camps and PSB officers and community fear. He liked having a foreign friend who knew so many things. Kwai asked Hai Pei-teh almost as many questions as Halpert asked him. But he was leaving China soon. Although Kwai affected to remain untouched by Halpert's rapidly advancing departure, in his heart he knew he would miss him very much. So much, in fact, that he had got the reluctant jour-nalist to agree to meet him two days a week during the last month of his posting – Saturdays and Mondays, Kwai's own strange weekend – and always at seven in the morning.

"I won't be able to make all those days, but I'll do my best," Halpert had told him. "I'm going on a little trip next week, so for sure I won't be here next Saturday or Monday."

On the park bench, Kwai smiled. Although today was the Saturday Halpert had said he would be away, he hadn't really deceived his cycling companion. Halpert sometimes changed his schedule. Kwai liked the unpredictability of foreigners. They were always changing their plans, always in a rush to go to the next place, always travelling.

Resting the back of his neck on the bench, he looked up at the trees. He was in no rush to go to *his* next place. The poplars were swaying gently in the hot morning breeze, and the sunlight dancing through the fluttering leaves seemed to him to be jewels from the Yung Lo emperor's treasure chest. No one knew how much he wanted to travel too, but if all the people who loved China fled to try their luck in the world, then there would be no love and no China.

The poplar leaves grew still, and he broke out into a loud falsetto and finished the Yung Lo emperor's song: "*Sun-dappled fruit hangs in the trees, its ripeness beckoning like Kai-lan's glance.*"

∾

In a matter of only a few days, Driver Koo had become an expert in all matters relating to the Northern Sung dynasty tomb site, at least as they affected the Kung-hsien County Communist Party Office. Which meant that he knew a lot about nothing, which was what he was meant to know.

His neighbours had asked about what was going on at what the locals called the Long March Agricultural Commune, and he was now a master of the oblique response intended to indicate knowledge so important and classified that it was inappropriate for the ears of the masses. "To know an answer is nothing," kindly old Party Secretary Liu had once said in the early fifties, "but understanding the question is everything." Too bad about Party Secretary Liu. He was exposed as a Rightist in 1956 and shipped off to labour-reform work in the Northeast, never to be heard from again. Koo would make sure nothing like this would happen to him. Ever.

What he did know for certain was that this was a Double Nine day – ninth day of the ninth month – and thus the potential for something momentous to happen was considerable. He had waited nearly an hour at the railway station for the arrival of the deputy vice-minister of culture, who was also director of the Cultural Relics Bureau. Then, as soon as Director Ng had arrived, without so much as a tea-break, they had headed to the tomb site where the archaeologists had been working. No stopover at the county office. No chance for an intimate talk in the Shanghai sedan since three local officials were dogging the director's every movement. Koo understood the syndrome: proximity to power was almost the same thing as power itself, at least as long as the proximity was maintained.

And now he had been waiting for nearly two hours while the official party was being briefed inside one of the site tents. Driver Koo had contented himself with random conversations with the security personnel. They were not ordinary security types and certainly not local. Koo figured they were on special duty for the ministry, but each time he tried to find out some more information, he was brushed aside.

"Must be something very important in the tomb to bring a leading comrade all this way?" he had asked at one point.

The youngest and most arrogant of the security officials, the only one who wore sunglasses, looked at Koo with withering contempt.

"Comrade driver," he asked, "what is your responsibility here?"

"My responsibility?" asked Koo, genuinely perplexed. "Why I have no responsibility here. I am just the driver."

"Exactly," said the officer. "That is exactly your responsibility. See that you do not exceed it."

Koo was not used to being put in his place, and – in fact – declined to be put there or feel any loss of face. The security officer was just another young asshole from Peking, so a half-hour later, he tried his luck with an older security official who had walked over towards the Shanghai sedan to divert himself from the tedium of waiting.

"They are certainly taking their time," said Koo. "How much longer do you think it'll be?"

"Oh, not much longer now," said the second officer. "It's a fairly complex briefing and everyone wants to show off to the boss. You know how it is. The director will probably go and take a look at the tomb's interior when they're finished. Maybe I'll finally get a chance to see what's inside. Everyone seems very excited."

"We always thought these old tombs had been robbed ages ago," said Koo with the air of an insider. "I guess they missed one. Anyway,

I hope it's true. It could be very good for tourism in Kung-hsien County."

The second officer looked at Koo properly for the first time. Then he looked over his shoulder. "Look, comrade," he said, "I wouldn't talk about this place to anyone. I know some of the local farmers are very curious, but if you are asked, I wouldn't say anything if you want to avoid unfortunate misunderstandings. This is an important project, very secret, and there already has been some trouble here."

"Oh, I know, I know," said Koo, both pleased and worried by the special confidentiality. "In my work, I get to know lots of things and I never talk about them. That's for sure. Just last year, when Comrade Peng was here from Peking — "

"Another time," said the security official, who was watching the tent where the briefing for Director Ng was taking place. He noticed that one of his colleagues had emerged looking for him, and he strode off. The director came out next, followed by a gaggle of other officials, who vied to be the closest to him without tripping him or falling over themselves.

"So which way do we go?" asked Director Ng. "Let's see this hidden room and these amazing artefacts that are three hundred years ahead of their time."

The second security official trailed along behind the pack, and when they reached the entrance to the tomb, he turned his head towards Koo and motioned for him to join them. Koo was pleased at the nod in his direction and started walking quickly towards the group. Then his highly developed instinct for self-preservation slowed his gait. Driver Koo had seen too many political ups and downs in his days, and he had survived them all by never being too closely associated with any event, any group, or any official. He understood and accepted that real power and great privilege always lay at the centre of things, but he also knew that it was at the centre where the risks were highest. It was safer to inhabit a more peripheral landscape, where there were perks enough for the likes of him.

By the time Koo got to the tomb entrance, he had taken so long that everyone else had gone inside. He stayed outside, assuaging any curiosity he might have had over the tomb's contents with the happy thought that if there were questions later about the appropriateness of anything, he could claim that he had not been involved.

Involved in what?

Driver Koo hadn't a clue, but he had his alibi ready.

∿

The night in Peking was a friend to Johnny Addo. The fourteen-year-old son of the military attaché to the Kenyan embassy suffered by day at a Chinese middle school where he had no friends and was regarded as little better than an ape recently descended from the trees. His aloneness was reinforced by his dislike of the two other African teenagers his age (from Ghana and Chad), neither of whom in any case lived near him in the San Li Tun compound. There were no other foreign teenagers of any age or race to pal around with, except during Christmas when dozens of mostly affluent white kids came from expensive boarding schools far away to be with their parents in Peking. Christmas was not a great time for Johnny Addo because he didn't fit into anyone's celebrations. Moreover, his mother and his brothers and sisters remained in Kenya because his father's posting was a short one – three years – and the Kenyan government declined to pay their passage or residence costs. His father had brought him because he was the eldest son and had hoped to grow closer to him during this unique posting. It hadn't worked out that way. Johnny was largely ignored by his father and usually left to his own devices.

In the daytime, when he came home from school, there were dozens of young Chinese children lined up with their grandmothers outside the compound's heavy metal security fence enjoying their regular afternoon entertainment: watching little African children play games inside the compound. Occasionally, when he walked by, the Chinese children would gawk and point at him, too. He felt like a chimpanzee in the Peking Zoo – an item of interest so long as he kept moving or sneezed or showed some iota of evidence that, however distantly, he was part of the vast evolution of mankind that led to the triumph of the Chinese race.

At night, though, the darkness shrouded Johnny Addo's loneliness and gave him respite. His favourite perch was on top of the long block of thirty-six garages behind Number Three Building in the San Li Tun compound. At this end of the compound, there was minimal public lighting – one exterior low-wattage bulb for every six garages. Usually, there was an easy sequence of footholds beside Number Thirty-six Garage, where abandoned shipping crates were stored, and he could clamber up to the top within seconds.

Johnny had found a dim and unfrequented fiefdom for himself, but he loved every square inch of it. No one ever contested his right to rule, and only once had he brought someone else there. That had been a mistake, never again to be repeated. It was seven months ago, the one time he had tried to strike up a relationship with the fifteen-year-old Ghanian from the Chiang Kuo Men Wai compound. But the Ghanian had thought it silly just to sit up there and look out. It would be much more amusing, he suggested, to go below and let air out of the tires of the diplomats' cars. Then, in the morning, he could have the real fun of looking out his own window as the owners fumed and fussed.

That wasn't Johnny Addo's way. He liked watching the passing scene, not the consequences of any actions of his own. Besides, he was too frightened of what his father would do to him if he was found out. It was enough just to know that he had a quiet place of his own in this strange and crowded city where everyone regarded him as an alien.

So, on a fine early autumn Saturday night, he took up his command position atop Number One Garage. It was the best spot by far on the best night of all. Saturday evening was party time at San Li Tun, and from here he could not only catch some of the action in the first three storeys of Number Three Building but could also see part of the adjacent public street and a whole flank of Chinese apartments immediately to the west. On those wonderful occasions when he found himself snooping on Chinese people who were themselves snooping on foreigners, he felt the kind of omniscience normally reserved for Greek deities or double agents.

Pleasurable as such special moments were, he was not dependent upon them for a satisfactory evening. The ordinary world around him was good enough. Out on the public street just beyond the compound, under the bright arc lights that the Peking authorities uniquely placed in the foreigners' districts, several curbside card games were being played by eager Chinese citizens who found the public lighting superior to the flickering twenty-five-watt bulbs in their one-room quarters. The games, usually played by older men surrounded by hordes of children, were conducted with great gusto, and the night air would regularly ring with triumphant shouts of "Ah! Ah! Ah!" as a joyous grandfather dramatically threw down his winning hand on the ground to the dismay of his opponents and the cheers of his grandchildren. From that safe distance where no one knew he was watching, Johnny Addo liked the Chinese and fantasized about floating down from his rooftop redoubt to take over the hand of a departing player.

But on Saturday nights most of the action came from within the compound. Already the noise level from the party in the apartment of the young first secretary at the Australian embassy was rising rapidly. The diplomat and his wife had once invited Johnny to a football game at the People's Stadium, the high point of his entire time in Peking. He longed to be asked again, but the invitation had come early in the Australian's posting, and as he got caught up in the round of diplomatic life, the shy African boy disappeared from his priority list. He and his wife could throw a lively party, though, and Johnny – directly facing their second-storey apartment across the garage alleyway – followed all the activity through three rooms of crowded people on full view.

The music blared across the back of the compound, and Johnny quietly gauged the irritation threshold on both sides of the security fence. He'd noticed that the Chinese were always the first to start whining about the noise because they went to bed earlier than foreigners. They came onto their balconies to glare with impotent anger across Johnny Addo's kingdom and hurl dark oaths into the unconcerned air. From other balconies, this time inside the compound, diplomats or their spouses occasionally came out to peer along the building to see precisely where the noise was coming from, in order to determine whether they were affronted or pleased at not having been invited. Tonight the noise was as loud as Johnny had ever heard it, and the partying even more frantic than the normal blot-out of Saturday-night revels.

Things were often done to excess in Peking. If someone arrived on a posting with a bit of a drinking problem, for example, within three months he would be a roaring alcoholic. If a couple brought some unsolved marital problems with them, the relationship was usually finished in the same time period. If, like Johnny Addo, you found your father austere and a little frightening, there was a horrible chance he could turn into a monster in the pinched, stressful life of resident foreigners. The syndrome enlivened the party scene, too.

Around 9:45 p.m. he heard the harsh bang of a garage door opening and a couple of shouts. The sounds came from below at the other end of the line of garages. He was sure of the time because he was constantly looking at the new watch he had purchased the week before from the Friendship Store, the bleak emporium reserved exclusively for foreign friends with friendly foreign currency. It was a Rolex-style watch, shamelessly and meticulously copied by the Chinese and sold for twenty-five dollars. You could also get a Parker 51-style pen for four dollars. Johnny had coveted the watch not because it was such a cheap ripoff of the Swiss original but because the fluorescent figures and hands glowed in the dark.

Any activity around the garages was unusual, and especially at night. As a general rule, the diplomats and foreign journalists of San Li Tun did not put their automobiles in their garages unless they were going to be away from Peking for a long period. Instead, they parked them as close as possible to the various entrances of their residences. Garages were used, if at all, to store trunks and suitcases or – among the affluent Western diplomatic families – large pieces of exotic Chinese furniture purchased for later transport home. The garages were padlocked, and when diplomats were set to leave for another posting, they often discovered that their padlocks were rusted shut and had to be sawn open. Occasionally, a foreigner simply forgot that he even had a garage and left China without retrieving what he had absentmindedly stored in it at the beginning of his posting.

Johnny crept along the flat roofs, whose surface of stone pebbles embedded in tar made a crunching sound if he walked too quickly or heavily. He had definitely heard a garage door opening and some voices, but as he came closer to the spot, he heard nothing but the party noise. He hadn't mistaken what he'd heard, he knew that. The door had made a squeal, and the shouts — heard over the party's music and banter — were like military orders in his father's regiment, more like human barks, but in what language he couldn't say.

It took him a couple of minutes to get to the middle of the complex. On his knees, he carefully leaned over the edge and scanned along the alleyway. There was no one there and nothing was stirring, not even one of the numerous rats that knew they were far safer with the disgust of foreign diplomats than they were with the cooking pots of their Chinese neighbours.

Something metallic on the pavement below caught Johnny Addo's eye. It looked beckoning. Abandoned metal objects intrigue most boys. Of any age. Of any race. He waited a few more minutes to make doubly sure there wasn't anyone about and then warily made his way to the top of the last garage and descended from one level of packing crates to the next.

Keeping close to the back wall of Number Three Building to be as far away as he could from the garages, he walked carefully down the wide alleyway. Although he was cautious by nature, Johnny Addo was not frightened. He always wore dark clothing on his evening patrols, and since his skin was the colour of night, darkness was his ally and fortified his nerve. He saw the open garage door when he was about ten yards away. But even now that he was standing directly opposite Number Nineteen Garage, he could still not see anything distinct except a steel wrench lying beside the open door. He looked up and down the alleyway one more time and moved out quietly from the shadows.

As he knelt down to look at it, he was surprised at the size of the wrench. He could have sworn what had shone up at him was much smaller. It was only when he reached to pick it up that he could see that half its bulk was covered in dark grease. Curious, he carried the heavy wrench over to the nearest exterior light. The grease, he saw, was not grease at all. It was blood, and the moment he realized this, he dropped the wrench and ran back to the wall of Number Three Building.

His hand was smeared with blood, and since he didn't want to wipe it off on his shirt or shorts, he rubbed it against the brick of the building. Now the cloak of night had ceased being his friend and he was torn between fear and curiosity. With some people, fear makes the soul grow smaller. This was not the case with Johnny Addo. He was shy, but ordinary fear acted as a challenge on him, and tonight it impelled his unwilling feet across the alleyway.

He had a thin penlight in his pocket, and when he was a few feet away from the open garage, he aimed it into the interior. The light was so weak it revealed nothing except the dark outline of large boxes. He stepped closer to the threshold and aimed the flashlight down. That's when he saw the feet – and the pool of blood.

Johnny Addo ran as fast as he could, down to the north end of the complex, around two corners of Number Three Building and all the way to Entrance Two, up the stairway to the second floor and along the corridor to the Australian diplomat's apartment. As he came bounding up the steps, he saw five or six people with drinks in their hands outside the open door of the apartment. One of the women instinctively drew closer to her mate. Perhaps she had heard too much about restless African youths.

"Something terrible in the back," he blurted. "I think a man is dead."

No one moved a muscle. Johnny Addo was breathing so heavily and talking so loudly that his startled listeners wondered if the young madman in front of them was on a rampage. The wife of the Australian diplomat, wearing a big party smile, came out into the foyer and saw the tears streaming down the boy's face.

"What's the matter," she said, her voice full of concern as she handed her drink to the first person on her left and quickly went over to put an arm around Johnny Addo's shoulder.

"Something terrible outside, madam. I think a man is dead."

By now, the others realized their lives were not in jeopardy, and one of the men went inside to summon his host. The Australian first secretary came out, and soon the foyer was filled with people. The diplomat sat Johnny down on the steps leading to the third floor and listened to his story. So did everybody else. The silence surrounding the man and the boy was broken only by the jingle of ice cubes in half-consumed glasses of Dewar's.

The Australian looked up at the crowd. "We better go down and take a look," he said. "Ladies, stay here."

"What do you mean 'ladies, stay here'?" asked a female voice somewhere in the midst of the crowded foyer. "We'll all go down. There's safety in numbers."

Out they all eagerly spilled from Entrance Two, united by booze, diplomatic immunity, Caucasian superiority, party-time solidarity, and – most of all – the excitement of the unexpected. When they rounded the second corner and started down the long alleyway, their loose formation tightened up. In the dim light, the group no longer felt itself nearly so numerous or so secure. By the time they all reached the open garage door, the fortifying effects of Dewar's had quite dissipated.

"My God," shouted Halpert. "I think it's my garage. What on earth is going on?" He broke loose from the group and strode up to the entrance. "If I remember correctly, there's a light switch on the left wall close to the door. Has anyone got a lighter?"

A half-dozen Zippo-style lighters were offered, and Halpert grabbed the closest. He thumbed the flint wheel to get a flame and soon found the light switch. When he turned it on, he heard a collective gasp from behind him. A woman starting sobbing, "My God, my God, he's dead, I know he's dead."

The Australian first secretary peered in and then recoiled.

"Oh Lord," he moaned.

Halpert looked around and saw for himself the twisted body, the blood glistening under the overhead light, and what was left of the head on the torso. It was so hideously smashed that had it not been joined to a human frame, he would not have tried to look for any of the familiar features of a face, like eyes or nose or mouth or ears. None of these were discernible.

Halpert did not recoil. Long ago in Vietnam he had learned how to steel himself in the presence of human carnage. He just kept staring, trying to make sense of what he was seeing. What on earth had happened here? Why was this body in his garage? Slowly, some of the other men approached the corpse, but each time they got a close-up of the pulped head, they also flinched. One man ran out and vomited against a closed garage door. And still Halpert remained glued to his spot. He noticed a large discoloured stain on the front of the dead man's khaki trousers where presumably the victim's bladder had exploded.

At what point he also noticed the silver ring, he could not say. All he remembered afterwards was that he saw the ring and that it did not occur to him till many seconds later that it was Gordon Wrye's ring on Gordon Wrye's hand that was connected to Gordon Wrye's torso upon which Gordon Wrye's bashed and unrecognizable face was still vaguely attached.

And even then, he did not move.

$$\boxed{4}$$

Whatever the cause, close proximity to the death of someone we know and love brings with it a period of intense unreality. As he knelt on one knee before the corpse of Gordon Wrye, Halpert did not feel grief, he did not feel anger, he did not feel nausea, he didn't even feel the supportive hand of the Australian first secretary on his shoulder. Nothing registered except disbelief. The bashed-in head, which looked a bit like a half-open, rotting watermelon, did not horrify him. He just fixed his eye on Gordon's ring. Dully, he remembered the way Gordon played with it when he got agitated. Then the seemingly disconnected realities came together: the agitation and the ring, the ring and the head, the head and the violence, the violence and the body, the body and the friend, the friend and their relationship, the relationship and the ring.

When these connections finally came full circle, Halpert did snap. Suddenly, he stood up and shook off the Australian's hand. Suddenly, it was unacceptable that anyone else should see the urine stains on the crotch of Gordon's trousers. Suddenly, it was time for everyone else to get the hell away from this spectacle. Suddenly, he turned to the party throng, still gaping at the corpse, and said as much.

Why don't they move, the stupid idiots? Of course, of course, I am the only one who knows the dead man is Gordon Wrye.

Suddenly, again suddenly, the burden of that exclusive knowledge became too much for him. He did not know what on earth to do except stand there, himself the stupid idiot, stupidly frozen to his position until the Australian once more put his hand on his shoulder and said, "Come along, old man, we should all get away from here and go back to the apartment. We have to figure out what to do next."

Halpert let himself be led away, and by the time he reached Entrance Two, two things were already quite clear in his mind. He would find out who killed his friend; and he would make the killer, or killers, pay. It was not normally in his nature to hate, and so the feelings of revenge that welled up during the short walk back to the Australian's apartment were an unfamiliar sensation. They restored the semblance of calm, and — more helpfully — the ability to think precisely.

Back inside, he didn't let the first secretary finish a sentence.

"The dead man was a friend of mine. I recognized the ring on his finger. He always wore it. His name was Gordon Wrye." Halpert's words were spoken softly, but his cold monotone further chilled everyone's souls. Even the Swiss embassy's cultural officer stopped hunting for the bottle of Dewar's and strained to hear everything Halpert said.

"He was a Canadian postgraduate scholar doing research in archaeology out of the University of Nanking, but was staying at my apartment during a brief visit. I thought he had already left to go to Hong Kong this morning. Someone should phone the Canadian embassy right now and tell them what has happened."

Halpert turned to the Australian and asked him also to call Colonel Henderson, the Canadian military attaché who was officially in charge of security at the embassy. "He's the person who should inform the Chinese."

But his mind was miles ahead of this perfunctory business. He was now certain about a few other things. Although he could think of no reason why anyone would want to kill Gordon Wrye, he was fairly sure whoever did it wasn't Chinese. There was only one recorded case since 1949 of a Chinese citizen murdering a foreigner, and that was a fatal stabbing on the street by a pathetically crazed factory worker who was soon subdued, arrested, and executed. Even if Gordon had been the most repellent and obnoxious foreigner ever allowed to reside in China, an expulsion was the worst punishment the Chinese would have in store for him. Looking around the room of friends and acquaintances who had gathered at the Australian's to say goodbye to Halpert, it struck him that Gordon – despite some of his notorious verbal rampages – was far from being the most obnoxious foreigner in China. Very far.

But he is dead! A man who loved China, who loved Chinese people, who was a brilliant scholar, who was a generous and thoughtful friend, who was exciting to be around. *He is dead, and it was a fellow foreigner or foreigners who killed him.* No Chinese were permitted inside the foreigners' compounds at night without special dispensation and prior approval, no Chinese could have got inside the compound without the help of foreign –

Sui-san! My God, Sui-san is still in my apartment. My God, my God, what am I going to do about her?

Sui-san had not been able to book a train ticket back to Nanking until early Sunday morning, but Halpert and Gordon had both decided it was safe enough for her to stay another night in Halpert's apartment, since the Chinese staff were not coming back until Monday morning. The bureau's old Volkswagen Bug was just outside Entrance Three, and Sui-san could go out the same way Gordon brought her in, crouched down on the floor of the back seat under a blanket. The sentries wouldn't see anything, even if they happened to glance through the rear window as Halpert's car sped through the gates. He and Gordon had worked it out that he would drive her to within a few blocks of the railway station. There she could be safely let off opposite the East Wind Hotel, where there were always plenty of foreign tourists and China Travel Service guides milling about.

He didn't know about that plan anymore, and he remembered Gordon's fears for Sui-san because her relationship with him was bringing her under increased scrutiny in their university department. More than anything, Halpert wanted to flee the party-turned-nightmare and get back to his apartment. The thought that he was the one who would have to tell Sui-san what had happened to Gordon had not yet occurred to him. He was in the grip of an emotion even stronger than revenge. Nothing at the moment was more crucial than getting back to Sui-san. In protecting her, he would actually be doing something useful. In protecting her, he would be doing something for Gordon. In protecting her, Gordon would feel closer. In protecting her, Gordon might not be dead. In protecting her, he could be Gordon, at least he could be Gordon until she was safe. Protecting Sui-san was suddenly the most important thing in the world.

He shook himself free from the centre of attention.

"I've got to go and see some people," he said and headed straight for the front door.

The Australian went after him.

"Look, old man, you shouldn't be alone tonight. You can have our spare room."

Halpert didn't even stop walking.

"I'm okay," he said. "I have to see some people. I'll talk to you later."

Then he broke into a run.

∾

He mumbled her name in a kind of manic litany the whole time he ran up the stairs, three at a time, to his floor. Normally, he never locked the door to his apartment, so he was momentarily surprised when he turned the knob and couldn't get in. *Of course, of course, it's locked because of her*. He fumbled in his jacket pocket for keys, and when he finally got in, he was practically shouting her name.

"Sui-san! Sui-san!"

He found her in the living room, in the corner of the large sofa, tightly clutching the blanket she had been sleeping under before she heard the frightening commotion at the front door.

"Sui-san!" he said as he walked clumsily over to the sofa and sat down beside her, heedless of the confusion of her semi-awake mind. "Sui-san! Gordon is dead. He's been murdered."

"*Gordon ʒai nar, Jamie?*" she asked, her eyebrows creased together in bewilderment. Sui-san's English was idiosyncratic but passable thanks to Gordon's influence. Love is a great teacher of vocabulary and grammar. But not right out of sleep and certainly not when an excitable foreigner was blurting things out too quickly.

"Where's Gordon? Gordon's nowhere, Sui-san. Gordon is dead.

Si-le! Someone killed him just behind this building. He's dead, Sui-san. He's dead."

She retreated even farther into the corner of the sofa and buried her head in the blanket. She did not moan or cry, but began rocking herself back and forth. Halpert wanted to reach out and touch her, comfort her, but he hesitated. He did not know what to do and so he asked a stupid question, at least stupid for the moment and for this person.

"Why would anyone want to kill Gordon? Do you know *anyone* who would want to hurt Gordon, Sui-san?"

Then the moaning started in earnest. It came deep from within her, and it was a noise unlike anything Halpert had ever heard. An animal sound. Low and instinctive. Now he could put his arm around her, and he was overwhelmed by her smallness. She seemed the size of a child as she lay enfolded across his chest, her sobbing so convulsive that he could hardly hold her. In a strange way, this relieved him. She was crying the tears he could not summon within himself, but because they were melded together into one entity, it was *they* who cried and *they* who grieved. In the unity of their sorrow, he felt some release.

After the violent sobbing subsided, they stayed still for a while before she indicated, with the slightest of movements, that it was time for Halpert to let her go. Sui-san got up and went off to the bathroom, and he was left there, slumped, feeling desperately alone and friendless. When she came back, he was ready to return to the first scene, but she was pushing on into Act Two. There was a look of sheer terror on her face.

"Jamie, Jamie," she said. She did not know if that was his family or familiar name, but it was the only name Gordon ever called him, so it was good enough for her. "Jamie, Sui-san have big, big trouble."

"What trouble? Was Gordon in trouble too? What do you know, Sui-san?"

"China trouble, Jamie. Difficult to say."

Eventually, Halpert got the scope of the "China trouble." Sui-san had been criticized by the head of her academic department three times during the past two months for various reasons, and it all stemmed from her relationship with Gordon Wrye. She hadn't told Gordon about the first two sessions, but after the third, when she was informed that her "case" was going before the political committee of the university for consideration, she knew she was in major trouble and felt she had no choice but to bring Gordon into her turmoil. Not uncharacteristically, he had exploded and said he was going to speak to the department head and get it all straightened out. Sui-san had pleaded with him not to make things worse, so over the ensuing few days he worked out a plan to solve all her problems and get her out of China.

"How was he going to get you out of China?" asked Halpert, a trifle hurt that Gordon, who usually told him everything, had not confided in him. Halpert also knew that Chinese citizens, even if they had the economic means, were not able just to fly away from either trouble or their country.

"Sui-san not know how. Gordon know everything. Sui-san going to Canton and Gordon do everything."

She was standing in front of Halpert, who was still slumped on the sofa. Her hands were on her hips and she was clearly agitated with fear. Halpert was amazed at her body language. It was taut, coiled and defiant, ready to strike out. She wasn't wearing a jacket, and her short-sleeved, pale-pink shirt accentuated her delicate bone structure. Even as he mentally staggered around, trying to make sense of what she was saying, he was transfixed by the tortured beauty of her face.

As best as he could make out, the whole visit to Peking had been a ruse to confuse the authorities in Nanking. Gordon was indeed supposed to be heading for Hong Kong, but through some contact or other, he was hatching something for Sui-san in Canton. She was supposed to take the train there the following morning and meet him. Somehow, they were both going to proceed to Hong Kong: he legally and she by means unknown. The only thing that was abundantly clear was that Sui-san had fled Nanking to avoid official wrath and there was no way she could go back. Her only hope had been Gordon's plan and now that hope was gone for good. If she couldn't go back to Nanking and couldn't get out of China, her fate was bleak. Only a month ago, an undergraduate from Peking University had been expelled for having a relationship with a resident foreign businessman. She was arrested, accused of revealing privileged information (not specified), and sentenced to three years of "reform through labour." The case was clearly designed to set an example. In the time-honoured Communist system of quotas for heroes and villains, other examples would be required throughout the country. Sui-san was being set up as Nanking's scarecrow.

At this point, when he didn't even know how to begin thinking himself out of the problem, the bureau telephone rang. He was so deeply troubled that he didn't hear it at first. After the sixth or seventh ring, he realized it was someone who was not going to give up, so he headed down the hallway to his office and picked up the receiver.

"Jamie, Jamie, Jamie Halpert, what the fuck has happened? The ambassador just called me and said Gordon had been murdered. This is a sick joke! Tell me it's a sick joke."

It was Alison. He didn't want to talk to Alison. He didn't want to leave the world of Sui-san and her almighty trouble until he had figured out some sort of strategy, however feeble. He had to do something to help her.

"It's horrible, I know. I just don't want to talk now. I hope you can understand. We'll talk in the morning."

"Like hell we'll talk in the morning. Jamie, I'm coming over right now. I'm on my way."

"*Alison!* Not tonight. Please don't come tonight."

He was about to yell when he realized that Alison lived alone in her apartment without benefit of Chinese staff, and *his* Chinese staff would all be coming to his apartment early Monday morning. If he could get Sui-san safely out of his place and over to Alison's, she could be kept out of harm's way for a few extra days. That might make all the difference in coming up with a solution.

"I'm sorry. Forget I said that. Come on over now. I really need your help."

"I'm halfway there already."

Only after he hung up did it occur to him that of all the foreigners in Peking who might be able to help Sui-san, perhaps Alison was the most inappropriate.

∾

Leading Comrade Fu was roused from his sleep by his worried-looking wife shortly after 2 a.m. on Sunday.

"*Lao* Fu, Old Fu, wake up, wake up. The director is on the telephone. He wants to speak to you immediately."

Old Fu tried to rouse himself, but it was difficult. Sudden awakenings always confused him and, besides, he still wasn't used to being called by his grandiose new diminutive, "Old" – even by his spouse. Old Fu had, until three months earlier, been *Hsiao* Fu – "Little" Fu despite being over forty, Little Fu despite fathering a son, Little Fu despite being the superior of many workers in the Diplomatic Service Bureau who reported to him daily, some of whom were called "Old." Then he got his promotion, which hurled him from number fifteen in the Diplomatic Service Bureau pecking order to number two. With it came his status as a "leading comrade" and the official post of deputy director.

Behind his back, they called him "the helicopter" because his promotion had propelled him from the ground straight up. Just like that. After his promotion to leading comrade, no one felt comfortable calling him Little Fu anymore, although it had always seemed such an appropriate diminutive for a man whose unctuous sycophancy to superiors had commended him to the director of the Diplomatic Service Bureau. But now he was the deputy director, and thirteen of those who had previously given him orders now sought his favour. It was they, more than anyone or anything else, who transformed his name, taking him from mundane Little Fu all the way to the acknowledged *gravitas* inherent in Old Fu.

The deputy director sat on the side of his comfortable sleeping platform and felt for his slippers with his feet. Unaware that he had put them on the wrong feet, he shuffled out of his apartment and down two flights of stairs to the communal telephone at the entrance of his building. Ten equally sleepy neighbours were crowded into the corridor. Phone calls in the night happened rarely; phone calls from very senior officials almost never.

"*Wei*," Old Fu blared into the receiver. "Hello, hello."

"Old Fu," said the voice at the other end of the line. "Come over and join us at the bureau right away. There is a very serious problem.

You better get Mai and Ouyang to come, too. They're in your building, aren't they?"

"Right," said the deputy director, who by now was fully awake and able to stare severely at the remaining hangers-on in the hallway. One by one, he glared them back into their apartments. In truth, they were all happy to go because they could see that Old Fu was still in charge and not in any serious trouble. If he *had* been, there was always the chance that they, too, might be in trouble simply as his neighbours. Significant promotions within the Chinese government or the Communist Party were always greeted with a mixture of excitement and dread by family members and friends.

Old Fu quickly returned to his apartment, dressed, and went down to the lock-up to retrieve his bicycle. After walking the bike to the next entrance, it took him only a few minutes to rouse his two subordinates. He told them that he was going on to the bureau ahead of them, but that they were not to delay. It was a matter of top urgency, he said, implying that he already knew everything.

As soon as he arrived at the seedy headquarters of the Diplomatic Service Bureau, he could see something was up. Lights were on throughout the east end of the second floor, and in the director's office, three of his senior colleagues were already sitting around the conference table.

"Ah," said the director grandly, "here's Old Fu. We can start now. Old Fu, there has been a difficult incident inside the San Li Tun compound. A foreigner has been murdered. The deputy foreign minister called me just over an hour ago. It seems clear that none of our citizens was involved, although the Foreign Ministry is conducting a formal investigation with the assistance of the Public Security Bureau."

The director's team of senior DSB officials were hanging on his every word. Even though he was only parroting what he had been told to say and do, he was investing those words with an air of authority and control that suggested he had just dashed in from the latest meeting of the Politburo.

"Old Fu, your immediate task is to remove the corpse from the back of Number Three Building in San Li Tun. There are a couple of

Canadian diplomats already there, and by the time your team arrives, I trust an official from the Foreign Ministry will be there, too. The body should be taken to the Capital Hospital. That's appropriate, isn't it? Take a foreign corpse to the foreigners' hospital."

This struck the director as mildly funny, and the slight crease of a smile on his face was quickly mirrored on the faces of his subordinates.

"And there better be a team to clean up the mess. Apparently, it's fairly disgusting. We also have another chore which is a little more difficult. This is a highly unusual happening, and the Public Security Bureau has asked all DSB workers in foreign residences and embassies — cooks, housekeepers, drivers, nannies, interpreters, everyone — to keep their eyes and ears open and report to you anything relevant they see or hear connected to this matter. It was a Canadian student who was killed, and he was staying in Peking as a guest of Correspondent Halpert. All your people should behave normally, especially the workers at Correspondent Halpert's apartment. We don't need any amateur investigators doing stupid things. If they simply perform their normal duties and report to you anything they think might be relevant, they will bring great credit to the Diplomatic Service Bureau."

The director paused and looked down at the table for a moment. His subordinates knew this pause. It was always the hint that the end was in sight, but not before the homily.

"I think that's everything for the moment," said the director, "unless anyone has anything he wants to add. I don't think I have to remind you of our duty in this important matter. We remain on the front lines in the defence of our beloved motherland. We work as a team with our own Ministry of Foreign Affairs and with our sister organizations from the security services. I want our bureau to remain on special alert for all this week, and longer if necessary, until it is appropriate to relax the extra vigilance. Is everything understood? Any questions?"

There never were any questions and had there been, the director would have been incensed. Old Fu himself had plenty of follow-up details to ask about, but he did not get to be deputy director by speaking out of turn. Anyway, he knew exactly what would happen next.

"If there are no questions," intoned the director, "let us get on with our work. Old Fu, would you remain behind, please."

As predicted. Old Fu knew the director wanted an update on the Chinese female still in the journalist's apartment. The Public Security Bureau was obsessed about her, and the director was under pressure. He knew that even the little new information he had would be gobbled up appreciatively.

Wrong, as it turned out. It was the director who had the latest information about the Chinese female. "However carefully you can manage it," he said to his deputy, "don't let your people make trouble for the girl if any of them come across her. This is directly from the top."

Old Fu's eyes widened and he immediately revised his earlier judgement. *Maybe her life isn't over quite yet.*

∽

However inappropriate, Alison turned out to be the best friend Halpert had in Peking. Perplexed and dazed though she was, she had never claimed proprietorial rights to Gordon Wrye and understood instantly the deep psychic wounds Halpert was trying to staunch by helping Sui-san. She had readily agreed to the plan of hiding Gordon's Chinese girlfriend in her apartment for a few days. The consequences for any foreigner who got involved in the "internal affairs" of China were serious, but Alison had no personal fear of them. She'd been posted here long enough to consider expulsion a reward, and she didn't even think about how being caught helping Sui-san escape might affect her standing with Canada's Department of External Affairs.

Leaving Halpert's building had been a bit more complicated than it should have been at 2:30 a.m. when no one was supposed to be around. They had gone down one flight of stairs when they heard people ascending below. Ducking down the second-floor hallway, they stayed behind an L-turn hoping that the latecomers were heading up to the third floor. Hearing their banter, Halpert recognized them as two fellow journalists and realized that they were going to his apartment. After the journalists had passed, the three rushed down the final stairs and got into Halpert's car.

There was a lot of activity at the compound's sentry post nearest Number Three Building, so with his car lights off Halpert slowly drove past it to the quiet exit near Number Five Building. After that, their departure was effortless. They made it to Chiang Kuo Men Wai compound in under ten minutes. The sentry wasn't even in view when they slipped past the command post, and he brought Sui-san to her temporary sanctuary with hardly a word exchanged. The terseness continued with Alison, who seemed to understand everything – even Halpert's reasons for not lingering. He wanted to spend the night in his own apartment. The germ of a plan was forming in his mind and part of it entailed being seen in his normal habitat, however upset he might be. As he drove home, he started making a mental list of things he would have to attend to.

First: Get hold of Bennett, the Reuters correspondent, to do a wire-service story on Gordon's death that could be sent to his own foreign desk. That should keep the editors off his back.

Second: Have assignments ready for the Chinese staff to keep them busy throughout Monday and Tuesday.

Third: Get as much currency as possible from his two accounts at the Bank of China on Monday, but not more than the bank snoops might think appropriate for a departing foreign resident who was making final purchases and paying off local debts. The remainder should be wired to his bank back in Toronto.

Fourth: Telephone the Canadian ambassador to let him – oh *Jesus!* yes – phone goddamned Toronto and get the editors to put off his successor's arrival – scheduled for Tuesday noon – until at least next Friday.

Above everything else: make it on time early Monday morning to Sun-dappled Park and pray that Kwai Ta-ping turns up.

His list was still expanding as he went down the hallway of his apartment to his office to write everything down. The telephone was ringing even before he got in the front door, but it wasn't his overseas line – he never gave out that telephone number locally – so he decided not to answer it. Nor would he take any more calls till the next morning. A few minutes later, when he looked up from his note-making, he saw Gordon's knapsack on the floor beside the sofa.

His latest burst of energy and resolve collapsed. The sight of the knapsack, bruised and frayed from thousands of miles of travel, waylaid him. He did not go and inspect its contents, nor did he put it out of his line of vision. He just stared at it for a couple of minutes and then laid his head on his desk and fell asleep.

~

An old Japanese security video camera of considerable bulk was set high up in the northwest corner of the lobby of the Peking Hotel. It used to be able to rotate, but hadn't done so for at least three months because no one knew how to repair it. It could not zoom in or back anymore either. As the Sunday noon-hour approached, the hotel's duty security officer was looking at the monitor, but he was having trouble concentrating thanks to the presence of two senior members of the Public Security Bureau who had descended upon the hotel without notice to eavesdrop on a luncheon conversation in Number Two Private Banqueting Room.

This was the only unusual event. Otherwise, the activity in the lobby was typical of just another normal day in post-Mao China. Staggering through the revolving door at the hotel's entrance, a group of tourists from Italy, whose bus had just returned from a visit to a commune on the outskirts of Peking, followed its leader to the main dining hall. Everyone was tired, hot, and confused. They were all Italians from the China–Italy Friendship Society, and over the last couple of decades, they had invested a lot in their belief that Maoist China offered a different and better way for the world to operate. They weren't Maoists themselves, these Italians. Most of them weren't even Eurocommunists. But they had their ideals, and from the other side of the world, the peasant-worker society of egalitarian New China had looked appealing.

On this, the first full day of their two-week tour, they had been taken to the Double Bridge Agricultural Commune, where they expected to see some of the minutiae of the Maoist miracle. Instead, they had found everything turned upside down, with peasants bragging about their new private plots and access to independent street markets and greedily discussing profits here and smart deals there. Only the Italians' tour leader, a wily old sleaze from Turin, knew what was in store for them. But then his company had been bringing friendly delegations of Italians to the

Double Bridge Commune for so long that he remembered when it was called the Chinese–Albanian Friendship Commune. He alone among these ideologically punctilious Italians understood the practical exigencies of adhering to the "correct" party line, and he alone exulted in the emerging changes. *If this keeps up*, he thought, *I may soon be able to conduct tours of religious sites for Catholic priests and nuns.*

Over at the reception desk, another tour leader – this one from the Netherlands – was screeching. She had just been informed that her group of seventeen agrarian specialists was being turfed out of the hotel two days ahead of schedule. She was hurling unheeded, if familiar, words at the concierge: "I insist on speaking with the manager," and "Do you realize the damage this sort of action will cause your country?" Even as she was baying into the great void of official Chinese imperturbability, her group's belongings, which had already been packed by hotel staff, were being brought down to the lobby. The rooms were now ready for a group of American newspaper editors, expected within the hour, at three times the rate the Dutch had been paying.

Eventually, the poor woman recognized the defeat that had been staring at her from her first burst of outrage. "Where can we go?" she asked in a voice somewhere between a whimper and a sob.

"Oh, you are very fortunate," the clerk told her with a bright smile. "The China Travel Service has found your group two nights' accommodation in a dormitory of the People's University. The students there took pity on your plight and have given up their rooms so that our foreign friends can have a place to sleep and eat. You are very lucky."

"Am I?" she said meekly and totally broken.

"Yes. It is a senior dormitory, so there will only be four people to a room."

As the woman retreated to her group to tell them the bad news, the Canadian ambassador pushed through the revolving door and headed to the back of the lobby for Number Two Banqueting Room. Up in the monitoring room, the atmosphere became even more tense.

"Here's our little man," said one of the two special PSB officers sitting at a table with ancient earphones on their heads. A hotel staff member tried to ply the officers with large cups of tea, but was waved away. The officers, hoping to hear new details on the incident at San Li Tun compound, had been awaiting Ambassador Messier's arrival at his monthly luncheon with senior members of the diplomatic corps.

The other four guests, ambassadors all, had preceded the Canadian. This informal get-together had been a regular fixture for over five years and was so highly esteemed that each of the founding ambassadors — from Canada, India, Sweden, the Netherlands, and Australia — passed on his seat to his successor. His or *her* successor, actually. For the second appointment in a row, the Swedish ambassador was a woman.

There were two hidden microphones in the room, both in lighting fixtures illuminating portraits of Chairman Mao and Chairman Hua. The microphone shining down on Chairman Mao's placid countenance was Russian-made and still worked. The microphone above Chairman Hua was a Chinese-made copy of the Russian design and wasn't working today. This had undoubtedly contributed somewhat to the tension in the monitoring room.

The two PSB officers, both fluent in English — the working language of this luncheon — could hear well enough with the old Russian mike and had begun to make notes the moment Ambassador Messier started talking:

VOICE ONE: "Gentlemen and dear lady, I must apologize for my lateness. I assume you have all heard there has been some unpleasantness. I nearly cancelled out of our lunch, but decided it was probably important to brief you on what has been happening."

VOICE TWO: "What a terrible business, Pierre. When did you first find out about it?"

VOICE ONE: "My security chief, Colonel Henderson, called me shortly after midnight. We got everyone up that we needed straight away. Very good response. Henderson was able to give us a firsthand description within the hour. He viewed the corpse, which was quite revolting, and he was also able to talk with several people."

VOICE THREE: "Yes, it was one of our people who gave the party. But you and I have already talked about that."

VOICE ONE: "Yes, yes. I'm very grateful for the co-operation, Ambassador. I mentioned it in my second dispatch. Our minister was awakened for this. He wanted as full a briefing as possible to prepare for press inquiries."

VOICE FOUR: "So what's it all about, Pierre? Have you found out anything? Have you come to any conclusions?"

VOICE ONE: "Look here, it's a very bizarre business. The victim is a Canadian national who loathes his own country and doesn't even bother to register at his embassy. He's a postgraduate student allied to Princeton University who should have been at his place of study in Nanking. All right, he's allowed to make visits to Peking. That's not so strange. But who is his host? His host is the Canadian correspondent for a Toronto newspaper who is a United States national. The journalist assured Henderson that the victim had said goodbye to him in the morning and was headed for a visit to Hong Kong. The Chinese foreign minister confided to me this morning that the victim had no exit permit, so clearly he wasn't heading for Hong Kong. Nor does the mystery end here. Throughout the early morning, our staff in Ottawa tried to locate his next of kin. The mother is apparently dead and the father seems simply to have disappeared. The father is as much of a mystery as the son. Next, we tracked down information from Princeton University. What do we find out there? We find out that the victim has followed a scorched-earth policy in his academic career. Princeton denies it has an association with him anymore. The University of Toronto, where he did undergraduate and some graduate work, denies him more times than blessed Peter denied Our Lord. I have a secretary who thinks the victim was a saint and I have not a few officers who think he was in the pay of a foreign secret service. So, dear colleagues, pretend you are me. What on earth do you make of this stew?"

VOICE THREE: "I don't know, Pierre. Did he have a Vietnamese-born girlfriend? Can we work the drug-cartel theory again?" *(Laughter)*

VOICE ONE: "Actually, I do have a bit of a theory. I believe our victim was up to no good, but I don't believe he was involved in criminal activity. My impression of him, and I don't mind saying it is one shared by a number of others who have encountered him, was that he was an arrogant poseur, but not untalented. I believe he was preparing some sort of book on China, a sort of update to the Simon Leys tirades. But obviously that was not why he was killed, and killed in such a brutal, *passionate* way. What I actually think is that we are looking at something very tawdry here. A variation on an old-fashioned lovers' quarrel, but this time with a bit of a homosexual overtone — " *(Many voices, indecipherable)*

VOICE ONE: "This is just a theory, but it makes sense. And the more I think about it, the more sense it makes. Ahhh. Shark fin soup. What a treat!"

VOICE FOUR: "But, Pierre, have you any idea who might have done it?"

Up in the monitoring room, the first PSB officer took off his earphones and placed them on the table with glum satisfaction.

"Let's go," he said to his partner. "Same old hot air. He doesn't know a thing."

5

"There's a weak and dangerous link in our operations," said Director Ng, late on Sunday night at a small meeting with his three most senior subordinates at the Bureau of Cultural Relics. Earlier, the four officials had been to a reception at the People's Art Gallery, where the ministers of culture of China and France jointly opened Peking's first exhibition of foreign paintings since the launch of the Cultural Revolution.

The French, naively supposing the Chinese would like to see some of the great masterpieces from the Louvre, had tried to interest the heirs of the Chinese Revolution with a sampling of spectacular canvases from the Impressionists to the contemporary. Officials from the Ministry of Culture had smiled politely and, equally politely, demurred. They were interested only in pre-Impressionist paintings that did not glorify either aristocratic or middle-class values, but at the same time — vaguely aware of the French Revolution — did not put wrong ideas into the heads of the masses. The curators of the Louvre had scoured their basement and came up with a herd of eighteenth- and nineteenth-century pastoral scenes, many featuring placid farm animals with occasional appearances from oppressed dairymaids and hay-makers.

This deadly rural phantasmagoria had ended up in the People's Art Gallery, and Director Ng, his official presence duly noted, left as quickly as he could. He paid as much attention to the art on the walls as he did to the disgusting-looking off-white sludge – beautifully ripe Brie, dutifully supplied by Air France – on the reception tables.

"There's a weak and dangerous link in our operations and I want it investigated immediately."

Director Ng sat back in his chair with a tight smile on his face and surveyed his colleagues.

"The journalist . . ." one of them said hesitatingly. "The Canadian journalist was on an official trip – "

"*Not* a Canadian journalist," interjected Ng. "A journalist for a Canadian newspaper who just happens to be an American national. And *not* just an American national, but an American journalist who used to work for the Washington *Post* newspaper in Vietnam."

"But he – "

"And it's the *official* trip that I want to know about. How could there be an *official* trip to Kung-hsien? Last year when the Foreign Ministry announced plans to open more of the country to foreigners, we were specifically asked if there were places we wanted put on a prohibited list. Did we not then place Kung-hsien on the top of that list because of the sensitive work we were planning there? Am I wrong?"

For the past two decades, arthritic spondylitis had gradually calcified all the bones in Director Ng's neck. As a result, when he wanted to look directly at his youngest colleague, he had to shift his entire body in the chair. It was done with such evident pain and impatience that the effect was devastating.

"Assistant Director Lu, am I wrong?"

"No, Director, you are right. And I have to say that I do not know the answer at the moment and I must criticize myself for not knowing. I will have the answer soon."

Ng was not about to relent. Not just yet. Lu was only a few months into his important new responsibilities at the bureau and still showed signs of institutional formalism and rigidity, whereas he had been pro-moted for other, more positive traits: an eye glued to the main chance, for example, and an ability to embrace pragmatic mendacity when it was called for. But Lu still needed concrete incentives, and Ng found that fear worked best.

"And I?" continued Ng. "I must criticize myself very severely for

83

putting so much trust in my colleagues. I must criticize myself for appointing people who did not immediately ask themselves obvious questions. Questions like: Why would a foreign journalist want to go to Kung-hsien at this particular time? Why would anyone in the Information Department of the Foreign Ministry even think of forwarding such a request when Kung-hsien had been placed on a prohibited list? Why would *anyone* in the Bureau of Cultural Relics approve such a visit? I ask myself these simple questions, comrades, and the more I ask them, the more uncomfortable I become. These simple questions lead to more complex questions. Such a succession of stupidity and error begins to look like something other than stupidity and error. Something that begins to look rather insidious. And the next thing I know is that I feel I am peering into a conspiracy."

Ng scrunched his neck into his shoulders to try to ease the latest pains, but only succeeded in giving himself a sharp twinge down his entire spine.

"*Fuck your mothers!*" he suddenly shouted, banging his fist on the table. "I want answers by noon tomorrow."

He slumped back into his seat and simply glared at the three. The oldest leaned forward with an earnest look of concern.

"What a sorry spectacle we are presenting to our hardworking director. I have already done some checking and you will be relieved to know that no one from the bureau has done anything wrong. The request for the trip by the journalist to Kung-hsien never came to us because the Information Department never passed it along. Someone in the Information Department wanted the journalist to go there and we'll have the name of that person soon. As well as the paper evidence."

"Paper evidence? What paper evidence?" *What a wonder is Deputy Director Wang*, thought Ng, whose pain receded at the smooth display of competence from his most senior underling.

"My understanding is that Public Security Bureau approval for the trip was based upon an application directly from the Information Department. Naturally, the PSB noted that Kung-hsien was prohibited by our bureau, but since our approval was initialled on the application, they saw no reason to prohibit the journalist."

"So then, who approved this trip on our behalf? I thought you said no one in Cultural Relics was involved?"

"Precisely, Director. No one was. Our approval was forged by someone within the Information Department. This will not in any way be difficult to track down."

The release of tension throughout the room was felt by everyone. Director Ng's smile was no longer tight. Assistant Deputy Lu figured he would see his family again, while the silent third member – the note-taker – rested his pen on his pad with quiet satisfaction.

"Very well then, comrades," said Ng, "we will meet again tomorrow on this matter. At noon, as I said. I would hope by then we would be in a position to recommend an arrest. The situation with the foreign journalist has become more complicated, and I do not want the bureau dragged into affairs that are not our concern. Old Wang, I would like to speak with you on another matter."

When the other two had left, Ng looked warmly, if a little quizzically, at his loyal deputy. Old Wang was the only man in China he could trust absolutely. Well, almost absolutely. After all, they had been through so many ideological perils together. Ng could count all the struggles at any hour of the day or night. Indeed, carefully enumerating how he survived nearly three decades of inner-Party strife often got him to sleep at nights when tranquillizers and painkillers failed to do the job. And for most of this journey, ever since 1957 in fact, Old Wang had been near him, a partner in survival. Now, once again, Director Ng had reason to feel gratitude for a relationship that was as hard as steel and as sharp as a warrior's sword.

"Have you actually located someone at Information whom we can safely blame?" asked Director Ng after the younger subordinates had left his office.

"Counter-productive and not necessary," said Deputy Director Wang. "Our new young assistant, Lu, is now more than sufficiently inspired. He will supply us with a suitable name by noon and we'll have a confession by the next morning. This is not such a complicated matter."

"No problems from the PSB?"

"Director, please!"

"My apologies, Deputy. Things have been happening more quickly than we are used to and I like to double-check."

"By the way, your Englishman's cheque has been cashed without a problem, and the money is in one of our foreign-currency accounts."

"Splendid. And what a nice consignment we will have to offer him to start our new relationship."

"Is everything from the tomb site going to him?"

"No. There's something of a problem. In addition to all the expected stuff, there is a set of fine blue and white porcelain bowls and vases that we shall have to retain for some time."

"Retain?"

"Because, Deputy, no one was supposed to be able to make porcelain at this high a technological level for at least another three centuries. The archaeological workers are in a frenzy about the discovery. I don't understand all the details, but it has always been accepted that the technology to keep kilns at a sufficiently high temperature to manufacture porcelain was not developed until at least the early Ming, and the blue colouring material is imported and wasn't supposed to be available till later either."

"Is this really a problem?"

"Not eventually, but immediately it certainly is. As you know, our bureau has pledged itself to raise thirty million American dollars by the middle of next year. There's no way we can do this with random sales from selected harvesting of the museums. The Sung site is a gift from heaven, one which we can exploit immediately and almost indefinitely. But at the moment, we don't need any anomalies or controversies. We don't need a lot of excitement inside or outside the country about historical breakthroughs. We don't need a lot of our archaeologists trying to figure out how the technology was developed so much earlier than we supposed. We especially don't need outside buyers re-examining traditional prices. And we certainly don't want a lot of Western archaeologists clamouring to get over here to make their own investigations. What we need are stable markets, brisk sales, and quicker returns. Without them, we have no hope of achieving our goals. Everything would have to be put on hold."

"Yes, yes, I see the point. These Sung discoveries, while potentially very lucrative, have limited potential. They may be the only examples of Sung blue we will ever find. No matter what prices they fetch, they are bound to bring down the price of Ming blue."

"Exactly, Deputy. Initially, they would bring the price down catastrophically."

"And since we have an unlimited supply of Ming blue, we would be undermining our own enterprise and failing in our duty."

"Exactly, and that being the case, how sure are we of keeping this secret?"

"Every member of our team at the site can be trusted. You know that, Director."

"I'm sure, I'm sure. Even so, I'd like some changes. I want the two archaeologists transferred to other projects. My sense from our visit there is that they are too excited by their find. I don't think they can help themselves and their usefulness in the immediate future is questionable."

"They won't be easy to reassign, Director."

"Oh yes, they will. Why don't you avail yourself of a little of our English friend's money and send them on a three- or four-month study mission abroad? Longer if you think necessary. They'll start salivating. And double-check to make sure there aren't any local weak links."

"Of course, of course. Now what will happen to the inconvenient discoveries?"

"We shall take them into special custody and protect them with our lives! They are only inconvenient today. Tomorrow, who knows? They may be able to pay for a nuclear reactor. There are special buyers out there. I'm sure we can count on Mr. Finch-Noyes to identify them. The trick will be to keep them away from museums. Deputy, we are on the threshold of a great new age for our old country. We shall not be found wanting in our duty."

Twenty-seven city blocks away, Hao Teng-kwa, a junior processing clerk at the Information Department of the Foreign Ministry, who had started his job barely seven months earlier, slept soundly at his married brother's apartment in the overcrowded southwest quarter of Peking. He did not know that it would be the last peaceful sleep he would have for several years. How could he know? His useful role as scapegoat wouldn't be ascertained until 9:30 a.m. the next day.

~

She was alone again for the second night in the foreign woman's apartment. Well, not exactly alone. Alison was sleeping in the bedroom, and Sui-san had tried to sleep on the sofa in the living room, but if her eyes had ever closed, she had not been aware of it. In any event, she was awake now and it was about 4 a.m. At her request, a light had been left on beside the sofa. She had not wanted to be in the dark anymore. Her world had closed in all around her, and Sui-san felt enshrouded within her own coffin. At least with the light on, she could still breathe – but only barely.

What was Gordon thinking? How could he have let this happen? Now there is no one to turn to. Can't go back. Can't go forward. Can't stand still. Can't deal with more than the minute ahead. But the minutes add up and it will be morning again. Then what? I would rather be dead than have this feeling inside me, this feeling of being completely alone, of being utterly unprotected. Of being dead without release. I should be dead, but how do I die? How do I die quickly with no pain?

In the kitchen to check out Alison's supply of knives, she spotted the photograph in the third drawer. It was sufficiently arresting to terminate the search for knives. How quickly the thought of suicide fades in those whose agenda turns out to be uncompleted. The picture was of Gordon, mugging for the camera. She thought it was an ugly picture to take, an ugly picture to keep: not formal, not proper, not composed, not fitting. She looked at his face closely and tried to reason out why he was making such a grimace, why Alison would want to keep such an ugly picture, and then – all at once – she understood completely and she could feel the waves of fear returning to her belly.

It wasn't jealousy. Sui-san was too deeply in trouble at this moment to succumb to anything as extravagant as jealousy. The fear arose from yet another assault on the fragile veneer of her collapsing world. Fate had planted impetuosity and determination in her character, and it had also conspired to use these traits to lead her into more danger than she had ever before conceived possible, more danger than even she and her family had faced during the Cultural Revolution, when her father was publicly humiliated, labelled "a stinking intellectual," and unceremoniously removed from his agricultural research position.

"It's true, I loved him. But don't worry, he didn't really love me. I was his friend in Peking. That's all."

Alison held back at the entrance to the kitchen, and although she spoke softly and with as much compassion as she could summon at that hour of the morning, Sui-san was momentarily terrified. The photograph of Gordon fell out of her hand and floated to the floor.

"So sorry," said Sui-san, bending down to pick it up.

Alison came over quickly. "You don't have to say sorry for anything. We just have to find a solution to keep you safe, and if I know our friend Halpert, he'll find some way. I can't sleep either. How about some coffee or tea?"

"I think Gordon was your very good friend, wasn't he?" asked Sui-san. It wasn't said with any slyness. Even though she knew the answer, she needed confirmation, to explore a little the new reality she had just stumbled across.

"It's just what I said. I loved him, but he didn't love me. I think maybe he loved you."

"Sui-san not understand. Gordon was your very good friend, but Gordon isn't loving you. How can this be? It is a contradiction."

"It isn't a contradiction. It's a fact. And now he's dead and both of us have to deal with that. What about some coffee or tea?"

Sui-san made a sort of nod with her head. It could have meant yes or no. Alison took it for yes because she was damn well going to have some coffee herself. In fact, Sui-san hadn't understood and her nod was simply meant to show that she was aware something was being said that required a response. What she had just decided was that, come what may, she would survive. At the worst moment during the public denunciation of her father, when people took turns to spit in his face and some of her own friends felt obliged to slap her to remove the taint of previous association, she had made a similar resolution. And she did survive. She would do so again. The decision gave her her first moment of peace in forty-eight hours, and suddenly she felt very tired. She walked silently back into the living room and, before the water had come to a boil, was sound asleep on the sofa. Alone in the kitchen, Alison felt something of the spirit of bitter loneliness and despair that had been roiling in Sui-san's stomach.

The first rays of dawn slid through her kitchen window, but Alison did not take too much notice. She thought instead about the small and enticing mole on Gordon Wrye's left shoulder blade. She also thought she couldn't live another day in China. This was not a contradiction either.

∾

Ambassador Messier also wakened early, shortly after 4:30 a.m. After lying in bed for about ten minutes, he got up and headed for the bathroom, closing the door as quietly as he could.

Feeling low when he dropped off to sleep a few hours before, he awakened to discover that his depression had transmuted into severe irritation. Irritation at his security officer, Colonel Henderson. Henderson had become too involved in the Wrye affair. Henderson was sounding off too much. Henderson was making a fetish of his murder-site inspection. Henderson was interviewing too many people. Henderson had sent too many Telexes back to Ottawa. Henderson was spouting too many theories. Henderson was . . . Henderson was becoming a damn nuisance. At one point Henderson had very nearly contradicted the ambassador in front of his own senior staff on a small point about Wrye's background. Messier had shot him a severe glance, but to little effect. *Nothing*, he thought, *penetrates that thick, robotic cranium, bloated by know-it-all self-esteem.*

In the early morning, minds are often translucently clear and resolve is at its highest point. Certainly Ambassador Messier, a can-do ambassador if there ever was one, now found the cutting edge of his affronted countenance as sharp as his Gillette-style, Chinese-made razor. While shaving in the bathroom, he decided to reassign Henderson to some other immediate task. Any task would do. By the time he was splashing aftershave lotion on his face, he had the preliminary strategy all worked out. Already scheduled to have his second meeting with the Chinese foreign minister in as many days, he would use this ace twice. It was not only important that his peers at other embassies understand the high level he was operating on, it was even more important for his staff to see that the person in charge was actually the person who was supposed to be in charge – not some cabbage-faced Anglo military upstart.

He also realized that it would probably fall to him to make the decision about the disposition of Gordon Wrye's corpse. This did not perturb him at all. From the communications between Ottawa and his embassy, he knew no one had been found who had a close family claim to the body. Unless a relative turned up in the next few days, the body belonged to the government of Canada, and Ambassador Messier intended to recommend that Gordon Wrye be consigned to Peking's crematorium. Why, he might even get to preside over a nice little memorial service at the embassy. What a very pleasant thought.

Pulling on his claret-coloured boxer shorts, he decided to call a meeting of his full senior staff for 4 p.m. to report on the latest developments, give a guarded account of his meeting with the Chinese foreign minister, and discuss what was appropriate for Ottawa to know. *Where the hell are my sock garters?* Colonel Henderson would be exempted from this meeting because he was going to have his work cut out for him with his new assignment – whatever it might be. Maybe a two-week observer's role with the People's Liberation Army while it was on manoeuvres in the Gobi Desert. Something like that would do very well. *A silk shirt, I think, but I won't wear a bow tie today. Don't want to be too conspicuous.*

Right now, he was personally going to check out the murder site. He needed some graphic details to flesh out his tale of "The Life and Death of Gordon Wrye," both for official Telexes to Ottawa and also for the dinner tables where he knew he was always expected to shine. This was a *Canadian* story and he was the *Canadian* ambassador and a little stroll over to the *Canadian* journalist's garage behind Number Three Building would not in any way be out of order. *But I'll wear a sports jacket*, he thought. *Nothing too formal. And my old trench coat.*

"Darling, where on earth are you going at this hour of the morning? It's not even five o'clock."

Madame Messier had spotted him fussing over his sleuth's wardrobe a few minutes earlier, but was resisting the effort to ask him what he was up to. He had been so agitated the last two days that she nearly said nothing, having resolved to disappear from his life until he returned to earth. In the end, though, curiosity overwhelmed her.

When he was telling a fib, Ambassador Messier was at his most unctuous, and the lugubrious vocal inflections he had picked up from his time at the London School of Economics in the early fifties came rushing to the fore.

"Now my dearest, put your sweet head back on the pillow. I have a lot to do today and want to get an early start. Goodness, you look lovely. I was trying very hard not to disturb you, so back to sleep you go. I'll see you when I see you. *Tirrah*, my love."

He blew her a kiss and off he went into Peking's smoggy dawn: more redoubtable than Miss Marple, cooler than Sam Spade, slyer than Smiley, more subtle than Inspector Dalgleish, but perhaps not quite as humble as Father Brown.

∽

7/8patsun 1-23shit 23-25/990?? 17shds wh/v cbt(exc) fl.dor/nomeld 6shdsfit 2mm'wall!!!!Kln??

Halpert read it again and again, but the more he read the more incomprehensible Wrye's note became. He had awakened shortly after 5 a.m., but did not want to set off for Sun-dappled Park for another hour. He would go early for his meeting with Kwai Ta-ping, but not conspicuously early. By six, the park would be buzzing, and if he dressed as he usually did for these meetings in the traditional summer gear of the masses (blue cotton pants, white short-sleeved shirt, plastic sandals, sunglasses, worker's cap), hardly anyone would give him a second glance, despite his height. It was more likely, he always reasoned, that he would be taken as a member of one of the Caucasian national minorities from the border area.

He whiled away the minutes after dressing and making some coffee by once again scouring Gordon Wrye's notebook, looking for any clue that might hint at a reason for his brutal murder. It was the fifth search. The notebook, a cheap scribbler, was the only thing out of the ordinary in Gordon's knapsack, which also contained his shaving bag, a couple of T-shirts, and a pair of black underpants.

Only seven or eight pages of the notebook had been filled. Apart from a few lists of things to do or buy in Nanking, the only entries were cryptic comments from what Halpert guessed was some sort of archaeological sortie early last July or August depending on how Gordon put his days and months. Other than "shit" meant shit, "*7/8*" was the only thing he had figured out. The reason he had got stuck at this particular juncture in the notebook was the exclamation marks. Four punctuation marks and suddenly billions of atoms reassembled in Halpert's mind. He could sense Gordon's exuberance, hear his outrageous laughter, see his somewhat bandy-legged gait as he strode ahead – always ahead – in search of some new adventure, smell his strong body odour, shrink from his angry, glaring eyes protesting at some iniquity or other.

A few minutes into this mournful reverie, after he had put the notebook down and thought vaguely of checking the time, something finally twigged. *990??* He fetched his copy of *Nagel's Guide to China*, the quickest and easiest reference crib he could think of. He opened the book and riffled backwards through the pages to the heading DYNAS-TIES. *There!*

> Shang Dynasty 1766–1111 BC; Chou Dynasty 1111–221 BC; Ch'in Dynasty 221–206 BC; Han Dynasty 206 BC–AD 221; Northern and Southern Dynasties AD 219–580; Sui Dynasty AD 581–618; T'ang Dynasty AD 618–906; Five Dynasties AD 907–960; Sung Dynasty AD 960–1279 . . .

It was only because he had read a little on the Sung dynasty, in preparation for his foreshortened trip to Kung-hsien, that 990 struck him as being a possible date. He still hadn't a clue what the note specifically meant, but now he remembered how keen Gordon was for him to go to the Sung site – insistent really – and the winking excuse he had made for not accompanying him: he had to show his new girlfriend a good time in Peking. If he had come, Sui-san would still be in trouble, but Gordon might be alive. Halpert winced at the horrendous consequence of a minor decision.

Abruptly, he realized he had lost all track of time and scrambled to find his watch. It was 6:20 a.m. Time to get going. He headed down to the ground-floor bicycle lock-up at the back of his entrance hall in Number Three Building, where he tried the door and found it unlocked, as usual. As he retrieved his bike, he absentmindedly glanced out the window overlooking the rear garage alleyway.

What the hell?

He rested the bike against the wall and took a closer look. In front of his own garage, where Gordon's body had been found and where the Chinese authorities had placed three portable metal fences like the ones used for crowd control at Chairman Mao's mausoleum in Tiananmen Square, he saw a man down on his hands and knees on the pavement, his wide flanks directly facing Halpert's window.

Oh my God, thought Halpert, as the man turned his head slightly and he recognized the portly figure of the Canadian ambassador. *He's even brought a magnifying glass.*

∾

The sentry didn't bother to look up when Halpert wheeled past him at the entrance to the compound. Within a few seconds, he was a block away and surrounded by a stream of Chinese cyclists who, even at that early hour, were either heading or returning from work. *So far, so good*, he thought.

Inside the command post, however, his departure was duly noted by the sentry, who immediately telephoned his superior with the information. Less than three minutes later, a Public Security Bureau traffic guard in a covered kiosk in the centre of the intersection of Lei Feng Street and Liberation Avenue was alerted by telephone to be on the lookout for a foreigner on a bike pretending to be a Chinese. "You'll spot him easily," he was told. "He stands out like a pagoda in a paddy field."

In this manner, Halpert was tracked right to the entrance of Sun-dappled Park, four miles from Number Three Building. Inside the park, there was no more need for telephones. He could be easily observed by any of the dozens of PSB "volunteers" stationed throughout the park, their job simply to be part of the passing scene and take note of anything untoward.

Halpert had discovered Sun-dappled Park early in his posting, before he had met Gordon, when he and his wife had been out exploring the city on their bicycles. It was the first time they had ever seen Chinese people relax or display themselves with any degree of spirited abandon. There were amateur painters lurking on stools in a cool grove of pine trees, quietly pleased with their imitation Impressionism. Old men sat on benches airing songbirds housed in intricately wrought palaces of bamboo, while their grandsons displayed chirping crickets in tiny cages fashioned from the stalks of sweet sorghum grass. Martial arts exercises, if they were good, always attracted a crowd of teenage admirers. And on that first visit, on the crest of a small hill, a blissfully happy tenor with his back to the risen sun had gloriously transformed "O solo mio" into evidence of counter-revolutionary tendencies.

Halpert came to see that among both the informers and the informed-upon, Sun-dappled Park appeared to offer a few hours of peace and calm at the beginning of every day. He eventually realized, thanks to Kwai Ta-ping, that this was a fantasy. The park was also a favoured place for the PSB to compromise dissidents. Nevertheless, even knowing the risks looming within, a day could be constructed and a life endured.

Halpert dropped off his bike at the lock-up and strolled to the foot of the tenor's hill. It was here that he usually met Kwai, but it was now nearly 7:30 a.m. and his closest link to the fragile democracy movement was nowhere in sight. He knew he had told Kwai he wouldn't be back that day from his trip, but he also knew Kwai always went to the park if he could, regardless of Halpert's schedule. He decided to keep walking, for fear of attracting attention by standing aimlessly still. He could set out in various directions and each time return to the same spot at fifteen-minute intervals.

Halpert was a bit smug about his association with Kwai, who was one of the few important Chinese contacts he had made without Gordon Wrye's help. He was briefly disconcerted to discover, months after their first meeting, that Kwai had sought him out after hearing about him from a mutual Chinese friend of Kwai's and Gordon's. But that inconvenient memory faded from thought soon enough.

Kwai's story, or at least as much of it as he told Halpert, was in several ways typical of many Chinese of his generation, the first post-Liberation generation. He had been born in 1947 into the family of middle-ranking Communist Party cadres. A ferocious Red Guard and a member of the dreaded Earth Faction at the beginning of the Cultural Revolution, he travelled freely all over the country on the Chinese railway system during parts of 1967 and 1968. It was during this exhilarating period of exploration and discovery that he experienced his initial doubts about Chairman Mao's vision.

Heartbroken by the poverty he saw everywhere and the regime's hypocrisy and brutality, he fell into open apostasy and was dispatched to the Northeast for his first dose of re-education. When he was released in 1971, after yet another round of inner-Party purges, he still believed that a reformed Communist government might yet redeem China. But by the time of his rearrest in 1975, a year before Chairman Mao died, he had become so disillusioned with the Communist Party that he resolved, somehow, to bring it down, single-handedly if necessary.

Traditionally, anyone in China who chose to oppose an emperor – of whatever dynasty or ideology – sought powerful allies. There wasn't any point to opposition if you had to stand alone, but allied to an influential faction, you could ride all the way to power. There were very few exceptions to this rule in all the long history of China. Within the first months of their friendship, Halpert realized that Kwai Ta-ping was an unusual rebel because he had the instincts of a martyr.

A careful martyr. Kwai had good contacts in the People's Academy of Social Sciences and even a few in the People's Liberation Army. He was able to raise money, indirectly, from his few shadowy supporters for his crudely printed but powerfully written unofficial publication, *Tomorrow*, sold (more or less) bimonthly. There was nothing he did unknowingly, and yet Halpert came to believe that Kwai's passion to rescue China meant that he was prepared to give up his life.

Soon after he was released from prison for the second time in 1977,

Kwai grasped the connection between what was written in foreign newspapers about China and what happened at the top. Looking to take up his cause again, he found it convenient to ally himself with the agitators hustling the masses to support the rehabilitation of Teng Hsiaoping. That's when he got hold of official documents incriminating Mao's last security chief, who still clung to office, printed them in his little journal, and while everyone waited for Kwai's third arrest for such foolish temerity, he had the unalloyed pleasure of being the public means by which the monster was felled.

Since then, he had kept his profile down, especially during the Sino–Vietnamese border war. He was enough of a tactician to know that the worst possible time to take his kind of stand was during a national crisis. He did not fancy bucking Chinese patriotism. Even so, he had been picked up at one point, but after an unpleasant three days of questioning and close scrutiny, he was released – following a perfunctory act of self-criticism – on the cognizance of a junior political officer at the People's Academy of Social Sciences, who pledged to help Kwai mend his ways. He was not entirely grateful to his brave academy saviour because he felt obliged to protect him from the contamination of such exposed proximity. That was the main reason he made the calculated decision to retreat from the front ranks for a while.

Halpert knew all this directly from Kwai, which was why his strategy to enlist the Chinese dissident's help on behalf of Sui-san was so risky. Kwai was lying low for the moment, and Sui-san's need was immediate. There was an even bigger flaw in Halpert's plan. If Kwai didn't show up soon at Sun-dappled Park, Halpert didn't know how to find him. The border war with Vietnam had abruptly terminated the democracy rallies where they had sometimes met. There were no more open sales of unofficial publications and no more Gordon Wrye to solve all his problems with a telephone call here or a little impromptu visit there. By eight, Halpert was in despair as the last of the musicians left for work and even the old men started to take their songbirds home.

Slowly he walked towards the park's entrance and passed through the gates. He didn't have a plan left and he was starting to panic. At the lock-up he fumbled in his pockets for the wooden token to give back to the bicycle attendant, a fat granny whose tiny feet exposed the binding they had been subjected to in her youth. She took the token with a low grunt, hardly looking up at him, but when he lingered in front of her, searching his pocket for a non-existent two-cent piece to pay for her guardianship, she waved her hand briskly.

"No, no, no," she insisted with presumed familiarity. "Foreign friends don't have to pay."

The peasant shirt, the sunglasses, the worker's cap, the blue cotton pants, the plastic sandals – none of this had fooled anyone. With the stripping away of his last conceit and the full realization that he was as obvious a stranger in China on his last week as he was on the first, Halpert's final emotional defences were routed. Not only had he no plan, he was also a fool. In utter despondency, he set off for home. Inside the park administration building, the duty security officer had already informed the PSB that the Human Pagoda was out and about on the streets again.

Halpert was swept slowly along the wide bicycle lane of the vast Stalinist avenue by the company of thousands of cyclists. When they pedalled, he pedalled. When they stopped, he stopped. When they started up again, he started up again. At the first large intersection, he stared dully at the traffic guard in the kiosk without registering that the guard was talking on a telephone, without even registering that there were telephones in the traffic kiosks. He didn't know that before and he wasn't capable of noticing it now.

The lights changed and the masses started pedalling, so Halpert started pedalling. When he got across the intersection and had been riding for about a minute, he heard a seemingly disembodied voice saying his name. "Hai Pei-teh, Hai Pei-teh, Hai Pei-teh." The name had been dreamed up by someone in the Information Department and, loosely translated, meant "The Unpredictable Sea." In time, the Information Department officials had learned his nature was the exact opposite of his Chinese name and had smiled at the irony of their early misconception.

"Hai Pei-teh. Hello, hello."

Am I dreaming?

Still pedalling slowly, he looked to his right. The cyclist immediately beside him turned his head and smiled. It was Kwai Ta-ping! Halpert's heart soared.

"Where were you?" Halpert spluttered in Chinese. "I waited and waited."

"And I had to wait through all your waiting because it was too dangerous to talk to you in the park."

Halpert's mind was now operating in top gear. First to fifth in four seconds. He realized Kwai had found a perfect way to meet him in a time of trouble. He could see ahead that they had a good five or six minutes before the next traffic stop. He also knew he had to be succinct and careful with his imperfect spoken Mandarin if Kwai was going to understand and offer help.

"I have some bad news," Halpert said.

"I know about it. I'm sorry for your friend. Many of my friends knew him and feel very sorry. He was a good friend of the Chinese people. Do you know why he had to die?"

"No idea. But, Kwai, listen carefully. I need your help and we don't have much time to discuss it."

"What help?"

"There's a girl. Chinese girl. She was Gordon Wrye's good friend. She's in big trouble. If she goes back to Nanking, she will be arrested. If she stays in Peking, she will be arrested. Now she is in the apartment of a Canadian, but soon she will have to leave. Do you have any contacts to help her get to Hong Kong, or anywhere out of the country? I can give you any money that will be needed."

"This is very big trouble, Hai Pei-teh. We don't know this girl. Maybe she is a PSB spy."

"No, no. She's a good girl. Her family had a very hard time. You know Gordon was too smart to fall in love with a spy."

"I don't know Gordon, Hai Pei-teh. You do. I only know about Gordon. Let me think for a moment."

They cycled on, and at one point Kwai drifted slowly back in the flow. For a panicky moment, Halpert thought he had been deserted. But Kwai Ta-ping, though susceptible to a certain amount of pragmatism, was neither a coward nor a fool. What Halpert was asking of him was extremely dangerous. Yet he knew exactly what to do, and his hesitation – including the slowing of his bicycle – was only an indication of all the possible consequences he had to consider. As the next traffic intersection hove into view, he turned to Halpert with a face full of concern and plots.

"Hai Pei-teh, can you get a lot of money very quickly?"

"Yes, I think so. Of course I can. How much and how quickly?"

"Maybe two or three thousand Chinese dollars and maybe one thousand American dollars."

"Oh yes, I can get that. I can get it this morning."

"Okay. Get that money and give it to the Chinese girl and bring her to the New China Bookstore on Wangfuching Street. Do you know the store? Just north of the Peking Hotel?"

"I know it, I know it. What time and why that place?"

They had reached the intersection and the conversation ceased. All of Halpert's rusty sixth sense was being deployed now, and he noted with alarm that the dumb traffic guard in the kiosk was on the telephone. *Am I being paranoid? Are they following my every move?* Kwai Ta-ping didn't have to fuss about such things. For the Chinese in Communist China, there is no call for paranoia. The conspiracy against the people is taken for granted.

"Around three o'clock. It's a good place. This afternoon the store is making available new books of foreign literature in Chinese translation. Hundreds of people will be there and it will be crazy, you'll see. You just have to bring her there safely. Let her carry the money in her bag, and when you see me, don't even say goodbye to her. Just go back home."

"How am I going to find her later? How will I know where to go and help her?"

"I will find a way. You know the English student Joan, don't you? Her Chinese boyfriend knew your dead friend. He's my friend."

"Yes, yes. I know who you mean. Joan. She's at the Peking Foreign Languages Institute."

"Maybe I will use her. Maybe not. I will find a way. So goodbye, Hai Pei-teh. I will see you at the bookstore, but we won't talk. The Chinese people will always respect you. You are our good friend. Goodbye, goodbye."

Halpert was confused. They were still cruising along on their bikes, at least a mile from San Li Tun and a couple of minutes from the next intersection. But when he looked around again to his right in order to thank Kwai Ta-ping, the Pimpernel was gone. By slowing his pedalling, he had allowed himself to drift inconspicuously backwards and become anonymously engulfed in the endless, relentless flow.

6

Halpert pedalled like a madman. Suddenly, the enveloping comfort of the masses of bicycles around him was a damn nuisance, and he tried to transform the bell on the Flying Pigeon into an ambulance siren. No one paid it any regard, and so his progress for the final half-mile to Alison's apartment was no faster for all his frantic gesturing. Only his impatience had speeded up.

Sui-san was still asleep on the sofa when he banged on the door, but Alison – who had never returned to bed – opened it quickly. There was an anxious look on her face.

"It's going to be okay," Halpert blurted out as soon as he was inside. "I'll come back here for her at two this afternoon. You should go to work and do everything normally. Maybe come back home for lunch to keep her calm. I've found a good solution, and I'll explain it to her when I pick her up. She better have a few clothes, Alison."

"Okay, okay. Just tell me one thing. Is it going to be very dangerous?"

"Everything will be fine. I've found a good solution. I've really got to go now. This is going to be a busy day."

He gave her a quick peck on the side of her cheek – so quick she thought he was going to take a bite out of her. And then he was off.

Pedalling the last few blocks home, he started making his mental lists again. *Bank of China. Phone Toronto. Phone the bureau successor in Hong*

Kong. Get the housekeeper started on packing all the ex's clothes. Bank of China . . . already know that . . .

By the time he burst through his front door, he was in an even greater dither than he had been at Alison's, and his astonished staff, who were all in the kitchen drinking tea and gossiping, were momentarily caught off guard. And this despite the careful prepping they had all received the night before from two officers of the Diplomatic Service Bureau.

Mrs. Liu, the housekeeper, darted off like a mouse to the laundry room. Old Chen, the cook, went back to the sink to clean the weekend dishes, piled haphazardly on the side counter. Young Hao, the interpreter and the most nervous of the quartet, made a beeline for the office to translate the day's headlines from *The People's Daily*. Only the self-confident driver, Old Hu, displayed an undeniable sang-froid. But then he had good reason: he was the political leader of this little unit and the one most determined to find out what he could, even if he didn't know exactly what he was looking for.

"Old Hu," said Halpert as he stuck his head into the kitchen for the second time in under a minute. "We're going to the Bank of China straight away. I'm just getting my papers and I'll meet you downstairs at the car."

"You come?" asked Old Hu, his sang-froid collapsing in an instant. This was unusual. Halpert never went to the Bank of China. Old Hu always went for him. Old Hu got the bureau cash every week and did all the other small business required of him without benefit of the boss's intrusive nose over his shoulder. Everyone knew there were long line-ups at the Bank of China and foreigners hired people like Old Hu to stand in them. Foreigners themselves *never* came. So this was something new, something to take note of, something to report, something to think about, something to cause irritation.

The bureau telephone rang, but Halpert ignored it, knowing Young Hao would take a message. As he was harrying his slow-moving driver out of the premises, the fast-moving interpreter came down the hallway from the office to announce grandly that "Toronto was calling."

"Tell them I'm out," said Halpert.

"I've already told them you were here, and they say it is a matter of great urgency."

"Damn it, Hao, can't you do anything right?" Halpert never barked at his staff. This outburst was new, too. Young Hao rolled his eyes in the direction of Old Hu as Halpert dashed down to his office to pick up the phone.

"Hello," he shouted into the antiquated receiver.

"Jamie, it's Jim Worrell, we've been very worried about you. Why haven't you been answering your phones? We have a lot of important things to discuss and you – "

Halpert decided he couldn't deal with this. In difficult telephone conversations between Toronto and Peking, it sometimes happened that connections were "broken" for no reason. This was going to be one of those times.

"Hello, Jim. Hello, hello," Halpert shouted into the middle of the monologue coming through from the other end. "I can't hear you. Jim, are you there? Hello, hello, hello – "

Halpert hung up the phone even as his editor-in-chief was protesting that he could hear Halpert "just fine." It would take over a half-hour to get a trunk call between Toronto and Peking reconnected and by then he would be long gone.

"Fucking Toronto," muttered Halpert. He was really irritated now. Old Hu was irritated too because his outings to the Bank of China allowed him to use the bureau car to shop at his favourite new food market in the southern district, thereby saving him and his wife endless bicycle rides, and also allowing him to buy in some volume. Besides, the line-ups at the Bank of China were not, in fact, quite so bad as Old Hu liked his employer to think. Not nearly so bad. A trip to the Bank of China could be made to last most of the morning and now Halpert would discover that it took only ten or fifteen minutes. *It's time for this foreigner to go home*, thought Old Hu as he shuffled down the stairway.

Halpert, who had run down the stairs two at a time, was on Hu's back before he had even reached the front door.

"Hurry, Hu," he said as he almost pushed him out the door. "I don't have any time to waste."

∾

It was only the second time Halpert had been inside the Bank of China. Presiding over the southwest corner of Tiananmen Square, the early 1920s mock-Gothic structure looked solid and imposing, like a bank should look. Inside, the high vaulted ceiling of the main hall and old marble floors made it feel like a bank should feel – like the big bank building he remembered in his youth in Boston on one of the rare outings with his grandfather.

There were a few pertinent differences, however, between the Bank of China in 1979 and the Chase Manhattan Bank in 1959. In the waiting area of the Bank of China, a large wall rack contained a multitude of Little Red Books in which Chairman Mao's brilliant, truncated *pensées* were made available in forty-eight languages. Another difference was aural: an incessant clicking that Halpert at first mistook for some sort of endless game of mahjong until he realized it was the sound of dozens of clerks fingering their abacuses.

Abacuses in 1979?

Yes, yes. You need an abacus to check out the results provided on the Japanese calculator. An abacus never lies. Calculators – well, it's best to double-check – especially ones made in Japan.

Old Hu's worst fears turned into reality. There were precisely four customers in the bank, but Halpert wasn't making any connection between the time Hu had always taken to do the bureau's banking and this desultory scene. He was a man on a hurried mission, and Hu could scarcely keep up with him.

They went to the nearest wicket, where Halpert told the clerk he was closing his two accounts. Most of the foreign funds he wanted to transfer back to his Canadian bank, but he would take two thousand Chinese dollars in cash, as well as a thousand in American currency.

The clerk looked up at Halpert for the first time from under a worn visor and shook his head. "Chinese money, no problem. American money, problem," he said in Voice of America English.

"Just give it to me, please," said Halpert. He was impatient now. This was a bank. It had his money. He wanted his money. *Do it!*

The clerk told Halpert that no one inside China was allowed to receive foreign currency from any branch of the Bank of China. This was the law and every foreigner entering China was told this. Moreover, the clerk added, Halpert would have made a declaration the last time he entered China about how much foreign currency he had in his personal possession, and he better make sure he had precisely the same amount when he left or else be able to show a receipt from the Bank of China proving the sum had been deposited.

Halpert groaned and insisted on speaking to the manager. He didn't stop to think that making such a fuss would draw undue attention to him on the one day he needed no attention drawn. He wanted his money and he wanted it now.

Reluctantly, the clerk went searching for a superior. Driver Hu was quite pleased with all this ruckus. He knew the rules even if Halpert didn't, and had the bureau business been carried out in the normal way, he could have spared Halpert the loss of the face. Ten minutes later, the clerk was back, at the elbow of a senior bank official.

To both the clerk's and Driver Hu's amazement, the official apologized to Halpert for the delay and handled over ten fairly crisp American hundred-dollar bills. In all his time at the Bank of China, the clerk had never seen such a flaunting of the rules, but his superior seemed to know who Halpert was and wasn't interested in the protests of his clerk, who nevertheless made a mental note of everything. For future use.

"That's more like it," said Halpert, who folded the bills – Chinese and American – into one fat wad and stuffed it into his right jacket pocket.

"Now, Old Hu, let's get back home. I still have lots to do."

∽

Halpert knew something was amiss the moment he entered the apartment. It was the suitcases. They were a dead give-away. And Mrs. Liu, the housekeeper, was fluttering about like a brood hen.

"Hi, Jim," said a total Caucasian stranger, who walked out of the living room as Halpert was closing the door. No one ever called him Jim. He hated the name Jim. *Who is this jerk?*

"It's Brian Patcheu. How the hell are you?"

Nothing.

"Brian Patcheu," he said again with a crooked smile. "Of the *Observer. The Toronto Observer.* You know, *your* newspaper. I'm the successor. Boy, have you been going through a rough time, I guess."

What the hell is he doing here?

"What the hell are you doing here?" demanded Halpert. "You weren't supposed to be coming till Friday. This is totally unacceptable. I can't do anything with you right now. I'm far too busy. Why didn't you phone from Hong Kong if you wanted to come early? I would have told you to stay put, as planned."

"Whoa, Jim! We've been trying to reach you by phone for two days, but you don't answer. Worrell told me to get up as fast as I could, and you are supposed to get out of here as fast as you can. For your own safety. I was told to tell you to go to Hong Kong tomorrow if possible and I'll arrange all the packing up. And don't worry about the transition. I'll figure out how to run the bureau. Jim, are you okay?"

"Will you stop calling me Jim. Call me James if you want. There's no one by the name of Jim here."

"Okay, okay. Man, are you in a bad way or what. Look, I'm here to help. You tell me what you want me to do and I'll do it. I've already told the interpreter to start arranging the travel applications, and the Information Department doesn't see any reason why everything can't be ready by noon tomorrow – "

"The fuck you have." Halpert could not remember ever being so angry. Had he been a less pacific soul, he would have punched Patcheu's over-eager face. The best alternative he could come up with was withering contempt.

"Look. I'm in the middle of something very important and I don't want you interfering. If you stay out of my sight till the late afternoon, it'll be safer for both of us. You can hang out with your friend the interpreter, and I'll get back to you later. Right now just buzz out of my life."

"Jim, I know you are under a lot of stress. I'm here to help. I'll just keep working on these travel plans for you. Don't give me a second thought. You do what you have to do. Oh, you might want to give these a gander. You're in the news."

He handed over some newspaper clippings that Halpert was about to scrunch up and throw back in his successor's face when he noticed the first headline: "MURDER IN PEKING: Mysterious death leaves diplomats in turmoil."

Shit, thought Halpert as he went into the living room to peruse the clippings. The first was from *The International Herald Tribune*.

"That's from the *Trib*," said Patcheu helpfully. "It's only four 'graphs, but it was above the fold on the front page. Wait till you read the account in *The South China Mail and Empire*."

Halpert tried to ignore him as he quickly scanned the first short article.

> PEKING (NYT) – The small, tightly knit foreign community here was rocked late Saturday night by the brutal murder of a 27-year-old Canadian archaeological student whose head had been bludgeoned beyond immediate recognition.
>
> Yesterday, Canadian diplomats confirmed that the murdered man had been identified as Gordon Alexander Wrye, a London, Ontario-born post-doctoral researcher accredited to the University of Nanking.
>
> His body was discovered inside a northern Peking diplomatic compound and diplomats said there was no known or apparent reason for the murder, although it is believed that Chinese nationals were not involved.
>
> It is the first murder committed inside a diplomatic quarter since the Chinese Communists took over in 1949. In this unprecedented situation, it is still not clear if there will be an official Chinese investigation. Officials at the Information Department of the Chinese Foreign Ministry have so far declined all comment.

Brian Patcheu had left the room to give him some privacy while he was reading. Halpert hadn't even noticed. He fingered the next clipping from *The South China Mail and Empire*, a racy broadsheet from Hong Kong that was far more chatty than the sober *Tribune*. Much more chatty. Far too chatty:

From our own correspondent

PEKING – The grisly murder of a young American university student here last Saturday night may have been the result of a vicious love triangle, according to informed sources.

A diplomat from a Western embassy, who asked not to be identified, told *The South China Mail and Empire* that Gordon Rye, a foreign anthropology student at Shanghai's prestigious Fudan University, had been murdered sometime during the evening after a turbulent argument during a party in a New Zealand diplomat's apartment.

"Rye was a notorious loner," said the source, "but he was known to like three-way sex. It is felt this got out of hand during his recent trip to Peking where he was staying with a close personal male friend. . . ."

Shit, shit, shit, thought Halpert. He couldn't read any more. He put the clippings down on the seat beside him and leaned back, running his fingers nervously through his hair.

And now, of all times, it finally hit him.

He knew his eyes were welling, but the urge to sob came from his gut, as if his emotions were located there. The sobs came convulsively, sob upon sob, sob within sob. There wasn't even time to breathe as his whole body was racked with the deferred grief. His successor heard all the commotion from two rooms away and came running down the hallway. But he hesitated outside the living room. As Halpert's wailing grew louder, Patcheu took a deep breath and went over to the sofa.

"Jim, old buddy, you have to get a grip on yourself."

God bless Brian Patcheu!

"I told you not the fuck to call me Jim."

Halpert got up from the sofa and stormed down to the office, followed closely by his unwanted successor. It was a goddamned insult he had to deal with this jerk before his appointed time and he was goddamned going to phone Toronto and tell them exactly that. Halfway through dialling the number, he paused, and then hung up the receiver. He was icy calm now.

"Brian," he said. "It's Brian, isn't it?"

"Yes, old buddy, it's Brian. What can I do for you? Please let me help."

"I'm sorry for the jumpy moods. Look, it's a good idea for me to clear out of here as fast as I can. I appreciate your help. What I want you to do is have Mr. Hao phone the Peking Hotel and get you a room tonight. The driver will take you there. I want to be alone today. We'll get my transport organized, and tomorrow morning I can go over some bureau details you should know and then I'll get out of your life. Right now I want you gone. I've got too many things to do. I hope you don't mind, but that's how I want to do it."

"Not a problem, Jim. I'll be back after breakfast tomorrow. And call me if you want anything tonight. I just want to help you. I can just imagine all the stress you're under now."

Can you really? Halpert thought as he grimly accompanied Patcheu to the interpreter's office at the very back of the apartment. *Can you really?*

∾

Director Ng was in a particularly good mood when his assistant informed him that the deputy director and two assistant deputies were waiting in his conference room to begin the noon meeting. After seven hours of uninterrupted sleep, there was only the slightest twinge at the base of his neck, and this was nothing compared to his satisfaction at a smooth-running department.

He had already talked to his senior deputy and knew Young Lu had matters more or less in hand. Now Director Ng was eager to discover if his initial instincts about his new subordinate were correct. It was one thing to do the immediate tasks; it was quite another to present a story that would hold up under intense scrutiny. The higher education of his assistant deputy was something Director Ng intended to deal with personally whenever it was appropriate.

As he picked up a file from his desk and walked briskly into the conference room, the director started to whistle an old army marching song from the hills of Yunan. The memory of those far-off happy days brought warmth to his heart, and he suddenly had a flashback to the first political struggle session he had ever attended, one at which a senior official was denounced because he had questioned some aspect or other of Chairman Mao's direction. *Where on earth did that fragment come from after all these years?* Director Ng smiled as he sat down. *Life was curious.*

"So, Deputy, have there been any new developments in this unfortunate matter?"

"Quite a few, Director. Perhaps we should listen to Assistant Deputy Lu's report first and then discuss what other measures we should consider."

"Excellent suggestion. So, Young Lu, I gather you've had a busy morning."

The junior official's brow was creased and he kept his head bowed in the direction of his open file on the table. He did not look up, and the rest could sense his nervousness. This was going to be a very enjoyable session.

"Director, the first thing I am pleased to inform you is that no one at the bureau was responsible for the illegal visit of the foreign journalist to Kung-hsien. A junior official at the Information Department took it upon himself to approve the visit. He was questioned closely this morning and denies that he forged our approval, but the documents went straight from the Information Department to the police, and when the official was confronted with this fact, he confessed his own complicity in that he was not thorough enough in double-checking. He was not able to provide a satisfactory answer as to what happened with the document after it left his hands. He has been suspended from work and is now in the midst of writing a self-criticism that we should have within the next few days."

For the first time, Assistant Deputy Lu looked up from his papers, waves of relief flooding his soul. He even managed a half-smile.

Director Ng had a half-smile on his face too. "And that is your report, is it?" he asked.

"Yes, Director. The supporting documentation is in this file. Do you want to see it?"

"Damn your supporting documentation. This is an unacceptable report. What the hell have you been doing this morning?"

None of this was said in a raised voice. The half-smile still adorned the director's face, and everyone who knew him well understood just how dangerous he was in this mood.

"I don't understand," stuttered Young Lu as he started to go through his papers. "I tried to obtain – "

"Answer me these questions, Lu. Straightforward questions that demand straightforward answers. Yes or no. Did you personally go to the Information Department to supervise the investigation?"

"Director, I made extensive preliminary inquiries – "

"Yes or no. Did you personally go over to the Information Department to direct the investigation?"

"No, Director."

"Thank you. If you didn't personally go over there, who may I ask questioned the young official?"

"The deputy director of the Information Department with whom I established a close liaison in this matter."

"*With whom you established a close liaison in this matter*. How pleasant. And in this wonderful new close liaison, may I inquire if you questioned anyone else? Did you, for example, talk to any of our special friends in the Foreign Ministry who supervise the work of the Information Department?"

"Director, I didn't think this was necessary after receiving such good co-operation from the deputy director at Information."

"*Didn't think this was necessary after receiving such good co-operation. . . .*"

When Director Ng repeated Young Lu's words, they were not simply laced with sarcasm. He said them directly to the note-taker, and in this way the sarcasm came with the ominous extra traffic of an official reiteration. Young Lu was close to collapse.

"*Didn't think this was necessary after receiving such good co-operation*. I see. Now let me sum up your report for you, Assistant Deputy. After whatever preliminary research you did, you made one phone call to the deputy director of the Information Department. Then you picked pimples on your ass for a little while until this helpful deputy director called you back and said, 'Oh dear, oh dear, it looks as if there has been a terrible mistake. One of our inexperienced young officers has not been vigilant enough, and we will remove him from his duties for a couple of days while he writes a self-criticism and accepts the error of his ways.' A very efficient and pleasant deal between two little emperors trying to keep their tiny kingdoms out of trouble. Is that a fair summation, Assistant Deputy?"

Young Lu could say nothing. His head was bowed low in shame and fear. Director Ng leaned back in his chair and stretched to ease his pain. His eyes caught his deputy's and there was a hint of a twinkle both ways. It was for the director to break the silence, but he was content to let it reign for what seemed an hour to Lu. Effortlessly, the director's tone turned conciliatory and paternal.

"Now, Young Lu, this just will not do. You are not on top of this matter yet. To begin with, you have dealt with the Information Department as if it and the Bureau of Cultural Relics were somehow equal departments within their respective ministries. You know very well that this is not the case and you also know the investigative power of your bureau. You should not be dealing in a friendly way with a deputy director. You should be making the director himself answer to you on short deadlines. Obviously, it is a matter of high state concern that a novice official in a nothing department feels he can override the security concerns of our bureau. There is no immediate possibility of reforming such a person. He is already three-quarters of the way down the road of counter-revolution. I do not want to read a self-criticism by this dangerous young man. I want to see a copy of an arrest order. Is this clear?"

"Yes, Director. I will report back as quickly as I can."

"Why don't you get working on it straight away?" said Ng, whose own head was now buried in his papers. He didn't look up as the deputy director indicated to Young Lu and the note-taker that they should leave the conference room quickly. After the note-taker had closed the door behind him, Ng looked up and smiled warmly.

"How did we do, Deputy?"

"Excellently, Director. I believe we have the makings of a fine official in Young Lu. I have listened to the tape of his conversations with the Information Department, and he really had the deputy director on the run. He's just learning to be a tiger. He hardly knows even how sharp our teeth are. The crucial point is that no one will ever be able to trace the journalist's permission to visit Kung-hsien back to our bureau.

All trails lead to the Information Department. Lu has done all of that perfectly."

"My impression exactly. He's going to work out well. I'm very pleased with him. Well done, Deputy. And how are things in the other matter?"

"Fine, so far as I can tell. You know there is always a certain unpredictability with foreigners, but usually nothing that we can't adjust to. The successor arrived this morning, so I expect everything will speed up now."

"And this successor? Will he cause trouble? Do we know much about him? What's he like?"

"Eager, like they all are at the beginning. But he's a business journalist, so I don't think we have to worry very much. Besides, he won't have the help of Mr. Wrye, will he?"

"No, Deputy. He most certainly will not."

And on that note, the two old comrades laughed as they added a new layer to a relationship that was already closer than lips and teeth.

∽

Halpert decided to take a northern route to the New China Bookstore, avoiding the busiest thoroughfares. He wanted to reach a street that went behind the Peking Hotel, where he could park inconspicuously and walk directly to the Wangfuching premises of the store without fighting his way through the bustling crowds on Peking's busiest shopping strip.

He had picked up Sui-san a few minutes before 2 p.m., more than an hour ahead of the time Kwai Ta-ping had told him to bring her to the large square in front of the store. Alison had told him that the old concierge of her building usually fell asleep at the desk just inside the door during the lunch hour, and if they were lucky they wouldn't have to set up a diversion.

The concierge was indeed asleep when Halpert arrived, and she was snoring loudly as the three of them left the building. Outside, where Halpert had left his car, Alison simply kept walking to the guard station exit and proceeded as usual back to the Canadian embassy. Inside the car, Sui-san donned one of Alison's large garden-party hats and pulled it down low enough so that no one outside could see her eyes. She was carrying her Mao jacket on her lap and was wearing one of Alison's bright floral shirts, so that all anyone looking in would be able to see was an exotic foreign lady with a wide-brimmed hat. They had had no trouble at the guard post, and Halpert was now keeping to side streets as much as possible.

Having a driver in Peking had made Halpert lazy about learning the city's geography. By 2:20 p.m. his careful plan to drive unobtrusively to the heart of Peking had come unstuck. He was hopelessly lost. Since Sui-san didn't know Peking at all and was extremely nervous as well, Halpert grimly kept driving, hoping to find some prominent building or landmark that would tell him where he was.

At the moment he spotted the triangular pennants flying at the top of the ancient Drum Tower in the northwest quarter of the city and realized that he had gone out of his way by at least two miles, he also noticed the dark-grey Mercedes-Benz in his rearview mirror. An official's car, perhaps. He knew he was in an area where many senior government and Party pooh-bahs lived. Just ahead he saw a reasonably sized neighbourhood laneway leading south, so he decided to turn off just to rid himself of the worrying feeling that he was being followed. Over the past year and half, the Public Security Bureau had been using its sleek new fleet of Mercedes to patrol the streets, and not unreasonably, Halpert's paranoia level was high this afternoon.

He drove down the laneway slowly. It was still the hour of the afternoon nap, so there were few people out on the street. He tried to keep up some light talk to relieve Sui-san's anxiety once he had explained what was going to happen. His banter had been so convoluted that she wasn't able to understand more than a few words, but she nevertheless kept assuring him she understood everything. He had been going down the laneway for about forty seconds when he looked into the rearview mirror and saw the Mercedes again.

"Shit!" he yelled. Sui-san didn't know what was up, but sensed the danger in the expletive. She sank as low into her seat as she could while Halpert picked up speed from fifteen miles an hour to a dangerous thirty.

The trouble with driving around the little laneways of Peking is that the forward vehicle has to take all the risks. Doors of houses open directly onto the street, and it is more hazardous to be cruising along a deserted laneway than honking your way through a crowded one. The car behind, on the other hand, lets the front vehicle explore the unpredictable territory, so as Halpert tried to speed up a little, the Mercedes was able to gain on them effortlessly. Within a few more seconds, he could make out the glint of sunglasses on the faces of the two men in the front seats. *PSB officers!*

He was on the edge of panic when he caught sight of the large, unattended night-soil cart pulled up tight to the side of a small dwelling. There was barely enough room for his Volkswagen Bug to inch by. In fact, he banged the edge of the reeking cart with his sideview mirror. But he got through, and felt enormous relief despite the overpowering stench that wafted into the car's interior. There was no way the Mercedes could get by. He sped on daringly, pushing the car all the way to thirty-five miles an hour. In his rearview mirror, he could see the Mercedes had stopped and one of the PSB officers was out on the street banging on the residence door.

Halpert was pleased for a second or two. The escape had been quite exciting, and the ensuing euphoria helped convince him that this was just a random check of a foreigner's car and had nothing to do with Sui-san's escape.

Inside the Mercedes, the driver was talking to his superior on the two-way radio. "He's going the right way now. At one point it looked as if he was going to end up at the Summer Palace, so we thought we better try to nudge him south."

༄

The scene that greeted Halpert and Sui-san after they had parked the car and approached the New China Bookstore was chaos — at least to outside eyes. There were about three or four hundred people in the square immediately in front of the premises, and an even larger crowd forming a semicircle around this inner crowd, which spilled out over the wide sidewalk and onto the street. Uniformed police vainly blew their whistles and tried to keep offenders from blocking the traffic, mostly to no avail.

Halpert was horrified to see all the white-jacketed police who were keeping well to the outside of the crowd. Why had Kwai chosen this as their rendezvous? It was ten minutes before Sui-san was supposed to be handed over to his friend, so the two of them stayed on the hotel side of the street and tried to make some sense of what lay before them. Halpert soon realized that Kwai had chosen a brilliant place, but this was only after he remembered that in a society as closely controlled as China's, the greatest moments of personal freedom come not in solitude or in secret corners – the most patrolled territories – but in vast, uncontrolled crowds.

There was, for example, that seminal encounter with the masses less than a year ago when he was leaving the enormous Workers' Stadium after a soccer game. As tens of thousands of people poured out of the stadium's gateways and formed a mass of moving humanity, a novice PSB officer on the sidelines took offence at a rude sign someone made in his direction. Impulsively, he left the safe company of his three colleagues before they could hold him back and went wading into the crowd to nab the offender.

Halpert, swept along with the crowd, had been within a few people of the young officer, who was quickly nabbed and hoisted up screaming into several bunches of arms, the whole crowd still moving forward. When his cap was hurled into the air, there was a giant roar. Then the white jacket disappeared, ripped off his back. Another roar. In quick succession, off came his shirt, his undershirt, his pants, and his undershorts. Only the shoes and socks failed to appear. Halpert was transfixed by the rough justice and pushed himself even closer to the scene, but when he saw what was happening, he was both repelled and astonished.

The naked man continued to howl as he was passed along the sea of eager hands. And as each group got hold of him, the young policeman was pummelled anew and practically had the genitals ripped from his groin. By the time he had been carried to the main gates, he had been transported to the edges of the crowd and was simply dropped on the ground, writhing in pain and clutching his testicles. It was several minutes before his colleagues could reach him, and by then his tormentors – nameless, faceless, and remorseless – had disappeared into the night.

There were more experienced police at the bookstore sale. Halpert spotted half a dozen carefully maintaining their vantage point a good twenty-five yards away from the periphery of the outer crowd. Three days earlier, the Peking Publishing Company had announced that for the first time since the onset of the Cultural Revolution, a wide range of foreign-language books translated into Chinese would be available for limited sales at its main outlet on the following Tuesday. First come, first served. Sort of. Promotion, marketing, and distribution were not among the primary skills of the New China Bookstore.

Within a minute or so, Halpert could see that the trouble was all rooted in the arbitrariness of choice. Although the New China Bookstore was making good on its offer of allowing the first five hundred customers the right to buy up to two books each, they had no say on which two books. A buyer simply lined up at one of the two wickets outside the store and paid for two foreign books translated into Chinese. If he had hoped to buy a copy of *Oliver Twist* and *Les Misérables*, he might be handed two copies of *Rob Roy*. The books were brought in cartons to the wickets by the storeclerks and, so far as the store was concerned, it was irrelevant what was sold to whom. They were discharging their duty to sell off a thousand foreign books in translation, thereby making good on the government's promise to permit the return of (approved) foreign literature to the masses.

Once the buyer had purchased the two books, the real game began. With his two copies of *Rob Roy*, he joined the milling crowd to look for someone who had two copies of *Oliver Twist* or *Les Misérables*. Location was very important. When an initial partner had been located, one of them had to stay put while the other went around and fetched another person who wanted to make a second trade. It was the responsibility of the scout to bring back the third partner to the first. If, however, the scout found the appropriate third partner, but he turned out to be someone with his own scout on the prowl, then an acolyte had to be brought in either to stand in for the second partner or to hunt down the second scout. This made for a great deal of walking around and shout-ing. To Halpert, it seemed like mayhem; Brian Patcheu, on the other hand, would have recognized the prototype of a healthy stock-market floor in the middle of a raging bull economy.

Halpert looked at his watch. It was 3 p.m., so he turned to Sui-san and smiled as much of a comforting smile as he could. "We should go," he said. She nodded and clutched her plastic Chinese airline bag extra tightly. It had more money inside than she had even seen before at one time. Times ten more.

Halpert had his hand on her elbow as they gingerly tried to push into the crowd. They hadn't even reached the sidewalk on the other side of the street when he became aware he wasn't holding on to anything, that Sui-san had simply disappeared. The panic returned. *My God. After all this, I've lost her at the last minute. What an inept idiot I am.*

As he looked wildly around, he caught a momentary glimpse of Kwai Ta-ping behind him. He was smiling, and when Halpert's eyes widened in dismay, Kwai started laughing and raised his arm high, his fingers clenched and his thumb sticking out in a heroic okay.

And then someone started pulling at his sleeve. It was a young Chinese man. Halpert looked at him closely, but did not recognize him at all. He shook his arm to break the unwelcome grip.

"*Ni yao shenma?*" he asked him. "What do you want?"

"Good foreign friend, do you not recognize me?" asked the Chinese in halting VOA English. "You promised bring me foreign magazines, give *Playboy* magazines."

Halpert, dazed for a moment, suddenly recognized The Slug. The Slug was his own little cross to bear, a persistent sleaze artist who first approached him nearly two years ago in Sun-dappled Park while he was waiting for Kwai. There were subsequent brief encounters. The Slug had tracked down Halpert's telephone number and usually called him at 3 a.m. Disconcertingly, Halpert came to feel The Slug knew more about his movements in the park than any of the local informers. At first, he assumed that The Slug had been instructed to compromise him, but in time he came to realize he was just a low-life opportunist who always had a shopping list ready for any encounter. The very last person in the world he wanted to see now was The Slug.

"Look, good Canadian friend, at the wonderful book from your country. I buy it for the memory of you."

The Slug held out the book so covertly Halpert thought he was being shown pornography. But everyone depicted on the dust jacket was fully clothed. It was a copy of *Red Flag of Courage: Canada's Own Dr. Norman Bethune.*

∾

The fair breeze of plans attended to and goals obtained was strong enough to blow away the sultry air of frustration and suspicion not only at the Bureau of Cultural Relics but also at the Canadian embassy. Ambassador Messier had summoned his senior staff for a confidential briefing at 4 p.m., an hour before the embassy's twice-weekly Happy Hour in the reception lounge, which all staff were expected to attend and be happy.

The Happy Hour was an innovation of the ambassador, who saw it as a useful institution to break down traditional barriers and to bring a sense of unity to the embassy's mission in China. As four of his five officers (all male) entered his office, he felt that buoyant sense of hierarchical satisfaction that comes from being on top of the situation.

"Well, gentlemen, since we're all here, let us proceed."

As Alison shut the ambassador's office door behind her, the first secretary (political) turned around. "Henderson's not here. Isn't he coming?"

Ambassador Messier smiled warmly, his bulging eyes dancing with serene satisfaction.

"No. Colonel Henderson sends his regrets. Now don't be too jealous, gentlemen. One of the happy results of my meeting with the Chinese foreign minister this morning was an invitation to Colonel Henderson to go on a military inspection tour of the Mongolian Autonomous Region. I don't need to tell you that this is a signal honour to our embassy. It's the first time since 1949 that this strategic area has been opened up to foreigners, and I told our colleague I wanted him to put everything on his desk aside and prepare himself for this most important assignment."

120

The first secretary (political) whistled inwardly and caught the eyes of the trade commissioner. *Hasn't our old ambassador been busy then! Henderson to the Gobi Desert! Imagine that!*

"Now, gentlemen, to the business at hand. I think we don't want anyone taking notes. This is a confidential briefing on my meeting with the foreign minister and an update on the Wrye affair. There's altogether too much getting out to the media, do you see, so I am placing a complete prohibition on any discussion of what I am about to tell you. I don't even want you discussing this with your good ladies!"

Everyone laughed. The ambassador, who was one of the biggest gossips in Peking and whose wife had never uttered an indiscreet word in her adult life, indicated that it was appropriate to laugh with that jolly little shake of the head that was his trademark at staff meetings and dinner parties.

He put his folded hands on the table and looked pensively down at them. This was an indication that it was time to be serious.

"Canada, and this embassy in particular, owes a great deal to the foreign minister. We have a potentially embarrassing situation on our hands. Very embarrassing. I have been shown some evidence from the Chinese side that our Mr. Wrye was in serious trouble because of . . . er, how shall I put it delicately . . . because of certain untoward sexual propensities. Now tell me I don't have to be more explicit, gentlemen. This is very distasteful for me."

Assuming, rather than waiting for concurrence, the ambassador pushed on. The hands were still folded on the table, but he was now looking up at his attentive officers. As he made his points, he made eye contact with each one of them in turn.

"Had not this ghastly murder taken place Saturday night, it is quite clear to me that *Doctor* Gordon Wrye would have been either arrested or expelled by the Chinese this week for indecent proposals and various disgusting attempted acts in Nanking. *With Chinese nationals*, gentlemen. With Chinese. God only knows what he was up to on his trips to Peking."

The first secretary (political) let his whistle of amazement sound out this time.

"I don't think I have to spell out the tricky situation such an awkward turn of events would have placed the embassy in."

"What's Mr. Halpert's role in all this business?" the first secretary (immigration) asked. He had met Wrye once in Halpert's company and rather liked both of them.

"That's a tricky one, too. I think with regard to Mr. Halpert, we shall all follow the example of the Chinese foreign minister and decline any speculation. Mr. Halpert will be leaving his posting tomorrow, a few days ahead of schedule. His successor, Mr. Patcheu, is already in Peking and seems a very good sort. I had an interview with him this afternoon. Halpert is in bad shape emotionally. This isn't surprising, considering some of the information I have been receiving. In any event, by tomorrow at this time, he will be gone for good from China, and gone for good from our care and concern. Soon enough, he will be back in Toronto and we can direct any further inquiries about Mr. Halpert to External Affairs in Ottawa. With his departure, the Chinese side will be drawing a line underneath the whole matter. I have been assured that there is no evidence whatsoever of any involvement by a Chinese national, and I have been further assured that the Chinese side will be discreetly monitoring all the foreign communities in Peking to try and track down the killer or killers.

"It was pointed out to me, however, that there was a very good possibility that the killer or killers have already left China. The Chinese side graciously showed me a synopsis of the flight manifests and passenger lists of foreign visitors over the weekend. There were three male tourists from London, Ontario, who left Sunday afternoon, one of whom we now know visited Wrye in Nanking University ten days ago. As you know, Wrye was born in London. The name of this visitor – and those of the two other travelling companions – has already been forwarded to Ottawa for follow-up.

"So gentlemen, sordid and melodramatic as this matter is, it is for our purposes almost concluded. Once we safely bid *adieu* to our colleague, Mr. Halpert, I think we would be wise to get on with the rest of our business for which the people of Canada are paying us."

He could sense the queries pent up all around him. He put up his right arm, the palm extended flat against the gapes of his senior officers.

"Gentlemen, it would be improper of me to say more at this juncture.

I have been made privy to details that are very unpleasant and should be passed along directly to our own minister and no one else. For ourselves, our duty is plain: we must be like the Great Wall of China, don't you see? *Comme un grand mur impénétrable.* I count on your support absolutely. This is a miserable business, but we must see it through properly. To your posts, gentlemen, the Happy Hour beckons."

∾

Driver Koo sat motionless in the front room of his small three-room home in Kung-hsien. He was waiting for the Shanghai sedan — *his* Shanghai sedan — to take him to the railway station. It would be driven by that wretch Chou An-wei, who he himself had taught to drive and then peremptorily dismissed as a possible alternative driver because of his bad attitude.

Everything had happened so quickly. Koo understood nothing and nothing made sense. On Sunday evening, he had been visited by the Party secretary of Kung-hsien County and two others. They informed him that he was being promoted and reassigned. The reassignment didn't sound half as ominous as the promotion. Promotion always caused trouble in New China. In a charming touch, the Party secretary had bought a bouquet of flowers that he presented to Koo's wife, who, as a result, became even more apprehensive than her husband. She was the one who summoned up the courage to ask where the reassignment would take them.

The Party secretary had smiled. How he was relishing this moment. When word had come to him from on high that Koo and Shen were, for reasons the Party secretary was not to know, inconveniently located in Kung-hsien, he could feel a thrill erupt all over him.

Inconvenient? The only connecting point between the two was peripheral service work they did for the archaeological team at the Long March Agricultural Commune. The Party secretary didn't know what the problem was, but this didn't affect his delight. He could tell his own tale about Koo. This arrogant peasant carried on as if he had more power than anyone else in the county, and yet no one dared to criticize him. And now, out of nowhere, came the order to move the insolent pest out. When the Party secretary was asked if there was some place that Koo might be pleased to be relocated, he didn't hesitate.

"I believe he has family from here posted to Lhasa," he had replied coolly. "Do you think you could find him something in Tibet? I'm sure that would please him."

"Really?" asked the startled superior. "How refreshing to find someone who would like to be posted to Tibet. That will be no problem whatsoever. Let me get back to you in a few hours."

It was all arranged. Driver Koo was to join the pool of drivers in Lhasa who would attend upon the political leadership of Tibet. It was clearly a promotion, plus he would get extra pay to compensate for the appalling altitude problems, the miserable local diet, the possibility of local insurrection, and the often unbearable loneliness for a Chinese national in this filthy military colony of Peking's.

And so it was a real smile on the Party secretary's face as he slowly formed the opening syllable of Driver Koo's new locale: "Ti – "

Koo's wife had let out a howl. "Not Tibet! What's the poor man done to deserve Tibet? Party Secretary, surely there has been some mistake. Old Koo is the most loyal member – "

"No mistake, comrade," said the Party secretary, who was displaying a countenance of paternal concern. "It is not for any of us to question the Party when it gives us an assignment. The Party knows best. Driver Koo's responsibilities will be considerably increased and I know you will be allowed a trip a year to visit him there. That is, unless you care to accompany him full time and perhaps I could make those arrangements for you. . . ."

Driver Koo's wife had drawn back and stifled her sobbing. Here was an aspect she hadn't thought through properly. Perhaps this new assignment might not be such a bad idea after all. Driver Koo himself was too stunned to take in much of anything, least of all his wife's defection. Somehow, his careful network had failed him. Somehow, he had been given no warning. Somehow, all the backdoor arrangements he had overseen throughout his years at Kung-hsien seemed to count for nothing.

Tibet!

"Birds eat you in Tibet. Big black birds eat your body."

That's all Koo could say. He'd heard his cousin report on the activities of vultures at the notorious Tibetan "sky burials." Actually, he had heard about it indirectly. Koo and his cousin hadn't spoken to each other since the cousin learned that it was Koo who had been responsible for his transfer to Tibet after the two had had a heated argument over a difficult family matter. Koo was that powerful in those days. He was this weak today. *Old tigers roar, but they have no teeth*, Eunuch Kung had once said about an ancient King of Lu. Poor Koo. He couldn't even roar anymore. As he waited in the dark room to begin his new assignment, all he could manage was a muffled sob as he thought of a Tibetan vulture slowly plucking out his eyes: first the left one, then the right.

7

Brian Patcheu had been busy. By the time he and Halpert met for breakfast at the Peking Hotel on Wednesday morning, he had co-ordinated all of his predecessor's departure plans, briefed the Canadian ambassador on Halpert's declining mental condition, phoned his editor in Toronto to give a full report, introduced himself to officials at the Information Department, and had Halpert's staff – soon to be his staff – all reporting to him. The only thing remaining was to get his man onto the airplane and out of his life.

Ambassador Messier had told Patcheu that it was customary for a considerable group of friends and colleagues to assemble at the Peking airport restaurant for a farewell party about an hour before departure time. This was a relic of the bad old days during the Cultural Revolution, when departing diplomats were required to run a gauntlet through screaming Red Guards all along the tarmac from the terminal exit right up to the stairs of the airplane. If you happened to be a diplomat or journalist from a country that was on Chairman Mao's hate list at the time of your departure, it could be a gruesome little stroll out of China. The Red Guards spat in your face; they might yank your hand-luggage away and empty it on the tarmac to expose the frivolousness or licentiousness of your life; they might even pull your hair if you looked angrily at any of them.

This special *envoi* was stopped when Lin Piao was purged and

President Nixon came visiting in the early seventies, but a residue of nastiness with officials lingered on, and so the policy of total support for departing colleagues continued. By 1979, it had become largely ceremonial, but Halpert's departure was clearly an event worthy of all the traditional honours – and scrutiny.

Rumours were circulating throughout the foreign compounds, and there were even people who thought Halpert was Gordon Wrye's murderer. They certainly weren't going to miss an opportunity to say goodbye. Others had heard that he was in the middle of a nervous breakdown, so that was worth observing, too. Then there were those who were fascinated by the notion of a love brawl between a homosexual trio and weren't going to miss the chance to shake hands with a man of passion and a pervert to boot. As the sounds of frenetic speculation raised the volume in the restaurant, the acerbic French cultural attaché, who hardly knew Halpert but was enjoying himself hugely, observed to his neighbour, "It's just like the old days, except that this time we get to play the Red Guards."

There were also colleagues from other newspapers and news agencies who turned up to make sure that the biggest pain in their professional lives was leaving for certain, not appreciating that with Gordon Wrye's death the journalistic competition they feared most had already departed. Still, getting rid of Halpert, belittling Halpert, discrediting Halpert, exposing Halpert, exterminating Halpert journalistically, was the goal of every Western journalist in Peking who had been posted there long enough to receive "a bullet" from the home office when Halpert/Wrye had scooped them yet again.

As Halpert's fame soared during his four years in Peking, his stock among his own tribe plummeted. After he was vindicated on the fall of the Gang of Four story, there were only one or two journalists left in Peking who would even speak to him, and they were just trying to cover their backs. Journalism does not always bring out the best in people.

Now that Halpert was on the ropes and his fortunes appeared to be in reverse, everyone wanted to tell him what a great guy he was. Ambassador Messier turned up, not only to make sure Halpert left but also to check on Colonel Henderson, who was to be on the same late-afternoon plane to Hong Kong.

Henderson was going to Hong Kong to be briefed by the CIA and given advice by the Americans on what to look out for. This tidy arrangement between a client state and a superpower was fully understood by the Chinese side. It was why, in the end, Colonel Henderson had been invited to visit the Mongolian Autonomous Region. The Chinese wanted the United States government to know – in the lead-up to full recognition between their two countries – that the Communist government was totally in charge of its borders. More than totally in charge: they had them steel-bolted into place, and God help anyone trying to adjust them.

There were several dozen people assembled at four tables in the airport restaurant when Halpert, looking haggard and withdrawn, arrived in their midst with the able Patcheu, who – it soon became clear – regarded the entire assemblage more as a welcoming committee for himself than as a farewell to his spent, nervous predecessor. A large huzzah went up when the pair was spotted. Other diners in the restaurant looked up and craned their necks to see what the fuss was all about.

"My dear Halpert, over here," said Ambassador Messier, who half stood up and motioned his victim to the empty seat beside him. "We've saved a spot for you. What an ordeal you've been having. I dare say, it must feel very good just to clear out."

Halpert had no powers of resistance to draw upon. He did as he was bidden. Had he been asked to write a self-criticism then and there, he would have done it. It didn't even bother him that the ambassador then shooed away one of his junior officers from the seat on his right side and motioned Patcheu to join him. The ambassador was still in a semi-erect position when he realized everyone else had stopped talking. In such a void, he knew his duty. He pulled himself up to his full height of five-foot-six and began a speech, as natural a thing for him as breathing.

"This is both an auspicious and a sad moment," said the ambassador. "It is certainly auspicious because we have been given the opportunity to show our esteem to one of our most respected colleagues, James Halpert. I would be remiss if I didn't also point out that it is doubly auspicious because we also have the opportunity to welcome his successor, Mr. Brian Patcheu. Welcome, Brian! I suppose it's all right to say this to a journalist just starting a posting here: *May you live in interesting times* — as our host nation puts it.

"But it is sad moment, too. Our departing colleague, who has witnessed and reported on so many startling and dramatic events over the past years, has been at the centre of a great tragedy, which we all know about. We all join together, James, in wishing that this unfortunate incident hadn't happened to mar your departure. But the fact that it has allows us to show you our warm feelings towards you personally and our regard for your remarkable achievements in what may well be the most difficult posting in the world. These are seven-league boots you are inheriting, Mr. Patcheu. I'm sure you are up to all the tasks, but I don't think it will come as any surprise to you to hear that we think you have a very tough act to follow."

The mandatory Hear, Hears! were muttered by a few. None by the journalists, of course, but diplomats are trained to say Hear, Hear! automatically whenever an ambassador, however insincerely, makes a compliment, clears his throat, and leaves a short, pregnant pause.

Halpert looked up at Messier in a daze. The small satisfaction he had gained for arranging Sui-san's safe exit and getting the hell out himself was overwhelmed by the nausea he felt in the presence of Ambassador Messier and his colleagues. He was praying that the philippics would end very quickly so he could make a dash for the washroom. It was a vain wish, and he had to cradle his delicate gut for another few minutes.

"We all come to this extraordinary country with different expectations and ambitions . . ."

Messier was now heading into familiar territory. Regulars at airport farewells featuring Canadians knew the rest of the speech almost by heart. They could turn off now and wait until the mention of Dr. Norman Bethune, which signalled the winding down, and then the quote from Robbie Burns, which was Ambassador Messier's loud and formal amen.

". . . and when we come to leave, we are all the wiser for this body of experience. When that outstanding fellow countryman of ours, Dr. Norman Bethune, first arrived in China in the midst of the bloody civil war, he, too, came with expectations and ambitions. But he soon learned that it was what he could give of himself that counted, not what he could get out of China. That is why he is venerated today throughout the length and breadth of this remarkable country. It is also why we Canadians have such an honourable legacy here. Now, our colleague James Halpert isn't exactly a Canadian, as we all know, but I'm sure he's been forgiven for that. But he has served his Canadian newspaper well and thereby also his adopted country. James, we all wish you well in the next phase of your career. The unhappiness of the last few days will surely pass. We wish you well and say to you with one united voice, 'Will ye nae come back again?'"

Halpert was by now well beyond nausea and was cruising in uncharted psychological territory. He longed to retreat to the washroom just to get his bearings. The ending of the ambassadorial valedictory ode was the signal for at least two other speakers to make short addenda, speeches Halpert couldn't stand to hear.

He stood up and briskly thanked Ambassador Messier. To everyone's immense relief, he announced that he hadn't even checked in yet and unless he did so rather soon he wouldn't be allowed to board the plane, and the poor ambassador would have to make his speech all over again. There was a bit of tittering and one loud groan. With a fixed smile, Ambassador Messier surveyed the tables to find the culprit and determine the punishment (if it was one of his staff: *bad reports to Ottawa*; if it was a journalist or non-Canadian diplomat: *no invitations*). With no culprit in sight and Halpert already gone, he turned to Brian Patcheu.

"Didn't you take him to checkout first thing?"

"Of course I did. Everything's in order. He wants a breather from this scene, for whatever reason. Leave him for a few minutes, then I'll go after him. We've still got over half an hour. I promise you he'll be on that plane. I've had my fill of him already and it's been less than forty-eight hours."

"Well, some of us have had forty-eight months, my young friend, so make sure you do get him on that plane or, by Jove, you'll have us to answer to."

"*By Jove!* What a wonderful phrase, Ambassador. I've never actually heard anyone use it before, and certainly not a Quebecker."

"Haven't you then?" said Ambassador Messier, who turned away and decided that Halpert's successor was a twit.

∾

Halpert had never before found the smell of a Chinese men's room welcoming. In fact, he didn't much like men's public toilets in the West either. However clean and well maintained, he thought them disgusting places and dreaded having to listen to anonymous dysfunctional bowels. He also disliked unzipping in close proximity to other men at stand-up urinals. Today, however, life in the men's room seemed less distasteful than the trivial ceremonies in the restaurant.

He had very little to offer the airport's cesspool on this occasion, but he unzipped anyway because it was the thing to do and he was trying to kill time. There were twelve urinals in a row, and he was the only one at any of them, so when someone came in and went directly to the first station on his immediate right, he was instantly apprehensive. From out of the corner of his eye, Halpert could see the man was Chinese, and his apprehension soared when he realized the man was positioned in front of the receptacle but was doing nothing: no zip, no fumbling, no flow.

"*Hai Pei-teh, nin hao!* Hello, hello!"

Hearing his Chinese name and the effusive greeting, Halpert's dribbling bladder ceased functioning altogether. Still holding himself, he turned his head in wild surmise to see The Slug, once again – as always – at the most inauspicious time.

"Hai Pei-teh, I come say goodbye to our good friend. You are the good friend from land of Dr. Bethune, and all Chinese people wish you the great success."

Halpert had zipped up by now and with The Slug's little speech, which formed a perfect counterpoint to Ambassador Messier's, he laughed for the first time in five days.

"What a good friend you are," Halpert said, at long last relishing the game of hypocrisy, "but I'm sorry I don't have any magazines for you and there isn't any time to visit the Friendship Store."

"Hai Pei-teh, nothing for me. Please, I give you the present to remember your friend in China."

The Slug looked over his shoulder to make sure no one had come into the men's room and then pulled a black-covered scribbler out of his bag. It was a slightly larger version of the kind Gordon Wrye used. For a heart-stopping moment, Halpert wondered if The Slug was complicit in Wrye's murder, and then he looked at the inscription in the notebook: "*To Canedian frend, Hai Pai-de, from the Chinese frend always! Good luck to the land of Docter Norman Bethune!*" Despite himself, Halpert was touched and put his hand on The Slug's left shoulder.

"Thank you," he said. "I mean it. Thank you very much. I have many Chinese friends who I will remember, and you are one of them."

"Hai Pei-teh," came the slow response, "you have no Chinese friends but me. Everyone else is a spy. Good wishes, Hai Pei-teh."

There were tears in The Slug's eyes. *My God*, thought Halpert, *what is happening here?* He couldn't decide if it was a moment of pure truth or the last ludicrous scene. At the same moment, Brian Patcheu came through the doorway into the washroom.

"There you are, Jim. Is everything okay? I've been sent to drag you back to your party. There's only a few minutes left."

Behind Patcheu, unbeknownst to him, The Slug waved goodbye to Halpert and went through the door.

"I'm coming," said Halpert. "Everything will be okay now."

"Of course it will, good buddy, of course it will."

∽

The momentary sense of relief Halpert felt by boarding the plane was knocked for a loop after he saw Colonel Henderson's unwelcome visage at the back of the trail of boarding passengers. He had sat down next to the aisle and placed a small travel bag and newspaper on the window seat in the vain hope of dissuading anyone else from joining him. He knew this would not work with Henderson and that he had to act quickly. Looking up, he saw an attractive-looking young Eurasian woman coming down the aisle.

"I'm sorry," he said to her as he moved over to the window seat. "I'm making this difficult. Here. This seat is free."

The woman's eyes widened as she hesitated for a moment, then she smiled, shrugged, and decided to accept the offer.

"Well, that was quite a fuss people were making over you in the restaurant," she said, settling in to her seat. "Tell me why you're so famous. I'm all ears."

Moving down the aisle and gesturing eagerly to Halpert to hold him a seat, Colonel Henderson was frustrated with only seconds to spare. The closest he would be able to get was two rows behind them and on the other side. As he passed by, he leaned over and across the woman to Halpert. "We really should talk, Jamie. Where are you staying in H.K.?"

Think fast.

"With friends. Where are you staying? I'll call you."

"The Peninsula, in Kowloon. I'm there for three days. How long are you staying?"

Passengers behind Henderson were starting to get impatient.

"Not sure at the moment. Better get your seat. I'll call you."

With Henderson safely out of the way, the woman beside Halpert turned to him with a broad grin. "That was a clever dodge," she said. "I see you know how to think quickly."

Halpert smiled. A slightly abashed, self-deprecating smile that usually appealed to strong women who liked to mother fragile men. There was no doubt about Halpert's fragility at this moment; nor was there any about the woman's forwardness. She put out her hand to him.

"I'm Julie Potlow, and I live in Hong Kong. Who and what are you?"

Halpert made small talk while he looked out the window. He wasn't so sure he was pleased to have such a confident and inquisitive companion, but he said enough in a sufficiently detached but polite way that she caught his mood of desolation and left him alone as the plane engines were started. Besides, she knew exactly who he was, and she had close to three hours to find out anything else she was curious about.

In the distance, Halpert saw most of the farewell gang out on the terminal balcony, some with drinks still in their hands. No one was waving to him. They had simply moved out there as part of the ritual, and perhaps also to make sure that he really did leave. Just before the plane turned to taxi towards the runway, Halpert noticed that the ambassador was already heading back to the balcony door. Directly beside the tarmac, Chinese peasant farmers were tending to vegetable crops, which for inexplicable reasons the airport authorities had allowed them to maintain.

As the plane took off, Halpert watched Peking shrink. Second by second, he observed his life during the past four years relentlessly contract into the few square inches of his scratched-up window. It was a weird sensation. Below him, nearly a billion people remained locked behind confined borders, most of them ignorant of the world beyond, most of them shackled to the endlessly rotating seasons of the earth, most of them no longer even specks on his immediate horizon.

And Halpert? What was he? He was free to roam. Or was he? He decided, just at that moment, that there was something terribly wrong at the core of his being. His best friend had been murdered less than a week ago and he could not at that moment even focus on him. He couldn't even remember what his friend looked like. *And this was the man for whom I've vowed revenge.*

What a farce. A week ago he was one of the greatest journalists the world had ever known, at least in his own eyes, and now he was a speck as infinitesimal as the disappearing Chinese below. Had he actually ever been in China? Wasn't the whole thing a big bloody joke? What of him was left behind? Four years in a six-thousand-year stream of continuous and coherent cultural reality. It was nothing. It was less than a speck. It was an iota of a speck. If even that.

"I expect you're glad enough to be rid of most of that lot."

She said it with such solicitation that he warmed to her all over again.

"The diplomats and journalists, I mean. Not the Chinese."

"My thoughts exactly," lied Halpert. Fleetingly, he wanted to be what she wanted him to be. Many an intimate airplane encounter has started with a lie that is beautifully sustained till landing, when both parties make their escape, never to be caught out in their fantasies. Halpert's brief fling with fantasy was that he was free and unattended, that there had never been a Mrs. Halpert, that he wasn't really a journalist, that he was stateless but unharried, that Gordon Wrye had never existed, that Sui-san . . .

The memory of Sui-san brought him back to reality. So did Colonel Henderson, who had left his seat the moment the seatbelt sign went off and, again, was leaning right over and across Julie Potlow, this time insisting Halpert join him in his seat.

"Jamie, the fellow beside me is quite content to switch seats. Why don't we do it now?"

Halpert looked up at him in total perplexity.

"Little man, go away," said Julie Potlow. "*Now.* Shoo."

Henderson looked at her in utter amazement. *How could anything so feminine and beautiful say anything so rude?*

"I'm sorry, ma'am," said Henderson. "You don't understand. This man is a good friend of mine and we want to talk. You won't have to move at all — "

"You are the one that doesn't seem to understand. Go away. Now. *This instant.*"

The colonel looked at Halpert, who smiled and made little body movements that said, "What can we do? Better just go back to your seat."

In confusion, Colonel Henderson retreated. He would lick his wounds, he decided, and rise again another time. After he left, Halpert leaned towards his saviour and whispered conspiratorially, "I owe you." She smiled and they said nothing more for ten minutes.

Can you fall in love instantly? Can you fall in love in the midst of grief and turmoil? Can you be in love with two people at the same time? Perhaps. For a moment anyway.

When she spoke again, she left Halpert nonplussed.

"I knew your friend Gordon."

Out of the blue, just like that.

"Not well. But we met a couple of times. Once in Hong Kong, when he did a bit of work for my father. And another time in Nanking. I thought he was rather wonderful, if a bit arrogant. Do you have any idea who might have killed him?"

This didn't fit into the fantasy Halpert had been constructing. Yet again, maybe it did. It wasn't really a question of trust. He had no reason to trust, or not trust, Julie Potlow. It was her assertiveness. He bowed to it with hardly a second thought, just as he had bowed to Gordon's assertiveness.

135

"Not even a hint of an idea. Well, maybe a hint. He was an archaeologist who specialized in ancient Chinese pottery, did you know?"

"I certainly did. My father used him to catalogue his collection of T'ang funereal vessels. We thought he was brilliant. I don't think we had ever come across an academic like him before. He adored speculation, absolutely wild speculation, and then he would bombard it with ruthless scrutiny. It was exciting listening to him analyse."

"And what did you do with him in Nanking?"

"Oh, when he was in Hong Kong, he arranged with my father to take us to the Imperial pottery works south of the city in Ching-tê Chên. We'd never been there, and my father was keen to see the ancient kiln construction."

"What does your father do?"

Halpert had lost the art of sequential questioning and was hopping all over the place. It did not strike him just then that he was more curious about this woman's background than about the potentially useful conjunction of their mutual knowledge of Gordon Wrye. He was always more of a feature writer than an investigative journalist.

"My father does many things. I suppose you could sum them up by saying that he is an investor. He is an Englishman who married a Chinese, so I suppose his cultural loyalties are divided. Sometimes, I think he is more Chinese than my mother was."

"Was?"

"Yes, she died when I was quite young. I work with my father on various projects. We get along very well."

While they were talking, he was slowly imbibing her. Scrutiny had started with the externals: the small jade and diamond earrings; the intricately wrought gold bracelet; the cool, light-blue linen dress, hardly creased. Then, what they adorned: the fine, sculpted face with slightly teasing eyes; dark, straight, mid-length hair that she kept out of her eyes with a cobalt-blue velvet band; a wide, generous mouth; pale skin; high cheek bones; delicate arms; the pampered skin on well-manicured hands that nevertheless took on different characteristics when she talked and gestured; small breasts – well, maybe not that small; beautiful knees, amazing knees, *extraordinary* knees – their alluring, slightly angular points lurking beneath creamy-white silk stockings. Halpert had never been aroused by knees before, but since he was so much taller than she was, those knees were the most prominent feature in his line of vision. He'd never seen Sui-san's knees, or if he had, he hadn't noticed them, so there was no chance to compare and contrast. *Sui-san, Sui-san, where is she now?* He dismissed the thought of her, ruthlessly. His mind was on Julie Potlow's knees, and the woes of Sui-san were very far from his immediate concerns.

"And what about you, Mr. Halpert? What's ahead for you?"

The Chinese Airlines staff were handing out free packages of cigarettes, free paper fans, and free candies. When a flight attendant tried to get this chatty couple to take her wares and they declined, she was sure they didn't understand.

"It's a gift from the people of China," she said, trying to educate them in good manners. "It is required to take them."

Halpert was brought up sharply into Chinese reality, but his travelling companion simply smiled sweetly at the attendant and said, "Well, if we must, we must." She took a few items and said thank you, again sweetly.

"Well?" she asked Halpert.

"Well, what?"

"So what's ahead for you. I trust you aren't going to belabour this poor world with yet another book about The China Experience."

"Well, actually, that's exactly what I intend to do. Is this a new crime against the people of China?"

"No, it's just a crime against poor forests and printer's ink. How long were you posted to Peking?"

"Four years. I think it's long enough to form an opinion or two."

"I dare say. Four years? The world may yet be saved. My father has a theory that only journalists and diplomats who have been in China for less than two years can write books on the country. If you stay longer than two years, you actually start learning something and it gets increasingly complicated to pontificate. 'A little learning is a dangerous thing,' you know? I expect your thoughts on China are very complicated now."

"I take it you don't like journalists very much."

"Not at all. Some of my best friends are journalists."

She laughed, and Halpert laughed with her, although he wasn't quite sure why.

"I don't have a lot of respect for much of journalism. Any time I've read an article I know something about, well . . . you know, it's almost a cliché. Lots of people say that. Close encounters with journalism tend to leave one pretty cynical. Has the business made you cynical?"

"No, I don't think so and that's strange, because I've seen a lot that should make me cynical about people. But I'm not. I still trust them. Ordinary people anyway, people who aren't trying to manipulate you for their own purposes. I could agree with you if you said that journalism sometimes brings out the worst in people, both reporters themselves and the people being reported on."

"All right, Mr. Halpert, I'll say exactly that and we'll be agreed. What a nice note on which to change subjects. What do you think — "

"My turn. What is it you're looking for? Are you a cynic? If you are, it's very disturbing in one so young."

The flirtation was getting serious here, and the plane had not yet even passed over the Yellow River.

"Well, I don't know what to say to that. I'm not cynical at all, or at least I don't think I am, but I do respect reality. In fact, I embrace reality. I hate sham and hypocrisy and ignorance and self-delusion. I like people who can get on with their lives and deal with things as they are. I never judge. I just try to understand the world as it is and despise anyone who lets himself get manipulated."

"Then you should love journalists."

She looked at him straight in the face and saw the half-turned corners of his mouth hold tight in mock-seriousness. Simultaneously, they both exploded into laughter. And then they were served a meal of glutinous, badly congealed rice, anonymous meat in an indifferent sauce, vanquished vegetables, stale cake, and a glass of madly over-sweetened pineapple juice.

And they laughed again.

～

A day later, almost to the late-afternoon hour, while Halpert haunted his room at the Hilton Hotel waiting for word of Sui-san and pining for Julie Potlow, the twelve-year-old Chinese bellboy of the Mandarin Hotel – resplendent in his dark navy-blue jacket with gold piping and brass buttons – slowly perambulated around the palmy aisles of the Soong Sisters Lounge. His ornate signboard, a fine piece of slate framed in rosewood and surmounted by two silver bells, was raised high on the pole he supported in a leather sling hung around his neck. He looked like a miniature regimental flag-bearer in a guard of honour. If people at a table looked up to read the board, he kept walking. If they ignored him, he stayed unobtrusively nearby and shook it gently till the twinkling of the bells made them look up and read what was written on the slate: *The Honourable Mr. Finch-Noyes.*

At the other end of the lounge, a Chinese trio – cello, violin, and piano – alternated their offerings between Schubert and Chinese love songs from the thirties. There was no clash of cultures. Everything sounded the same.

"I say, that's me," shouted a voluble gentleman at the table near the trio where the bellboy had finally arrived.

"Telephone, sir."

"Sorry, people," said Desmond Finch-Noyes to his senior staff at the Hong Kong office, who had assembled at the Soong Sisters at his behest. "I trust this will only take a moment."

He followed the bellboy to the main desk outside the lounge. An immaculately groomed young Chinese clerk in a dark grey flannel suit leaned a little over the counter and talked in a confidential whisper. "It's a Mr. Potlow, sir. He says it's an important matter."

"Rather," said Desmond.

"The second booth is free Mr. Finch-Noyes. I'll put the call through right away."

Desmond closed the door of the booth and picked up the receiver.

"Potlow? It's Desmond here. Hello, Potlow, are you there?"

He bellowed into the phone, but it was the Chinese clerk who responded.

"Just a moment, Mr. Finch-Noyes. I'll put Mr. Potlow through now. Go ahead, sir."

"Potlow, is that you?"

"Hello, Desmond. Sorry to interrupt, but I thought we should get this little matter cleared up because I think we have a deal."

"Excellent news. What's the problem?"

"I appreciate that you are not proposing that we use your own family's bank, but frankly I would be more comfortable with some place other than Baring's."

"Nothing wrong with Baring's. Absolutely top notch. Royal Family still uses them. Chose them because I thought they'd put your mind at ease."

"I'm happy enough for the Royal Family, dear fellow. I just find the profile a trifle high for what we want to do. And in this case, I'm not so keen on the English connection."

"But the point is I know people at Baring's. I trust them."

"Precisely. I'd prefer a little more anonymity. This is a joint venture between the two of us. I've had some research done. I think one of the those little Canadian trust companies would fit the bill."

"I don't know them at all."

"Neither do I, and that makes them just fine. They're more than solid. Backed up by government guarantees and all that. There's one called Prince Edward Trustco that I think will suit both our purposes. As it happens, my daughter is heading up to Toronto after she finishes in New York and could establish some contacts."

"I suppose. I don't really like not knowing their people though, do you read me? I think it will make things more complicated than need be."

"My dear Desmond. We *want* them complicated, at least in terms of a final repository."

"You're right. Prince Edward Trustco, do you say? Wonder if the family uses them too? I expect it'll be fine. What about all those transfer arrangements with the Bank of China?"

"The last people we have to worry about are the Bank of China. They may be the only truly reliable bankers left in the world."

"I suppose you're right. It's good then? Subject to checking out these Canadian johnnies, everything's worked out swimmingly and we can proceed?"

"Exactly, Desmond. It's a whole new world."

"Rather."

~

When the call finally came, at 1:30 a.m. Thursday, Halpert was lost in a dream of rage at his ex-wife. She was pleading with him to let her start having children, and he was howling at her that she was irresponsible and selfish. In the midst of the howl, he shot out his arm to reach for the ringing telephone.

"Hello?"

"Hello, Mr. Halpert. It's Joan Paget."

"Joan *who*?"

Halpert was faking alertness. He wanted to get back to his dream because he had another great point to make at his ex-wife's expense.

"We've met, Mr. Halpert. At the Canadian embassy. I'm at the Peking Foreign Languages Institute. I'm Kwai's friend."

"Oh my God, *Joan*! I'm so sorry. I've been waiting to hear from you. Where are you?"

"I'm in Hong Kong. I think I owe you the cost of this trip, so I should thank you."

"Forget that. What's your news?"

"Kwai says to tell you that the girl is okay and that by next Sunday she should be in the Cambodian refugee camp in Aranyaprathet."

"Where?"

"It's in Thailand, Mr. Halpert. I don't think we are supposed to know too much about Kwai's connections, but he seems to have found a way to get the girl out of China via Vietnam and Cambodia. He told me it was the best way."

"So how am I supposed to find her?"

"I don't know, Mr. Halpert. I suggest you better get over to Thailand and out to this refugee camp. Aranyaprathet is a village near Bangkok. I'll spell it for you, if you like."

"Dear God, what am I supposed to do there?"

"I assume you'll still recognize her, won't you?"

Halpert was fully awake now and had finally detected the note of cold perfunctoriness in his caller's voice.

"Joan, is everything all right?"

"I don't know, Mr. Halpert. I certainly hope so. Kwai is a very fine man, and you have put him considerably at risk with this little escapade. This lady is worth it, I take it? Kwai trusts you implicitly, you know. I hope that trust isn't betrayed."

"For God's sake, Joan. How could you say such a thing? This woman was Gordon Wrye's special friend and her life was in danger."

"Gordon Wrye was a prick of the first order, Mr. Halpert. So I'll just say this once again. I'm praying Kwai's trust isn't betrayed. I really don't have anything more to say to you. I hope it all goes well."

She hung up.

Halpert was still holding the receiver when he realized there was no return to his dream.

PART TWO

June 1989

8

Susan Liang Halpert stood at the corner of Bay and Front streets holding a hand up to shade her eyes from the early summer sun. She looked at her watch. It was nearly 10:30 a.m. and there was no sign of Mrs. Li. The bus was scheduled to begin its tour of Toronto, but she had asked the driver to wait a few minutes, assuring him it would be worth his while. The driver smiled. He had learned to like Chinese people who assured him something would be worth his while.

At 10:40 a.m., just when Susan was starting to look into her purse to find a ten-dollar bill to tip the driver and tell him he had better go ahead, a long white limousine pulled up to the side entrance of the Royal York Hotel. Mrs. Li came bustling out before her chauffeur had a chance to get around to the other side and open the door for her.

"So sorry, so sorry," said Mrs. Li, who was about fifty-five and a little plump. A nicely rounded face gave off such a warm smile that Susan would have forgiven her anything. She was an extraordinary woman, Mrs. Li. Of Manchu ancestry, she was, as Susan knew, connected to the final dynastic oligarchy to rule China, although her family had gone to Hong Kong after the fall of Pu-yi, the last emperor. She was born and brought up in Hong Kong and had imbibed all its values and exuberance – and anxieties.

What Susan didn't know was that Mrs. Li had married beneath her — a previously married Guangdong peasant on the make — and for a period of time her family would have nothing to do with her. But she had had the last laugh. She had chosen her husband, Huang Dafu, with a careful eye to the future and figured he had vision and ambition enough to carry even her desiccated tribe into the twenty-first century, whatever it would hold out for them.

She had given him two more sons and a daughter to add to his two sons from the first, dissolved marriage. And Big Huang — as he came to be universally known — had not failed her. Now he presided over a string of sweatshops stretched out between the New Territories on the Kowloon side and the most remote inhabited islands in Her Majesty's soon-to-disappear prize colony. Thousands of Hong Kong workers, who manufactured European brand-name clothing for the export market, depended upon Huang Dafu not only for their jobs but for most of their reason for living. Industrial philosophy, camaraderie (in the form of popular company-sponsored mahjong clubs), holiday villas, even birth-control assistance came his workers' way along with their weekly pay cheques. He had also become an important figure to the colonial administration because of the influence he exercised over the labour unions. In this complex fashion, Big Huang became one of Hong Kong's guarantors of social and entrepreneurial peace.

On several occasions, he had had to act quickly and ruthlessly, and his decisiveness had led to the return of stability and a quantum leap in Hong Kong prosperity. It had been so easy for him each time.

The problem was always the same: worker discontent. The moment Big Huang got wind of it, the moment he discovered a home-grown rabble-rouser making his people unhappy with their lucky lot, he ordered a three-pronged campaign that took less than a week to bring about total victory. Every time.

First, he called upon the governor of Hong Kong to give his border-patrol guards a much-appreciated leave for a few crucial days. All of them.

Then, well-greased senior officials in the neighbouring mainland city of Guangzhou were alerted that Big Huang could do with a few thousand eager young male workers between the ages of nineteen and twenty-five.

Next, the border patrols on the Chinese side also disappeared and, within twenty-four hours, the new labour recruits were already signed on in Hong Kong. With these measures in place, Huang would fire his entire workforce of 120,000 and hire them back the next day – minus a cautionary two or three thousand. Even the most loyal employees would find their salaries reduced by a nominal – and again cautionary – percentage.

The whole effect was effortlessly salutary; a wizard touch that bonded everyone on both sides of the border. Only those fools fighting for fairness got shafted, but then they never saw the bigger picture, never understood the bottom line, never had a clue about the delicate balance that kept Hong Kong such an enticing profit centre.

Mrs. Li knew most of this history directly. In the early years of their marriage, Huang Dafu confided in her often; later, less so, but only because their everyday interests had diverged as she became more interested in the world beyond her husband's authority. She had to be nimble these days because that world was shrinking fast. Big Huang had become rich beyond even his own calculations, and his vast holdings, which were handled by a team of advisers headed by a son from the first marriage, spawned equally lucrative investments in North America and Europe.

With the historic announcement by Britain and China that Hong Kong would be returned to the all-embracing arms of the motherland in 1997, Big Huang hadn't even had a night's restlessness. His sweatshops had become the model of what the Communist government wanted to set up in a so-called New Economic Zone on the other side of the Hong Kong border. Being pragmatic post-ideological Communists, they liked a man with Huang Dafu's grasp of realism. They had cooperated with him before, even during the Cultural Revolution, so the prospect of his entrepreneurial acumen and China's limitless labour pool fit together as close as dollars and cents – or wrists and shackles.

Like most of Hong Kong's outsized entrepreneurs, however, Big Huang had no intention of being locked into an uncertain future.

Business was business; reality was reality. So, among many other family initiatives throughout the West, he dispatched his good wife to Toronto to purchase a house for one of their children – it hardly mattered which one, but probably the daughter – to establish a Canadian domicile. Mrs. Li knew no one in Toronto, although her husband's Canadian investments were handled by Prince Edward Trustco, whose officials could be counted on to roll out the red carpet. They had hired her a limousine and escort service, and that was why Susan Halpert was waiting for her charge on a June Friday morning.

Susan had been getting steady freelance escort work from Paulsen's Livery since the Hong Kong invasion of the Toronto real-estate market began in the mid-eighties. Paulsen's didn't have a strong comprehension of China's different regional dialects, which was Susan's luck.

Mandarin was her mother tongue, and her Cantonese – the dialect of Hong Kong – was limited. But it worked out in the end. Most rich Cantonese-speaking Chinese from Hong Kong wished that they could speak more Mandarin, and pretended that they could. In fact, Susan mostly used English during her escorting work, and Paulsen's was none the wiser. During a good month, the work could pay very well – especially if she sufficiently ingratiated herself to her wealthy charges to elicit a generous gratuity. It supplemented Jamie's modest newspaper salary.

"So sorry, so sorry," said Mrs. Li as she came puffing along the sidewalk to where Susan was standing with the tour bus driver. "Go to bank. Take too long. Too busy, too busy."

She was carrying a large attaché case covered in alligator hide, which Susan offered to take before they boarded the bus. Mrs. Li hesitated and then shook her head and abruptly handed it over. "Okay, okay. But careful. Money, money."

Susan smiled as she took the case. It *was* heavy, whatever Mrs. Li was carrying in it. But Susan wasn't thinking about the weight. She was hoping that she hadn't made a miscalculation about taking her charge on a standard bus tour of Toronto. When they had talked the day before about her itinerary, Susan had expected to take Mrs. Li around the city herself in one of Paulsen's vulgar vehicles – the kind Hong Kong people seemed to like.

But she had detected in Mrs. Li something quite different from her usual customer. She was not weighed down by a designer watch or encrusted with the usual lazy-lady jewellery. Mrs. Li's small share of spoken English, translated briskly from Cantonese complete with Chinese grammatical construction, was refreshing in contrast with the slyly indirect conversations of most wealthy Hong Kong Chinese. And Mrs. Li had said she wanted to see the *real* Toronto rather than being cocooned inside Paulsen's stretched-white horror.

"What if we went on an ordinary bus tour of Toronto with other visitors?" asked Susan. "It might be fun."

"Good, good," said Mrs. Li enthusiastically. "See people. Toronto people. Good idea."

And so, while Paulsen's driver kept the White Maria in attendance at the Royal York Hotel at $200-an-hour, Big Huang's wife presented her $7.50 ticket and boarded a green and gold contraption tricked out to look like a turn-of-the-century omnibus.

"Hi, everyone. I hope you folks are in a real great mood because you are about to see a good-mood city. Toronto is a world-class city, folks, and I want you all just to sit back and relax and enjoy the ambiance."

Susan led the way to a rear window seat and was about to put Mrs. Li's attaché case in the storage area above the seat when she was asked to give it back.

"I take. I take," said Mrs. Li with a laugh, reaching up to get it from Susan and placing it on her lap. "More good here."

"We're starting off our tour this morning in the historic heart of Toronto's business district. Any folks here from Montreal? A couple, eh? Sorry, folks, Toronto took over from Montreal as Canada's commercial centre a couple of decades ago and has never looked back. Eighty-five per cent of the new jobs created in this country last year can be located to within eighty miles of where we are driving right now. That's real economic clout, ladies and gentlemen. That's why Toronto has the highest real-estate prices in the country. That's why we have a thriving restaurant and theatre dist . . ."

"When you leave China?"

Mrs. Li's question to Susan came right out of nowhere as the bus lumbered up University Avenue and turned right on King Street West to take in the banking district. Susan already realized Mrs. Li understood far more English than she spoke, but since her own English had been learned so painfully and she had always been worried about making blunders, she was somewhat in awe of both Mrs. Li's self-confidence and her happy indifference to correct grammatical structure.

"In 1979. My husband is American-born, but we are both Canadian citizens now."

"Good, good, good. Canada good country. China very bad country. Communists very, very bad. You have children?"

"No, we don't. My husband would like to have children, but I'm not so sure. I don't think this is such a wonderful world to bring in more children."

Mrs. Li looked at Susan in astonishment. "Children good. Lots of children, lots of good. Communists say only one boy. No girls. Family with no girls bad, bad, bad."

Susan smiled in spite of herself. "Oh look, Mrs. Li. This is the newspaper building where my husband works. He's probably there right now."

"If you look to your left, you will see the premises of *The Toronto Observer*, Canada's most respected daily newspaper. It was founded in 1837 by the son of the English governor and that's when Toronto was called York. Muddy York, in fact, because the streets were so . . ."

"You make baby tonight," said Mrs. Li, patting Susan's lap. "Quick, quick. You not young anymore. How old you are?"

Susan laughed again. "I'm not that old, Mrs. Li. I'm thirty-three. These days, lots of women don't have their first baby till they are my age."

"Too old, but no choice. Make baby tonight. Husband be very happy. Good, good, good."

"Oh, I don't think anything will ever make my husband truly happy. He wasn't born to be happy. But he's a good man. He's a good husband."

They passed Toronto's two city halls, old and less old, and headed west on Dundas Street. "We'll soon be in the heart of old Chinatown, ladies and gentleman. You know, Toronto is the most multicultured city in the world. It's the biggest Greek city outside of Greece. It's the biggest Italian city outside of Italy. It's the biggest Polish city outside Poland. It's the biggest Chinese city outside China. You name it. We're the biggest . . ."

"Man stupid," said Mrs. Li. She had been listening after all. "Hong Kong bigger Chinese city. Taibei bigger Chinese city. Singapore bigger Chinese city. Why he say stupid thing?"

"Probably because he doesn't know how to talk any other way."

"Back to baby. You have special problem? I know good Chinese medicine – yo! yo! yo! – what trouble?"

The bus had come to a sudden stop. Within seconds, all the traffic on Dundas Street between Spadina and Beverley had been engulfed by a surging, happy crowd of Chinese wearing white headbands and shouting out slogans. There were signs in Chinese and English everywhere: PROTECT THE STUDENTS and WE ARE WATCHING and LONG LIVE DEMOCRACY. The crowd waved to people in the tour bus, who, momentarily disturbed by the demonstration and abrupt halt, quickly caught the prevailing spirit as the demonstrators gave them the thumbs-up sign.

"China trouble," said Mrs. Li, "always China trouble. No good, no good. Make baby fast."

Susan looked at the faces in the crowds surging past the bus. Mrs. Li was right. She *was* getting old. All the faces looked so young. She was just eleven when the Red Guards came hunting for her family in Nanjing. The same laughing faces, the same thumbs up. Different signs though. And that time she knew so many of them, faces of her father's students, faces of her older brother's friends, faces of her mother's cronies. Except in 1967, when she and her family had been dragged out of their compound house, all the laughing had stopped, as if on cue, and the screaming abuse started. It had lasted for seven hours, and when it finally ceased, her father was bleeding from head to toe. They dragged him off, crippled, with a placard around his neck, never to be seen again. Then they pasted red paper labels over their doorway accusing the family of counter-revolutionary tendencies, and everyone shunned them, and her childhood ended forever until the moment Gordon Wrye came into her life and made her laugh for the first time in eleven years, for the first time since her childhood ended, for the first time in her adulthood.

"Good, good. China trouble over," said Mrs. Li as the bus resumed its tour and headed north towards the University of Toronto.

"This is Canada's biggest university, ladies and gentlemen. Over eighty thousand young people come here every day to be turned into the leaders of tomorrow. This is the university where insulin was discovered, so they say. Did you ever hear about Marshall McLuhan. Yes? Some of you have? Well, this is where he hung out, but I have to be honest with you, wonderful as our university is, Bobby Hull never went there. Oh look over there, ladies and gentleman. We're about to pass Queen Victoria Museum. You know they call Toronto 'The Queen City,' and royalty is a big part of our history. The Queen Victoria Museum houses some of the finest historical artefacts anywhere in the world. If you go there, they say to be sure to see the Chinese exhibition. There's an entire Ming tomb on display, the only complete Ming tomb on public view outside of China. Now I don't know a 'ming' from a 'ring,' but I'm told by smarter folks than me that this is a real must-see. . . ."

Susan's pensiveness put a damper on Mrs. Li's comprehensive advice on conception ("pill no good, make very sick"), but as the bus headed east along Bloor Street and north on Sherbourne, she became animated again.

"We're about to enter Rosedale, folks. This is one of Toronto's oldest and most prestigious residential areas. House prices here range between half a million and over five million dollars. You heard me right! Five million! This is where Lord Thomson of Fleet lives. Have you heard of him? He owns most of the newspapers in the world and he lives right here. We'll be going past his home shortly. You know a lot of Hollywood movies are made in Toronto now and this is the part of town the Hollywood stars like to stay in. . . ."

"Nice houses," said Mrs. Li. "Very nice. Look that house. Very nice."

Susan looked, but wasn't quite sure which particular house Mrs. Li was referring to, so she simply nodded diplomatically.

"Yo! yo! Look that house! That house for sale. Very nice. Tell driver to stop. *Stop! Stop!*"

She shouted so loudly that all the passengers on the bus turned to stare at her.

"I'm sorry, is there some trouble?" The guide was as perplexed as everyone else, but the bus *had* come to a stop, and Mrs. Li was gesturing animatedly to Susan to join her in the aisle so they could get off.

"Come, come. Nice house."

Totally mystified, Susan followed obediently. When they got out on the street, she looked back at the guide, who was gaping at them.

Mrs. Li looked up, too.

"Nice ride. Very nice. We say bye-bye now. You go. Go, go, go. Give money. Nice ride."

Susan smiled the strange smile she always did when she didn't understand what on earth was going on. The driver smiled back. The guide smiled. Susan reached into her purse and took out a fifty-dollar bill and went briefly back onto the bus to give it to the driver. "I guess we're staying here. Goodbye and thanks."

"Goodbye and *thank you*," said the driver. The door was closed and the bus moved on. As it disappeared along Elm Avenue, Susan and Mrs. Li found themselves all alone on the sidewalk in deepest Rosedale. The only sound to be heard other than birds and air-conditioners was the hedgecutters being wielded by a Jamaican immigrant. A decade earlier, he would have been Chinese.

"Mrs. Li, if you want to look at houses in Toronto, I can easily arrange for a reputable agent to take you around."

"No agent. You my agent. Want to see this house. Very nice house."

Susan looked at Mrs. Li's quarry. She didn't have a lot of opinions on houses, or at least not on their different styles. She'd not been brought up to appreciate them, and her highest aesthetic statement in this regard was gratitude for a simple roof over her head, especially one that also featured flush toilets, running hot water, and was warm in winter.

The house that had attracted Mrs. Li's interest was small in comparison with its immediate neighbours, but the front garden was pretty and the main entrance welcoming. The for sale sign listed the name of the agent and a phone number to make an appointment for a viewing. It took Susan a few seconds to realize that Mrs. Li fully intended to march up to the front door then and there.

"I think if we walk for a little while, I'll find a phone booth and we'll get the car to pick us up. I can arrange for you to see this house this afternoon, I'm sure."

"We go now," said Mrs. Li, who then proceeded up the flagstone pathway to the front door, attaché case in hand. Before Susan could even catch up to her, she had rung the bell.

A few seconds later, a man in his late middle-age answered the door. He was wearing a tweed jacket, an open-necked shirt, and a loose Paisley patterned cravat. There was a gold and bloodstone crested signet ring on his little finger. The club look.

"Yes," he said as he peered at the two Chinese women. "Are you agents? We told them we don't permit viewing of the house in the morning."

Susan was about to say something when Mrs. Li took her breath away.

"No agents. Buy house. Talk now."

"My dear lady," said the club man. "Perhaps you don't understand how we do business in this country, but if you – "

"How much you want?"

"*Excuse me?*"

"How much you want?"

"I'm sorry. This is very distasteful. For your information, the asking price is six hundred and eighty-five thousand dollars, and if you are interested in making an offer, perhaps you would be so kind as to get in touch – "

"I give you seven hundred thousand Canadian dollars. We talk now."

He was about to shut the door in their faces when he noticed Mrs. Li's eyes were twinkling as she patted her attaché case meaningfully. There had been just enough accounts in *The Toronto Observer* about rich Chinese in a hurry to make him pause before he hurled his highest insult the ladies' way. Whatever ensued, he decided, this was going to be a great yarn and, besides, he was now intrigued. Mrs. Li had that effect on people. And besides, again, his overpriced house had been on the market for nearly eleven weeks with hardly a nibble.

"Would you care to come in?" He put out his hand. "My name is Michael d'Ecrivan. I don't believe we've met."

~

Promptly at 11 a.m., the organ in the assembly hall of the Shearer Academy boomed out with Handel's triumphal march, "See the Conquering Hero Comes." The boys all stood up, and the procession of teachers and specially invited guests for the annual Prize Day ceremony, led by the headmaster, shuffled down the central aisle to the raised dais at the front.

Halpert had missed the ceremony only once in the five years since the Gordon Wrye Prize for Outstanding Achievement in International Studies had been inaugurated in 1984 and that was only because his father had died in Boston. The prize, which was a leather-bound copy of an appropriate book with the school's crest on the cover, along with a cheque for one hundred dollars, was funded by Halpert. The head-master had suggested the idea to Halpert during the weeks he had haunted the school after his return from China, when the obsession over Gordon's fate had led him on a disorganized investigation into his friend's history in Toronto.

As Halpert sat in a place of honour on the dais after the strains of the opening hymn ("Lord, thy mercies yet unfolded, / Cheer the heart and light our way") had faded away, he surveyed the faces of the teenaged boys and their parents at the academy. The school was not that old. It had been founded in 1953 by an English-born teacher at Upper Canada College who had become distressed at what he considered was the private school's unfocused direction in its tutelage of the sons of Toronto's gentry. And so, with the backing of three wealthy families, he founded his own institution based on a special understanding of boys' needs during the difficult teenage years.

Gordon Wrye had been a full-scholarship student at this pre-dominantly WASP establishment. Now, as Halpert looked out at the four-hundred-odd faces assembled before him, he noticed that in 1989 close to half the student body was non-white. The majority of the non-whites were racially Chinese or Korean, with a smattering of sub-continentals and Middle Easterners. He knew Gordon had loathed the school, but he felt he would be amused by the transformation of its racial configuration.

"O universal Creator," intoned the headmaster at the podium as he read the updated school prayer, "who is known in many lands by many names, be with us today in all our challenges. Give to us the wisdom of Solomon, the rectitude of Confucius, the empathy of Christ, the patience of Buddha, and the determination of the Prophet Muhammad. Help us to be faithful stewards of thy noble planet, Earth, defending its fragile environment even as we protect all thy endangered creatures. We ask this in the name of all that is holy under Thy comprehensive gaze. Shalom. All praise. Amen."

Halpert's gaze wandered to the honour rolls printed on finely carved oak boards festooning the walls of the hall. Gordon Wrye's name appeared three times, once as top scholar of the leaving class and twice as The I. K. Shearer Medallist for Leadership. His was the only name to appear more than twice on the gold-lettered boards, and this year the school had finally opened up a new section to include the previous four winners of the Wrye prize.

Halpert was glad he had introduced this small gesture to Gordon's memory. There were now so many painful things that his name aroused in Halpert's mind – Kwai Ta-ping's arrest, show trial, and twelve-year sentence to hard labour; his messy divorce and his confused, compli-cated, and mostly loveless marriage to Susan; his abandoned book and almost-aborted career – that the annual rite of purification which this prize-giving represented was almost the only happy fixture in his life.

More than halfway through the ceremony, Halpert shook himself out of his daydreams as he heard the start of his cue. Many of the silver trophy cups, books, medallions, and plaques – all heaped up in front of the headmaster's chair – had already been handed out.

"It is now time to present the Gordon Wrye Award for Outstanding Achievement in International Studies," said the headmaster. "This is quite a new award, and I'm happy to report that it finally has a proud place on the honour rolls of this school, as you can see if you look up to the right there beside the middle window."

Everyone looked up, including Halpert. The names of the previous prize-winners were instructive of the new reality at the Shearer Academy: 1985 *Robert Stapells*; 1986 *Fong Ai-qing*; 1987 *Sampson (Tsui-sen) Lee*; 1988 *Mufestar Ali*. If Halpert's haphazard investigations had been the inspiration for this prize, the headmaster was the driving force. He wasn't at all surprised that Gordon Wrye had been murdered, for whatever reason, but he retained a warm spot for the memory of this engaging, busy boy primarily because – in a certain sense – Gordon had been responsible for getting him his job in 1966.

After the saintly Shearer had retired, the school's board of governors had chosen another Englishman, a shy and intensely intellectual Anglican priest, to be the second head. That was in the fall of 1965. Less than a year later, the new headmaster found himself serving a two-year prison sentence after being convicted of indecent exposure and attempted buggery on a minor. His accuser was Gordon Wrye, although the teenager's name had been kept out of the newspapers thanks to court injunctions against the naming of minors in criminal cases.

The priest's wife had had a nervous breakdown, and a year later his fifteen-year-old son committed suicide. It had been a terrible mess. It might have gone unremarked had there not been a mole in the school who supplied lurid details to a racy new tabloid, *The Toronto Mirror*, eager to make a name for itself with just such stories.

Mercifully, the public's memory is almost as short as a journalist's. The third and still reigning headmaster had earned his spurs during his first years by a conspicuously masculine approach to his tasks, and by obliterating all memory of his predecessor, whose name and record had been consigned to the dustbin of history. In the Shearer Academy, he was a non-person.

"Gordon Wrye first went to the People's Republic of China in 1975," read the headmaster. This was a little commemorative essay he and Halpert had worked out five years earlier, to be read out each time the new recipient was announced. "He went there with all the friendly instincts of inquiry which had been fostered by the Shearer Academy during his years of study here. We should ask ourselves today what it was in this young man's life which made him identify so strongly with the Chinese people, to the very point of making the ultimate sacrifice. It was nothing less than the restless spirit of international inquiry and understanding. In honouring the memory of Gordon Wrye with this annual prize to the student who has shown extraordinary aptitude in international studies, we also make good on our school's commitment to global harmony."

The headmaster paused, looked up from his text, and made an emphatic turn of his head in Halpert's direction.

"Once again, we are fortunate to have the patron of the Gordon Wrye prize here to present it to this year's winner. James Halpert, as you all know, was the distinguished foreign correspondent of *The Toronto Observer* who lived and worked in China at the same time as Gordon Wrye. They were good friends, and he remains our closest link to one of the finest Shearermen who ever lived. Mr. Halpert will now join me at the prize table as we give the 1989 Gordon Wrye Prize for Outstanding Achievement in International Studies to . . . Kim-yan Sun. Mr. Halpert, if you please."

God, how Halpert hated to hear that phrase "distinguished foreign correspondent." It was another person being talked about, someone Halpert scarcely knew anymore. What he did know at this moment was that it was close to noon and he had only an hour to get down to the *Observer* to begin his shift as copy chief on the national desk. If he was really lucky and someone notable died, he might also get a chance to write an interesting obituary.

∾

Geoffrey Cameron switched on his terminal in the middle of the *Observer*'s newsroom. *If that bitch doesn't buy this outline*, he thought to himself, *I'm quitting*. Cameron was one of yesterday's golden-haired boys, an abrasive investigative journalist who, in his prime, had loved to dig into the muck in life to get the stories other journalists were either too frightened or too lazy to touch. Some of his pieces didn't pan out. Many of them, actually. But those that worked had worked very well. He had felled cabinet ministers, destroyed the reputations of chief executives, and sent at least a half-dozen bottom feeders to prison.

But his hit-and-often-miss work was no longer appreciated at the *Observer*. The old and forbearing editor-in-chief had been pushed into early retirement, and it was a toss-up what his successor loathed more, Cameron's story ideas or his huge expense accounts. Both seemed to her to be equally grotesque. One thing was quite clear within the first few weeks of the current regime: the new editor-in-chief had no intention of presiding over a newspaper that businessmen either feared or despised.

Cameron had been reassigned to general news. He was incapable of stopping his old ways, however, and on his own hoof he would sometimes investigate a potentially corrosive story and try to sell it to the news desk. Occasionally, but increasingly rarely, he was successful – at least if it wasn't a business story. This time, it was different. This was a *real* story, and the business angle was minor compared to the exposure of international corruption:

MEMO
TO: HILARY FAIRE
FROM: GEOFF CAMERON

Cameron paused. He wanted to make this one work. His last two had been rejected out of hand, and among the things he stood accused of was jerking the story line too dramatically without any real proof. He despaired of the new crowd ever understanding how an investigative journalist operated. Support was needed before the final proofs were in. Support was needed to finance all the difficult undercover work. Support was needed to pay for trips, and this one would require trips to New York, London, Hong Kong, and Singapore. *Oh hell, just write the damn thing*.

Re: Finch's Fine Porcelains (Toronto) Ltd.

The firm of Finch's Fine Porcelains (Toronto) Ltd. opened for business here four years ago. It is part of the worldwide English firm of Finch Importables PLC, now based in Singapore. By 1986, it had become one of the prize shops in town thanks to the housing and property boom and the propensity of Toronto's wealthy classes to use decorators with whom Finch's has especially warm relationships.

The Toronto branch is located in the upmarket Scollard Centre on two floors connected by a wide interior circular staircase. There is no general admittance. The most the public are permitted to see are two small windows, each featuring rotating displays of stunningly beautiful porcelains, and a locked glass door leading directly to a receptionist. The advice on the door is "By appointment only," and it is part of Finch's studied snobbery that it does not even supply an accompanying phone number.

I have a contact who works there and he has told me many strange things about this company. Let me start with the most straightforward of the strange things: Why, for example, does Finch's bother to pay the high rent for the public visibility of the Scollard Centre when the public is banned? The answer has two parts: (1) the low-key, deliberate arrogance helps to maintain not only the appropriate mystique but also the exorbitant prices for its antique porcelains; and (2) the entire Scollard Centre complex is owned by 788642-1984 Ltd., which in turn is owned by Potlow Investments of Hong Kong and St. Peter's Port, Guernsey, which – thanks to some sort of Potlow partnership with Finch's Importables PLC – means that the rent is merely a bookkeeping item.

The staff at the Toronto branch comprises a manager, two salespeople, one bookkeeper, and the receptionist. In any week, I am reliably told, there may be only one or two invited customers, other than the professional decorators. The sales staff of two handle the decorators and are often out on site assignments. The special customers – and some weeks there are none at all – are invariably seen by the manager.

My source has good reason to believe that there is an

entirely secret line of merchandise for these special customers, merchandise that is not revealed to the sales staff.
My source further believes that some or all of this special
merchandise, which it is assumed comprises a variety of
porcelain antiquities, has been brought into the country
illegally – or, at the very least, improperly declared.

I have found all this out on my own initiative, and I now
need the newspaper's support in developing the story. I
have good reason to believe that the illegal merchandise
originates from China and that I will find similar covert
selling operations at other branches of Finch's. I therefore
request permission to travel to New York, London, Hong
Kong, and Singapore. Singapore is where Finch's now has
its headquarters and it is there that I would like to confront
the owners with my research, which won't be complete
until I check out the other branches.

I have done a detailed costing of such a trip which is
attached and I request approval as soon as possible so I can
make my plans. This is an excellent story for the *Observer*
which will get the newspaper wide international attention.
It's also a shoo-in for a National Newspaper Award.

I also request some dedicated backup here at the newspaper and would like Halpert to be my research and copy
editor because of his China background. When he was
posted to Beijing, he wrote several fine features on grave-
robbers (I believe the illicit antiquities have been stolen out
of China under the noses of the authorities), and Halpert is
more knowledgeable about Chinese antiquities than anyone else on the newspaper's staff.

Sorry for the length of this memo, but it is a complicated story that I haven't got to the bottom of yet. As I
said, I am looking forward to your earliest possible positive
response.

∾

Even while Geoffrey Cameron was tapping out his memo on a Friday afternoon, the small staff at Finch's Fine Porcelains was awaiting the arrival of Dr. Julie Potlow, vice-chairman and senior director of Potlow Investments, who had flown in unexpectedly from London the night before, en route to Hong Kong. She had telephoned Toronto just before her plane left Heathrow to ask that all the staff wait for her appearance around noon, so there was an undeniable tension in the air.

Undeniable and understandable. One of the reasons Mr. d'Ecrivan had ultimately warmed to Mrs. Li earlier in the morning was that the property and housing market in Toronto was on the skids. He knew it in his gut because the asking price for his house had been uncomfortably, if discreetly, lowered twice; but like most other home and large-property investors, he resisted the full, looming catastrophe. He and all the other high-flyers simply couldn't afford to embrace reality. So much of the borrowed cash they were floating around in depended on an ever-expanding market. While they were fully prepared for little fluctuations here and there, the notion of an out-and-out collapse was as unthinkable as . . . well, as unthinkable as the notion that the Reichmann brothers might go bankrupt.

The taxi drivers knew better, of course. They were always the first to suffer. People in hock to the banks for millions of dollars, or even merely hundreds of thousands of dollars, had already decided to tighten their belts by holding back on eight-dollar taxi fares. It made them think they were still in control. Next in line to the taxi drivers in feeling the pinch were newspaper and magazine owners, who, almost overnight, saw their ad lineages mysteriously plummet. Then came the proprietors of exotic merchandise – like antique Chinese porcelains – the purchase of whose wares could be put off as indefinitely as that superfluous addition to the summer cottage.

The two salespeople at Finch's had seen a precipitous decline in business during the previous two quarters. Even more ominously for the future, three of their most active decorators had recently relocated to Vancouver. So when they got the word that Dr. Potlow – difficult Dr. Potlow, purposely intemperate Dr. Potlow, impossible-to-placate

Dr. Potlow – was staging a surprise visit the following day, they were not expecting "good service" bonuses.

What did arrive surprised even Mr. Stavert, the manager, who was the most accustomed to his employer's summary ways. At 12:10 p.m., a mail courier delivered a large brown manila envelope addressed to the manager. He opened the envelope to find a smaller manila envelope, stapled to which was a memo from Julie:

TO: M. L. Stavert, Esq.
FROM: Dr. J. Potlow
RE: Redundancies

> Changing sales patterns necessitate the closure of Finch's Fine Porcelains (Toronto) Ltd. You are to give the staff immediate notice. Severance cheques in conformity to Ontario legislation on closures are attached. Potlow Investments will retain your services (with bonus), dependent on smooth closure procedures. Severance cheques are not – repeat *not* – to be handed out immediately, but are dependent on written acceptance of our offer and an orderly departure from our premises. You retain responsibility for stock and completing pending sales (if any). Report to A. Fisher, New York branch, re: shipping remaining stock. Expect to hear from you at above office by Tuesday at the latest.

Alone of all the employees, Stavert had been anticipating exactly this communication. Alone of all the employees, he appreciated its cool, businesslike tone. That was because, again alone of all the employees in Toronto with the exception of his trusted bookkeeper, he knew that the closure had nothing at all to do with the recession and everything to do with a general "quieting down" of all special sales. He was perfectly safe. He knew too much.

That's why he was now smiling warmly at his concerned colleagues, who had been trying in vain to discern the contents of the missive from his initially expressionless face.

"Ah well, then," he said. "It seems that Dr. Potlow is not coming here after all. Why don't you all go for lunch and I'll see if I can get to the bottom of this."

The staff's relief was almost as palpable as the manager's optimistic guess at what bonus might be in store for him. He didn't get to manage a Julie Potlow enterprise by being a dreamer, however, and as soon as his staff left, he made immediate arrangements to have the locks changed before they returned.

∾

Halpert pushed through the heavy bronze doors at the main entrance of *The Toronto Observer* on Bay Street. The metalwork, which had always been so scrupulously polished, hadn't been touched for weeks and was looking dull and dirty. *Bad sign*, he thought, *more cost-cutting*.

Since he had returned to full-time work at the *Observer* after a fruitless leave in 1980 to write his book on China, the size of the newsroom staff had declined by nearly forty per cent. The most recent downsizing had been the worst, with over sixty staff members either forced out through early retirement or made to feel so miserable and insecure by the editor-in-chief that even the prospect of unemployment seemed preferable to the daily demolition of their souls.

"Hi, Charlie," he said automatically to the security guard at the reception desk in the front hall.

"Say, Mr. Halpert, quite the doings in your old neck of the woods, eh?"

"Charlie?"

"China, I mean. Says on CNN that the army's going to come again for sure and those kids better get on home."

"Now, Charlie, you know better than to trust television news. Only believe what you read in the *Observer*."

They both got a chuckle out of that one.

The *Observer*'s coverage of China over the past couple of years had been a disgrace, but Halpert – powerless to do anything about it – had so distanced himself emotionally from its field of irritation that most days he never bothered to follow the dispatches of his third successor, a whiz-kid product of the University of Toronto's Department of East Asian Studies who spoke Mandarin like a native but disliked talking to ordinary Chinese people. He preferred to talk to officials and scoured the beat simply to find the proof to theories he had come by before he had ever set foot in the Middle Kingdom.

Yet the correspondent had turned out to be the right man in the right place under the right editor-in-chief. Shortly after Halpert rejoined the *Observer* in 1981 as a senior feature writer and roving correspondent, his old editor-in-chief, Jim Worrell, was pushed out, and he found himself reporting to M. (for Mary) Hilary Faire, the cleverest office strategist the poor old *Observer* had ever nurtured.

Halpert hardly remembered her from the few months he had spent at the newspaper in 1975 before taking up the post in Beijing. She had been editor of the editorial page then and apparently known for her common sense, as well as for her loyalty to Worrell, who had so admired Halpert's careful, cogent dispatches from Vietnam for the Washington *Post* that he decided to import him.

In the end, it was Hilary Faire's dagger sticking most prominently out of Worrell's back when he was forced into retirement two years ahead of schedule, but her appointment as the first woman to lead Canada's oldest English-language daily had still been hailed as innovative, daring, and anti-sexist.

"Hi, Arch," Halpert said to his Number Two on the copy desk as he settled into his slot and started searching around in the computer for the digest of the top national news stories of the day. "All quiet on the domestic front, I trust?"

"Mulroney's wacking off on his Quebec pecker again. The Montreal shipyards are getting the frigate contract which should have gone to Halifax. Usual shit. All the excitement's in China today."

"Right," said Halpert, tuning out. He was hunting through the international obit file to see if there was someone freshly interred who could ignite the tiny remaining spark of journalistic initiative he had left. He hadn't done such a bad job in the feature-writing post, especially considering the mental state he had been in. But he knew he was in trouble after Hilary Faire had taken over, when she moved him out of features and assigned him temporarily to the lowly task of drafting a new style guide for editors to follow when using Chinese names for places and people.

"I can scarcely believe we are still using the old system," she said to Halpert after summoning him to her office and keeping him waiting for over a half an hour. "It's antiquated and inappropriate, like so many things at this newspaper."

This had been the first opportunity Halpert had had to see the inside of the editor-in-chief's office since Jim Worrell's days. It was utterly transformed.

In place of the overstuffed bookshelves on the back wall, there was a vast abstract canvas whose colour variation ran all the way from grey to grey-blue. She had replaced Worrell's comfortably cluttered desk and worn-out, bulging In basket with a black lacquer table on top of which was . . . *nothing*. This was genuinely arresting. No paper at all, not even an inter-office memo. No bric-à-brac. No Roladex. No photographs. No telephone. *No newspaper anywhere*. It was a command centre, stripped down and battle-ready.

The two visitors' seats in front of the desk were fragile-looking designer chairs, also in black, and were pushed so close to her desk that it seemed necessary to ask permission to pull one out and take a seat. Permission was rarely granted, and when it was, no one ever wanted to linger for long. Or so Halpert was told. He, personally, had never been asked to sit down since Hilary Faire had been appointed editor-in-chief.

"So," she continued at that first office encounter, when Halpert had stood so awkwardly in front of her gleaming, unobstructed desk, "I made some inquiries and discovered you were the one who recommended we retain the old system when all the rest of the world was adopting the new one. And now we're the only one left. Someone showed me your original memo from 1983. I couldn't understand your reasoning at all. Perhaps you could summarize it for me now?"

"I think the old Wade-Giles system of romanization is easier for the reading public to decipher. There's quite a few letters in this new Pinyin system – like 'x' and 'q' – which don't correspond in any way to the sounds we habitually associate with – "

"I think, Mr. Halpert, you can let me take on the burden of the

readers' concerns. That's what I get paid for. I would like you to prepare a style sheet for the new system which we can use on the copy desk.
I don't want a half-assed job, either. It should be comprehensive and
comprehensible. I also want you to write a tight account of why we are
making these changes which we will run with the first dispatch deploy-
ing them. I'd like it by this time next week."

Hilary Faire's greatest skill as a manager was in deconstructing any
sense of confidence or security an underling might have erected. Ten
minutes earlier, Halpert was not in particularly good emotional shape,
but he had been holding on.

His self-esteem, or what little he had of it, mostly came from the way
his colleagues regarded him. They knew how devastated he had been
when he heard about the arrest and trial of the Chinese dissident, Kwai
Ta-ping. The charges against Kwai had clearly lacerated Halpert: aiding
and abetting the escape of an unnamed traitor; working "hand-in-
glove" with foreign provocateurs; selling state secrets to Western journalists. The specifics of the show trial were secret, but the result was
public: twelve years in the labour-reform camp system. Twelve years
without remission.

That was in 1981, when Kwai was thirty-four. In 1993, when he
might re-emerge, he would be nearly forty-seven. Jim Worrell had
given Halpert a few weeks of leave, for Halpert's own sake and out of
respect for what he had done for the *Observer*.

Now, in less than a couple of minutes, he had been stripped of any
lingering respect. Suddenly, he was being treated with contempt and
ordered around like a copy boy. Perhaps another journalist would have
been tempted to pick up one of the visitor's chairs, raise it high over his
head, and bring it smashing down on the black lacquer table. And then
storm out of the *Observer* forever. That thought didn't occur to Halpert.
Worse, it took him a while even to comprehend the new world he had
just entered. Like someone who tugs at a sore tooth to make sure it is
still there, he lingered in her office for more punishment.

"I'll be happy to do the style sheet," he said. "You may be right, and
sticking to the old system has become a lost cause. Probably we should
retain some of the most used old spellings, like 'Peking' and 'Canton.'

I'll look them all over, but I can't get it done this week. I'm scheduled to go to Vancouver tomorrow to do a feature on Asian contributions to the World's Fair, so maybe you can look for it a week Wednesday."

"You don't get it, do you?" said the editor-in-chief. Earlier, she had turned her swivel chair away from Halpert when she dismissed him from her presence. Now she turned back to take aim at her target once more.

"I'm not interested in your views on any of this. I simply want you to do it. And I've cancelled your trip to Vancouver. It's absurd to have someone travelling out there for minor features when we have a very well-paid correspondent twiddling his thumbs with not enough to do. After you get the style sheet done, we'll discuss your overall assignment and see if we can't find something more suitable for your talents. You can go now, Mr. Halpert."

And so, instead of travelling to Vancouver, he did this:

Peking = *Beijing*,
Canton = *Guangzhou*,
Mao Tse-tung = *Mao Zedong*,
and Teng Hsiao-ping = *Deng Xiaoping*,
but Shanghai is still *Shanghai*!

Chou En-lai = *Zhou Enlai*,
Ch'ing Dynasty = *Qing Dynasty*,
Sian = *Xian*,
and Nanking = *Nanjing*,
but the good old Sung dynasty can still be *Sung*!

Lee = *Li*,
Lin Piao = *Lin Biao*,
and China is really *Zhongguo*, but here at least we'll draw the line and stay the same.

It was just an introductory memo to prepare deskmen for the coming changes, but Hilary Faire told Halpert not to issue it.

"Not very clever, I'm afraid, Mr. Halpert. Frivolous in the extreme, and possibly insidious. Is this the sort of stuff your much-touted fame rests upon?"

No, thought Halpert. *No, it's based on nothing more than fraud, but no matter what you say or do Kuai Dabing will always be Kwai Ta-ping to me. Always, always, always.*

∾

It was 7:45 p.m., almost time for Halpert to go home. Someone on the foreign desk kept dropping off printouts of wire stories on the increased troop movements in and around Beijing. Halpert wished he wouldn't. He knew exactly what was going to happen. Well, if not exactly, the gist anyway. Troops would come in. Lots of deaths. Outrage round the world. Then, soon enough, business as usual. He had read all the analytic thumbsuckers written by his third successor – initially dismissing the significance of the democracy activists, then insisting that they would triumph, and now criticizing them for an inability to see beyond anarchy. He wondered why the third successor had not yet been appointed to the Politburo.

"Our Miss Faire has approved a leave of absence for your noble successor in Beijing, starting next week," Arch Crawley observed sarcastically to Halpert as they both started clearing their desks.

"You're kidding," said Halpert. "The place is about to explode. What's the leave for? A book?"

"Yah. Madam's memo says he has 'an impressive offer' from some publisher – where the hell is that memo, the wording's very nice – oh yah, here it is. Now get this: 'an impressive offer worthy of the quality coverage he has been providing *Observer* readers.' Like it?"

"Knock it off, Arch. I don't care."

"I know you don't care, that's why I tell you. Did you see the other memo?"

"What other memo?"

"Dum-de-dum-dum time again. Full meeting of the newsroom in the cafeteria on Monday afternoon to, I quote, 'discuss the latest innovative measures in cost-cutting and newsroom efficiency.'"

"I don't care about that either."

169

"Well, excuse me, Mr. Don't Care, but some of us would kind of like to keep our jobs."

"I need my job, too, Arch, but I'm not going to get into an almighty lather about something that is not at all clear yet."

"Are you kidding? They've been hinting about this for months."

"All right, dammit. I'll deal with it when I have to deal with it."

"Ooo-kay. We're a little touchy tonight, I can tell. So let's change the subject. Did you hear who she's fucking now?"

"C'mon, Arch, let it alone."

"No, I'm really serious. This may be important for all our futures. I was told — I won't say by who because I know how distasteful you find gossip — I was told that she's going postmodern, giving up on bedding broads for a while and has taken Brendan to her chilly breast."

"Who?"

"Brendan Corey. That sucky-assed wimp she hired to write the Business Periscope column last month and who we all took for a prize faggot."

"How can anyone be such a bigoted asshole as you and still judiciously edit the national news? How can a guy who is reputed to have a quarter ownership in a brothel in Bangkok even bring himself to walk through these doors every day and work in this female-dominated, fag-loving, ideologically confused cesspit?"

"I ask myself the same question all the time. And every time I come up with the same answer. I must have balls of steel. It's the only explanation."

"See you Monday, Arch. Have a good weekend."

As Halpert tried to leave the newsroom, Geoffrey Cameron came running over to him. "James, I need to speak to you. I need a real favour. I've taken your name in vain with Hilary because I want you to be — "

A young female editor came up to the two of them and interrupted Cameron midsentence. "Mr. Halpert," she said, "CNN is reporting major troop movements on Tiananmen Square. It's pretty awful. A bunch of us are watching it on the library's set. Do you want to join us?"

"No thanks," he said wearily.

He looked at his watch and realized that the next day's edition of the newspaper, which once had five mighty editions a day and now had only one, was beyond recall. The presses, which no longer stopped for man or woman and certainly not for the news, were even at that moment disgorging the daily analyses of trends and developments which were already months old.

Halpert smiled at the young editor.

"At least we won't have to read about it in tomorrow's paper."

Then he turned away from her and Cameron. "I'm going home now, Geoff," he said, heading out the newsroom door. "Can we talk about this later?"

∞

Susan was lying on the bed, staring up at the ceiling, when she heard him come through the front door of their apartment. He didn't shout hello and she didn't acknowledge his return. They had ceased these simple exchanges over six years ago, barely two years into the marriage. She noticed it at first, but Halpert didn't. He just stopped doing it one day, and that was that.

She had laid out a cold supper on the kitchen table, but he came directly into the bedroom and went straight to the closet.

"Oh, there you are," he said. "What's the matter? Have you got a headache?"

"No," she said, looking away from him. Her eyes had begun to well up. "Jamie, this trouble in China. It frightens me."

He was hardly listening as he pulled out a couple of cardboard boxes of old files.

"Why? No one can harm you. Where is that damn thing? Oh, here it is."

He snatched the file and headed back out of the bedroom.

"As far as I can tell, everything's happening in Beijing. I haven't heard of any real trouble in Nanjing, so your mother should be okay."

She kept her head turned away.

The caller had phoned scarcely a half-hour ago. She had been expecting to hear from Mrs. Li about the itinerary for Saturday. Instead, she heard a low male voice.

"These are difficult days for our motherland. We will need your help again. Be ready."

That was it.

He had spoken in Chinese about China, of course. No one had ever referred to Canada as a "motherland." Not even as a joke.

9

Halpert was already browsing through the file before he got to the kitchen table. There was no order to its contents. Like his life, it was a mess. Started out of desperation late in 1980 when he realized that the two desultory chapters of his China book were leading nowhere and what he really wanted to do was write a biography of Gordon Wrye, it had seemed at first like a liferaft. He had married Gordon's woman, he was taking out citizenship in Gordon's country, and he was living within a few blocks of Gordon's school and university. Writing a life of Gordon Wrye might make sense of everything, might be better than revenge, might ease his heart, might let Halpert get on with the rest of his life.

He had started systematically enough, beginning with Gordon's boyhood in London, Ontario (the mother was dead, the father had simply disappeared, but a great-aunt remained), then moving on to his boarding school (the headmaster was more than eager), to Cranmer College at the University of Toronto (Professor Emerita Sybil Johnson, his graduate thesis supervisor, had become Halpert's closest friend in Toronto), and finally to St. Aidan's Anglican Church.

The file he had retrieved after so many years contained random, handwritten notes and typed transcripts of recorded interviews. Far from being a liferaft, the file had dwindled into a talisman of failure. When his book publisher got wind of the changed project, he demanded repayment of the $25,000 advance. This was a problem, since it had been used as part of the down payment on a small house he had bought for Susan and himself in the Beaches district. So, six months after they had moved in, they were forced to sell, at a small loss. He had been able to return only $15,000 to the publisher, with the promise of monthly repayments stretched over two years to make good on the rest.

Then the accounts of Kwai Ta-ping's arrest and trial began to come in, and he succumbed to something approximating a nervous break-down. It was only thanks to Jim Worrell, and perhaps also to Susan's quiet constancy, that he was able eventually to soldier on. But the book on Gordon Wrye was still-born and when, with perverse compensating logic, he suggested to Susan that they make a child and she had resisted, the notion of being among the walking dead first occurred to him. It vaguely intrigued him to see how long a corpse could carry on.

He looked at the food Susan had laid out for him. Cold noodles, cold chicken, cold vegetables. All purchased cooked and long cold. All waiting for the microwave. He didn't complain. He didn't even want to complain. Out of the vortex of his lack of feeling and her terrible lone-liness, something unspeakably bleak kept them together. They hadn't made love for months, and the few times they had earlier happened only when he got looped and didn't really know what he was doing, or at least wasn't thinking about it. If he thought too much about making love to Susan, the image of Kwai Ta-ping in prison surfaced, which was not in any way erotically stimulating. Yet they were tied to each other by a tight knot of inchoate despair and dependency, and the only way they could deal with this absurd state of affairs was never to discuss it, never to explore or analyse it, never to admit its reality.

He got a beer from the refrigerator and took himself and his file to the living room and the large chair beside the sofa. They had moved to this one-bedroom apartment on St. George Street, north of Bloor, after evicting themselves from their house in the Beaches. The rent was cheap. It was close to the subway and shopping. It was near Gordon's university. And, to both their consternations less than a year after they moved in, it was also kitty-corner to the new Chinese consulate-general that bought the old Ontario Medical Association building. After a large staff of diplomats, clerks, and spies had moved in, the Chinese closed all the blinds on all the windows. They had not been opened since. Susan and Halpert thought of moving, and then thought better of it when they pondered their debt and the rising rents. So they stayed and usually avoided walking in front of the Chinese citadel.

∽

TRANSCRIPT
Dr. Sybil Johnson
Professor Emerita, Cranmer College
Toronto/12 Nov 80

H: When did you first meet Gordon?

J: Oh, I remember it vividly. Did you know he'd been imposed on me?

H: How do you mean "imposed"?

J: Just what I say. Imposed. Forced. No choice given. The head of my department said he had this brilliant bad boy and wanted me to whip him into shape.

H: Why you?

J: Well, I have this reputation, you see. An old dragon lady. I suppose the head of the department was frightened of me, so he decided Gordon Wrye would be frightened of me, too. It didn't quite work out that way.

H: I'd like to come back to how you first met him in a moment. You referred to Gordon as "a brilliant bad boy." I know he was brilliant, but why "bad boy"?

J: That wasn't my phrase. It was <u>his</u> reputation.

H: Based on what?

J: Based on his undergraduate career. The mid-sixties were a very difficult time for the university. It wasn't just China that had Red Guards, you know. Gordon was a very active campus politician and he was a natural leader. If you mention his name to a few of the old trouts who still turn up around here – the former president, for example, or the provost emeritus of this college – you'll see them groping for their nitroglycerine pills.

H: What things did he do that got people so upset?

J: Well, let me give you a picture of Gordon when he was in his element

175

during those days. It wasn't the first time I met him, but it was the first time I actually saw him in action. It must have been during the fall term in 1967. Gordon and some other student activists had organized themselves into a kind of Committee of Public Safety — I invoke the French Revolution carefully. They weren't exactly a self-appointed group, you see, but I think it's accurate to say that the elected student council wasn't given much choice other than to approve its existence. The idea behind the group was that the university's curricula were all out of date and hopeless, and Gordon's group — with the help of student funding — would organize a different sort of education. Or at least they would set an example for the university to follow. That's how the teach-ins began. Huge gatherings in Varsity Arena. Gordon's group would invite special speakers from all over the world on the subjects he decided were most pressing. Not surprisingly, given Gordon's interests, China was the subject of the very first teach-in. And that's when I saw him in action.

H: You went to the teach-in?

J: I certainly did. Every professor interested in preserving his or her scalp turned up. It was quite funny, looking back. There was intellectual and professional blackmail involved, and I wouldn't care to point out the number of my male colleagues who made themselves absolutely ridiculous by dressing down in bell-bottom jeans and shirts open to their navels. They were trying to shed their years <u>and</u> their doctorates.

H: Didn't the female professors dress down, too?

J: Well, I suppose some of us did, but you see there were so few of us in those days, it hardly mattered. It was the tenured gentlemen of this comfortable club we call a university who were scared right down to their shoelaces. And Gordon didn't disappoint any of them. He made them shiver in terror. He'd flown in Han Suyin to give an overview of the Cultural Revolution, and she was very popular with the students. He'd carefully chosen the most blimpish-looking English sinologist he could find to argue the anti-Communist line. You've lived in China, so you might appreciate the moment. Dr. Han came dressed in a smartly pressed Mao suit. She looked like a beautiful version of Mao's wife. Poor old Professor Swithin came in his heaviest tweeds, complete with waistcoat and watch-chain. He was a comic figure before he opened his mouth. And whenever he attempted to explain that all this bizarre Red

Guard activity was destroying Chinese culture or hurting Chinese agriculture or destroying the universities, <u>the whole time</u> Han Suyin would shake her head in quiet, dignified dismay, as if to say, "You just don't understand; history has left you aside; the future is for the young." That sort of thing, you see? The students lapped it up.

H: And what was Gordon doing while all this was going on?

J: Looking like the cat who swallowed the canary. He didn't have to do very much because he was so well prepared. He had it all organized with his group. Han Suyin was apotheosized as the messenger of Chairman Mao himself. She could have told the students to swim across Lake Ontario and they would have marched twenty abreast all the way to the lake singing "The East Is Red" or some such nonsense.

H: And the English professor?

J: Crucified! They just crucified him. He was made to represent everything backward in education. He became the perfect symbol of the Universal Reactionary. Gordon's finest moment that evening was when he had to take over the podium from Professor Swithin because the students were howling so much the old boy couldn't make himself heard — even through all the massive loudspeakers on the stage.

H: What did Gordon say?

J: He gave a lecture on freedom of speech, if you can believe it, on the higher purpose of the teach-ins! It was almost Churchillian. So the students let poor Swithin talk and they listened to him in malicious silence. This was when Dr. Han did all her head-shaking. And when he was finished, they maintained the silence. They just sat on their hands. Oh, it was quite deadly.

H: So, from this, I take it you weren't very impressed with Gordon.

J: Not at all. It was the times, you see. I'd be a ripe old hypocrite if I told you today that I didn't get some measure of dark satisfaction from watching the discomfiture of some of my male colleagues that night, including Professor Swithin. You see, some of us on the faculty really were quite fed up with the way everything here seemed suspended in aspic. We longed for a more open relationship with our students and far more flexibility in creating new courses, so that while I no doubt tut-tutted along with the rest about all the excesses of the rabble-rousers, I was rather cheering them on.

H: So. Let's go back. When did you first meet Gordon Wrye?

J: Well, as I said, he'd been imposed on me for his master's thesis, but I don't think I put up too much resistance. I was genuinely intrigued. I already had in my hands his proposed project, which he'd left in my mailbox before we met. He wanted to investigate the development of early Sung dynasty kiln construction in the area roughly between Xian and Kaifeng. He was already fascinated with the ancient technology of making pottery, you see, and this was a perfectly orthodox line of inquiry. What was unorthodox was to inform me about it the way he did. He needed my permission to pursue any project whatsoever. That's the way we are supposed to work at a university. I was his assigned supervisor and he was the student. His letter to me wasn't simply premature and arrogant. It was extraordinarily presumptuous. It was written colleague to colleague.

H: So you were expecting a row when you started?

J: Looking forward to it! I come by my reputation honestly, you see, and I had this feeling that here was a really bright, extraordinarily bright, student and that if I did my job correctly, he could be directed into scholarship of real and lasting value.

H: So how did you first meet?

J: I sent him a very sharp note and told him to meet me in my office the next day at 10 a.m. promptly – or else.

H: I suppose he was late?

J: Gordon Wrye? Nothing as predictable as turning up late. What he did was find out my address and come to my apartment building that night. I guess he waited until one of the building residents came in or went out, because he never rang up. I wouldn't have let him in, I assure you. I have a nice old chime clock in my apartment, and as it struck ten o'clock he knocked on the door. I thought it must have been one of my neighbours, so I opened up without looking through the peephole and there he was, smiling from ear to ear. I thought at first that he was drunk.

H: What did he say?

J: Just the cheekiest thing you could ever imagine. "They say you are the wisest woman on the campus, Professor Johnson, so I came along to test the thesis." Can you imagine?

H: What did you say?

J: I did what any proper lady would do and certainly what an academic in my position, facing such a spectacle, would do. I told him he was a fool, and not just a fool but a trespassing fool, and that if he didn't leave that instant, I would call the police and the next day I would make sure the university authorities were made aware of what he had done. And then I tried to close the door.

H: Tried? Did he use force?

J: No. Not at all. Not a bit of it. He made me laugh, you see. He made me laugh at myself and my little speech and at the silly little melodrama we were enacting.

H: It must have been a memorable punchline.

J: I can't remember what he said. I just have this vivid, vivid memory of his beguiling cheekiness and that big smile. Whatever it was that he said, it drew me into his world and that wasn't, well, it wasn't unpleasant, really. My own world – I mean my world outside of scholarship – was not so very exciting. So I asked him in.

H: I'm not so sure I should be dwelling on this little scene anymore.

J: Oh, heaven's, nothing like _that_! I was old enough to be his grandmother. If I had only been as old as his mother, it might have been a different story. Anyway, we had a nice cup of tea and a little chat that didn't end till after midnight, and when he left, I wished he had stayed longer. That was the first meeting.

∾

NOTES
Miss Louise Cotter
Great-aunt
London, Ont/9 Oct 80

• Gordon's mother's aunt, 85
• Barnable's Leisure Life (pretty dreadful old folks' homes, codgers left in wheelchairs in hallway, bathroom smells <u>awful</u>, staff perfunctory)
• Mind up and down, drifts off after a couple of minutes, gets tired v. quickly

• Basics confused! g.w.'s mum dies when he is twelve, later when he's a baby/died of what? can't find out/if I push, Miss Cotter just goes quiet/unnerving

• "Beautiful boy" – about twenty times "beautiful boy"

• Altar boy at St. Paul's Cathedral! London <u>Ont</u> has a St. Paul's Cathedral, a River Thames, and a kind of ersatz Buckingham Palace called "Eldon House"

• Father? Nothing. She remembers nothing, or says nothing/goes into story about g.w. at a church picnic when he was/what age? maybe young teenager, hard to tell/story concerns Gordon and "little China-boy" who was being bullied/g.w., newborn St. George, rushes to defend, but doesn't fight/puts his arm around China-boy and makes speech/grown men in tears, etc, old girl very proud/real Christian!!

• Not much else/little things: sensitive about his small stature/always interested in old aunt's display chinaware/beautiful singing voice before it broke/went away to boarding school in Toronto/stayed with Miss Cotter on holidays . . . <u>Where's father?</u>

∾

TRANSCRIPT
Dr. Richard R. Thornton
Chief Curator
Queen Victoria Museum
Toronto / 22 Nov 80

H: I take it from our phone conversation that you didn't hold a very high opinion of Gordon Wrye.

T: No, I wouldn't say that was accurate. He was a brilliant young man, no question of that. We wouldn't have hired him for the Greene Project if he hadn't had the very highest recommendations and aptitude. So that wasn't a problem. The fact of the matter was that he was a cheat and a liar. I know you were close friends and that what I might say could prove hurtful, but you are the one who insisted on this conversation and if you ask anyone who knows me, you'll be told I'm not inclined to make things prettier than they are.

H: I'm not looking for a pretty story, as I told you. I'm trying to put together pieces in a jigsaw puzzle. I already have some of the pieces. You have some more. So I want to know about your relationship with Gordon, and I want to know what happened during that summer, what year was it?

T: The summer of 1972.

H: Yes, that's it. The summer of '72. I want to know what happened, in your own words.

T: All right. But I want you to understand some background. Look at this. I've brought something from our collection for you to see. You can hold it, but be careful. It's very old. Maybe don't lift it too high off the desk. But feel it. Feel its weight and look at its colour and textures. Tell me what you see and feel.

H: Well, it's not "exquisite," as they always seem to say in the porcelain business.

T: Not exquisite at all. Rather humble, I'd say. Go on.

H: Well, I won't lift it. I'm sure it's very old, but I'm not at all versed in Chinese pottery beyond the rudimentary.

T: This isn't a test. I don't expect you to identify it. I just want you to describe what you see and feel.

H: Well, it's a sort of pot. There's a wide, open top with a rim that's turned in a bit. And it's got . . . what should I say? It's got a nice round shape which gets narrower at the bottom and then flares out into this very solid base. And on one side there's a little handle with two holes in it, or something . . . oh, and on the other side, too.

T: Lugs, we call them.

H: Two pairs of lugs. I suppose you could put a rope or some such thing through them and make a handle.

T: Exactly! Well done. It's an earthenware pot or jar that was discovered in Anyang, and it was made sometime between the thirteenth and eleventh century BC during the Shang dynasty. But you're not finished. There's only two others like it in the West, and possibly three inside China, but there's something special about all of them. Do you think you can guess it from this one? Tell me a little about the texture and colour.

H: The tummy is lovely and smooth. And there's a glaze over most of it, except at the base. I've got a little colour-blindness problem and can't differentiate between some greens and brown, but I'd guess this glaze is probably greenish, with a fair bit of yellow. I can certainly see the yellow elements.

T: Excellent. Now let me tell you. The extraordinary thing about this jar is that it has any glaze at all. You are holding the oldest discovered glazed vessel in the world. We still don't know exactly how they did the glaze. It may simply have been the result of experimenting with ash in the kiln, stirring it up so lots fell on the pot and was transformed into a glaze. Or perhaps the Shang potters were trying out some other non-leaded substances to produce the glaze. We just don't know. What we do know is that this pot represents an extraordinary advance in technological development. It means that as early as the Shang dynasty, the potter knew how to get the temperature of a kiln up to over a thousand degrees centigrade, that he could maintain this heat, and that he wanted to maintain the heat to create a glaze which would make all his earthenware pots impermeable, which expanded their use and longevity.

H: Did Gordon work with this jar?

T: No, no, no. I simply brought it out here to try and explain the core significance of a museum like this, and also to point out what an important institution the Queen Victoria Museum is. Both these things are essential to understand before you can appreciate how destructive Mr. Wrye was when he was here. A museum houses many objects, of course, but it also houses mysteries. We have objects from the past whose creative provenance we still don't fully understand. We have complete collections, and bits of collections, and objects which fit into no collection and are just huge question marks. Of all the museum's collections, Mr. Halpert, none is more impressive than our Chinese collection. We have the best set of religious statuary outside of China. We have the most comprehensive range of porcelains from all periods of Chinese history. We have a stupendous gallery tracing the technological advances of ancient China – from the making of porcelain, to silk production, the issuance of paper money, and the invention of explosive material. And, as the centrepiece to the collection and the symbol of the whole museum, we have a complete tomb from the Ming dynasty. And I mean <u>complete</u>. With stone guardian animals, sepulchre, coffin, funereal pottery, jewellery, clothing. We've even got the mummified cadaver of the Ming general, in uniform, for whom it was built.

H: I suppose this has all been assembled over the years.

T: Yes, to some extent. But the bulk of the Chinese collection actually was obtained for the museum at the beginning of this century by one man, an Anglican missionary-archaeologist named Greene. Cedric Greene. He was remarkably knowledgeable, and he only sent us back the very best. After he left China, he came back to Toronto and was appointed the provost at Cranmer College. He set up their splendid archaeological department, which has now been absorbed into the main university. But he started it. And he catalogued the whole of our collection and is the main person responsible for our international fame. And I'll tell you something else, which is very instructive. When I went to China two years ago, I visited the caves in Loyang where Greene had acquired much of the Buddhist statuary you can see today in the West Gallery downstairs. In the largest cave there, you can tell exactly where he had been. The statues were very carefully sawn out of the rock, and in each place where he took something, the Chinese authorities have placed a small sign in five languages naming Greene as the monster who stole the patrimony of China.

H: A bit like the Elgin marbles in the British Museum. I don't really think you can blame people for wanting the return of their cultural artefacts.

T: You don't, eh? Well, I'll tell you something else. The little signs attacking Cedric Greene occupy about a dozen niches in this vast cave in Loyang. No more than a dozen in a cave that used to have at least three hundred carvings of all sizes. Bishop Greene went around and took representative examples of groupings. He was meticulous in making sure that he took nothing singular, nothing that there wasn't as good or even better left behind.

H: But still he took them.

T: Yes, he took them, and thank God he did, because in two days in early 1967, Red Guards went into the caves of Loyang with sledgehammers and axes and simply smashed ninety-five per cent of what was left. There are now just stumpy mounds all around the walls between

183

the little propaganda notices attacking Provost Greene. And when the stupid guide made all the predictable noises about Bishop Greene's "theft," I asked him who was responsible for the ferocious, tragic destruction of all the rest. "Oh, that," he said with a shrug. "That was done under the pernicious influence of Lin Piao and the Gang of Four." And that was okay, I gather, because Lin Piao and the Gang of Four were no more and everything was bright and happy again. Fortunately, this museum can still give the world a hint of the past glories of the caves in Loyang.

H: This is all really interesting, but I better stick to my subject here. Surely Gordon appreciated what the museum represented and was housing?

T: Appreciate? I suppose he did, in his way. We had a commitment to working with the archaeology department of the university, although in those days we were almost penniless. The funding agencies had started turning up their noses at the great institutions in the country and were cutting back dramatically on grants. Still, we found a bit of money in the budget to hire two summer students. Wrye was one of them. I personally gave him his project. I wanted him to get started on the first comprehensive recataloguing of the contents of the Ming tomb. I was counting on him having the benefit of all the subsequent discoveries and research since Greene's time. The project was dear to my heart because in the early autumn of that year we planned to launch our first major fund-raising campaign, using the Ming tomb as a symbol, and the whole future of the museum depended upon it. At that moment, nothing was more important than finding a new way to keep our operations going and finding new sources of funds for acquisitions.

H: And Gordon frustrated this ambition somehow?

T: Frustrated? He killed it, or damn near did. It was unbelievable. There's a process here, you know. I expect to get weekly reports on everyone's work, and it was part of Wrye's responsibility to keep me fully abreast of what he was doing. He started in early May, and after one terse, and rather rude, report, weeks went by before I could get him to come to solid brass tacks with his work. He was charming and all that. A number of my staff members liked him, but it was all very undermining because he mocked people – good people – whose work he thought was old-fashioned or stodgy in some way. In any big institution like this museum, there's always something of an audience for that sort of thing. In any event, the catastrophe hit us two days before the launch of our campaign in September, the week after Wrye left our employ.

H: What catastrophe?

T: A stupid little news story in the back pages of <u>The Toronto Mirror</u>. One column of newsprint and five paragraphs long. The story underneath it was about Adolf Hitler in Paraguay or some such place! That was apparently worth seven paragraphs. The rest of the page was devoted to an advertisement for Honest Ed's Warehouse. I remember the entire page quite vividly.

H: What did the article say, for heaven's sake?

T: The headline read: "STUDENT DEBUNKS MUSEUM'S MYTH" and described how an unnamed student researcher had proved beyond any doubt that the Queen Victoria Museum's famous Ming tomb was a fraud, that it was actually from the later Ch'ing dynasty and that most — if not all — of its contents were assembled from all over China rather than being part of the one tomb.

H: This was the result of Gordon's summer research, I take it?

T: Oh yes. The day he left, he turned in his report. Everyone was so busy getting ready for the launch of the campaign that no one even thought of looking at the summer students' project reports. Of course, if we'd had even a hint of what he was up to, we would have been able to deal with it properly. But he gave no hint. Not at any point during the summer and certainly not when he handed in his paper. Just this big arrogant smile and a handshake and a thanks for the job and all that. I tell you honestly, Mr. Halpert, it's a very lucky thing I have the iron-clad alibi of being in my office right here the day Gordon Wrye met his end. Otherwise my name would be at the top of any suspects' list. I'm sure I said to lots of people that day that I'd kill Wrye if I ever got my hands around his neck. I hope this doesn't distress you.

H: Surely a five-paragraph tabloid news story couldn't bring down a museum like this, and besides, things don't look so bad today.

T: They don't look so bad because of all the damage control we managed to do. That little story got expanded into a front-page exposé in the <u>Observer</u> the next morning. We had to put off the launch of the campaign indefinitely in order to repair our image. The <u>Observer</u> story was picked up by the foreign news-wire agencies. We had a hell of a time! And do you know who supplied the <u>Mirror</u> with the original story? Well, obviously Wrye did. He was a snitch, as well as a cheat and a liar.

H: Well, but was he right?

T: That's completely beside the point. In fact, most of his research was subsequently proved accurate, but it wasn't as damaging as he made out. The tomb was built for a very early Ch'ing general, but he'd been born at the end of the Ming dynasty, so it was a perfectly honourable mistake by Provost Greene. And when we checked Greene's original notes, we found he had made it quite clear that some of the tomb contents he had assembled were not from this one tomb, but from others in the vicinity. Subsequent curators fudged the point a bit. We could have accommodated all these updates. In themselves, they weren't a terrible threat. What I am talking about is the total betrayal by a young colleague who was welcomed into our midst, who understood fully the economic pressures the museum was under, who knew perfectly well that the entire financial campaign was being symbolized by the Ming tomb, even to the point of using one of the stone entrance lions as the campaign logo on all our appeal literature and notepaper. What kind of colleague would jeopardize all that? What kind of person could whistle his way out of this place having put everyone's jobs at risk, as well as all the work of all these years? Gordon Wrye was a little bastard, and I guess I'm sorry he met such a bad end. But I'm not that sorry.

H: Is that really the way you still feel after all this time?

T: Well, maybe if you had asked me point-blank a week ago I might have said something slightly more temperate, but dredging all these memories up leaves me feeling exactly the way I felt back then. So, yes, that's the note I'd like to end on. Gordon Wrye was a little bastard.

∽

Halpert put the transcript down and leaned back in the chair, stretching his tall frame. He could hear Susan in the bathroom. It was just past

11 p.m. He stood up and went to the window. Across the street, he saw the red flashing lights atop three police cruisers that had taken up positions outside the Chinese consulate-general. He went into the kitchen and got another beer out of the refrigerator. Absentmindedly, he looked at the calendar on the kitchen wall and saw that he didn't have to go to work on Monday because he'd agreed to do a double shift the following weekend. He frowned. He didn't like having three free days in a row.

He went back to his chair and picked up the file folder again. While he was leafing tentatively through another long transcript, a small white envelope fell out onto the floor. He reached down to pick it up and realized it was his notes from an encounter with Father Bell. He could feel his gut seize up as he put it back into the file, and then took it out again, then put it back, and – finally – took it out again. He had written three sheets of lined scribbler paper with a hard lead pencil, and he had trouble reading them.

∾

NOTES
Father William Bell
Retired auxiliary priest
St. Aidan's Church
Toronto / 2 Dec 80

• 7 a.m. communion service, middle of the week / four other people in church / no music, just three old birds, me, fragile priest at the altar
• no formal sermon, but short five-minute talk from altar / quite moving / our faith in christ begins at the foot of the cross / can't begin anywhere else, has to begin in the full acceptance of catastrophe / not just our sins and weakness we bring to the foot of the cross but our entire understanding of humanity / without embracing the reality of evil, we can never understand the nature of The Good / have to accept that nothing is ever sacred in this world, everything susceptible to decay and corruption / god sent his son yet world not only denied him also tortured and killed him / not ultimate sacrilege, just symbolic of ordinary

everyday world/same world we have to find our own way to understand evil and hatred and how to transmute it/cannot do this without starting at the foot of the cross and listening to jesus shout to god, "why have you abandoned me?"/we also are both abandoned and loved — abandoned by our natures but loved by god's example in jesus/only at the foot of the cross can we begin to understand task in life is to begin all journeys embracing the abandoned love represented by christ's sacrifice/first steps away from the cross are always accompanied by both sorrow and hope

• v. simple delivery style, voice still has traces of english accent, whole demeanour weary but unrattled/v. moving

• coffee hour afterwards/wait till old ladies leave/tell him about book project/expressionless/tell him i know he was the priest g.w. accused of sexual assault/expressionless/explain about murder/expressionless/still says nothing/ask him if he will talk to me/NOTHING/absolute quiet in room/ask if he's okay and he smiles/really nice smile/nods head several times/no he won't talk to me about g.w. except to say g.w. was "most perfect embodiment of evil" he had ever personally encountered, before or since/not g.w. himself, but g.w.'s "capacity" for evil/facing such evil he had learned it could have no power over him/<u>never</u> frighten him again/said this knowledge for him had been a great gain/source of peace of mind

∽

TRANSCRIPT
Dr. Sybil Johnson
Professor Emerita, Cranmer College
Toronto/17 Nov 80

H: You've read Gordon's notebook. Can you make sense of it?
J: So, I have to repeat everything again for your silly machine?
H: Yes please. You started taking off, and there's no way I can remember everything properly.
J: Fine fate for me! I am a retired professor of the history of technology

and I'm going to end my life ensnared by wires and microphones and tiny little machines. There's justice in everything, you see.

H: The notebook.

J: What about some more tea? I made these biscuits specially for you. I think you only took one out of politeness, which I do resent. Old ladies have better things to do than stand around a stove. Our time is getting limited.

H: They're wonderful biscuits. What about the notebook?

J: Well, as I just told you, it seems fairly clear to me that Gordon made a very important discovery. You can follow the pattern quite easily. He was obviously out on a field trip last August near Kaifeng. I think I counted six place names, so he was having no trouble getting round. So far as my colleagues know, all these places are still off limits, so Gordon had really discovered a way to get to the places he wanted to see. The last place – P'a-ts'un – well, it's really important. I was near there once, in 1936, believe it or not. It's a terribly important place, you see, because that was where the technology under the Northern Sung was really taking off. Not just in the manufacture of pottery but all sorts of other developments. And I say "manufacture" purposely, because under the Northern Sung, pottery production starts to be a big, important business. The production starts to get systematized. You get officials involved, and taxes, and production quotas, and standardized procedures. And under the Sung, the Chinese became great exporters, you know. It is a _very_ dynamic period.

H: We're talking tenth and eleventh century AD here, aren't we?

J: I'm going to break you of that nasty journalist's habit of saying "we're talking – "

H: Did Gordon take all this bullying without complaint?

J: Well, he was a real scholar, so he didn't use jargon. And I don't bully people. I'm a teacher and I do my job.

H: Yes, ma'am. Now what about the Northern Sung and Gordon's notebook?

J: Well, that was his field, his period, you see. He had a theory based on analysis of kiln designs that the potters of the Northern Sung were probably the first to make the great technological breakthrough that produced the blue and white porcelain we have always believed had to wait another few centuries till the Ming arrived on the scene. I don't mean that dynasties made the breakthroughs. The development of pottery is spread over millennia, and the development of porcelain over centuries. But Gordon was brilliant in this field precisely because he had no problem working intensively in his rather narrow speciality, while at the same time keeping the whole picture in front of him. We scholars prefer the studies of individual trees generally, rather than the study of forests. You can get lost in the forest, but you can always embrace a tree. More tea?

H: No thanks. Really. Actually, can I use your washroom?

J: Oh, of course. It's just down the hallway. First door on your right. And the light's outside the door. If you dare mention all the old lady paraphernalia there, I'll never speak to you again.

H: I won't, I promise. Be right back.

H: Why do you need that ramp by the bathtub? You walk perfectly well.

J: None of your business! What a beast you are! You promised not to mention it. Old people put on a lot of effort to keep up a good front. Our dignity is very important to us. Now, I believe we are discussing Gordon Wrye.

H: We are. A long time ago you were deciphering his notebook for me, but we seemed to have strayed off the track.

J: But straying off the track is the most fun of scholarship, or at least of real scholarship. That was Gordon's speciality, you see. Now back to the blue and white porcelain. Its manufacture during the Ming is what set the world on its ear. When Ming porcelain started appearing in Europe, people were amazed. They couldn't believe how fine it was, how beautiful, how strong. They tried to reproduce it, but didn't come anywhere close to discovering the secret for centuries. And they certainly tried to find out the secret through spying and bribery inside China, but the authorities made very sure no foreigner got anywhere near any of the Imperial pottery yards. There wasn't really a recipe for it, you see. It was the result of enormous numbers of years of trial and error. You went to Ching-tê Chên, south of Nanking, didn't you?

H: I did. With Gordon.

J: Well, then you saw those vast mounds of centuries-old pottery failures. Trial and error, trial and error. If the kiln temperature fluctuated too much, all the contents being fired would collapse. Throw them out. Start again. If the mixture of clays and kaolin was not just right, no porcelain. Throw it out! And the mounds keep rising. Those mounds are wonderful playgrounds for archaeologists because they take you into the heart of a craft that turned into a huge industry. Did you know there were potters' guilds in China well before the time of Christ? And all the time the innovators were trying out new ideas and when the experiments failed, they threw them out and started again. Well, as I said, Gordon had a theory based on fragments of circumstantial evidence that the technology to manufacture the blue and white porcelain that so dazzled the West was known during the period of the Northern Sung. The problem he faced was that no piece of Sung blue and white had ever been identified. And the prevailing view has been that it couldn't possibly have been manufactured then because the cobalt blue used to decorate the porcelain under the glaze had to be imported from the Middle East. The earliest known blue and whites are the David vases, which we know were manufactured around the middle of the fourteenth century. They were strictly for export, and the blue and white porcelains continued to be manufactured strictly for export because the Chinese found the designs very vulgar at first. Suitable for foreigners only!

H: Why did Gordon think the procedures and ingredients for blue and white had been discovered three centuries earlier?

J: Well, he knew that during the earlier T'ang dynasty, cobalt blue had been imported and used as a colourant in the glaze, rather than for actual decoration. It's a very significant difference. He was also very familiar with the gradual development of what we call porcellaneous pottery – that's pottery with many of the ingredients of true porcelain, but not developed to the fine level we associate with blue and white. The key, he felt, was in exploring kiln construction because it was only when potters learned how to fire the clay to extraordinarily high temperatures – well above fourteen or fifteen hundred degrees centigrade – that you could successfully manufacture the blue and white.

H: Hold on. I'm getting confused. What does the note say? 7/8patsun 1-23shit 23-25/990?? 17shds wh/v cbt(exc) fl.dor/nomeld 6shdsfit 2mm'wall!!!!Kln?

J. That's right. Now this entry that intrigued you with the exclamation marks, well, that's it. It's a real eureka! Somehow he found a "trial and error" mound from a Sung pottery yard, which is pretty exceptional all by itself. Now here, take a look. There's the date. Seventh of August 1979. There's the site in P'a-ts'un. He's been working his way down one of three mounds and twenty-three feet down, from an era he feels confident enough to put in an estimated date, 990 – with two question marks – he has found seventeen shards of vitreous, off-white porcelain with cobalt-blue decorations. Some of the shards fit together well. The wall of whatever the object was is classically thin, around two millimetres. And he's so excited he puts four exclamation marks because he has made the most important discovery in his field since it became a field of study. And what do we have right after his shout of triumph? He writes "Kln" with a question mark. That's his specialty: kilns. He hasn't found the kilns yet, or the kiln site. Maybe he won't, but that's where his mind immediately went. Oh, my dear Mr. Halpert, Gordon could be alive right now and sitting with us. I feel his presence so strongly with this note.

H: It really is a major discovery?

J: Absolutely! Nobel Prize stuff. I doubt very much if the Chinese Communists wanted someone from outside to make such a discovery. I'm afraid we might be very close to the reason he had to die. If we hear about this discovery in the next year or so and see that it is attributed to Chinese archaeologists, I'm afraid we'll have our answer about who killed him and why.

H: You may be right. What a terrible thing, to die at the edge of such a discovery.

J: Terrible, terrible. But you know, Gordon had another theory. He said he hated those trial and error mounds. Well, at least, that's what I call them. He called them mounds of broken dreams. He was convinced that if he discovered proof that the blue and white technology was known during the early Sung years, he would also find proof that it was somehow forbidden, that the potter and his breakthrough would be buried because it upset the system of taxation or export or something. That's where the comprehensiveness of Gordon's vision was so wonderful. He understood the whole remarkable cycle of pottery.

H: Which is?

J: The clay comes from the earth. Nothing more than a handful of dust. And when man the agriculturalist needed receptacles for water and food, man the creator figured out how to take the earth and mould it into something useful. It comes from the earth and goes back to the earth. And then the artisan-potter appears and we start to see decoration. Already a simple technology exists, but the potter pushes on and on. He doesn't like the way it crumbles after being baked in the sun, so he figures out that he can make it stronger by using fire. And after he concocts whatever sort of primitive kiln, the potter is unhappy because he doesn't like the thickness of the clay, so he tries other materials from the earth. He also finds out that if he throws the clay on a wheel, he can make his vessels thinner with his own hands. And still the restlessness. Even with this tougher, thinner earthenware, there is far too much absorption of liquids and his pots retain smells and oils and can't be used for anything other than what first went into them. And so the potter experiments with glazes, probably by accident, probably by ash falling on the clay during firing, but this glaze armours the vessel and makes it impervious to its contents.

H: And somewhere along this line, aesthetics become important.

J: Exactly. Before you know it there are rich people who like a certain look and want to make sure poor people can't have it. They invest pottery figures with superhuman qualities and they want their company in their graves for the next world. But, of course, there are generals and emperors who want to have better things than ordinary rich people, and they have bureaucrats who can oversee manufacture and levy taxes. And then the potter finds that he is no longer working alone, that he is very important in the social structure, that his skills are valued alike by the common man and the emperor. But at the very moment of his triumph, when he is master of his craft, an artist of supreme aesthetics, a technician second-to-none in history — at that moment he looks around and sees everything is lost. Middlemen have taken over his craft, failed potters have turned themselves into bureaucrats and guild bosses. He must join organizations, the emperor wants him to turn out not a dozen or two pots and figures but a thousand thousand, and the only way that can be done is to create vast communities of potters and streamline the operation so that our universal potter is turned into a kiln operator here, a glazer there, an expert at throwing clay here, a decorator there. What came from the earth and returns to the earth has been transformed not just into a symbol of man's instinct for invention and beauty but also man's dreadful propensity to accumulate and stigmatize and seek power over other men. Creativity <u>and</u> corruption. They are partners – the one striving to survive the other; the other longing to subsume everything in its path. This is the story of our civilization, from beginning to end. It starts with just a handful of dust and it ends back in the dust. How we travel on the journey in between defines what we are. Gordon understood this perfectly. Forgive me, Mr. Halpert. Sometimes old ladies talk too much.

∽

Professor Johnson was still alive, but had succumbed to Alzheimer's two years earlier. Halpert went to see her, more or less faithfully, but she didn't know who he was. Her mind was dust already, and it was only a cruel fate that kept her body from returning to the earth.

Susan stood in front of him, and for a moment after he lifted his eyes and looked at her, he had no idea where he was. She was in a white nightgown and was hugging herself, arms crossed over her breasts.

"What's happening, Jamie? The drum?"

"What drum?"

"The drum outside. Can't you hear it? It's been banging for nearly half an hour."

He looked at his watch. It was past midnight. He got up and went over to the window. Over at the Chinese consulate-general, there were now at least ten police cars, all from the special detachment of the RCMP assigned to protect foreign embassies and consulates. Some officers were erecting crowd-barrier fences to block off the sidewalk. Halpert could see, squatting on the ground just the other side of the fences, a Buddhist monk in an orange robe, bald head gleaming under the street-lights. He had a stick in his right hand and he must have been bringing it down on a drum that Halpert couldn't see. A very loud drum. The police seemed to pay him no attention. Directly across the street, on the same side as Halpert's apartment, about thirty or forty people were standing in a group.

There was a time when a sight like this would have sent him scurrying down to the street. Not now.

"It's nothing," he said to Susan. For the first time he noticed how swollen and puffy her face looked. She had been crying. "Come on, Sui-san. Let's go to bed."

$$\boxed{10}$$

When the telephone rang at 9:30 a.m. Saturday in the Halperts' apartment, Susan had already left to meet Mrs. Li. She had had to walk to Avenue Road to hail a taxi because the police had closed the streets to traffic for three entire blocks around the consulate-general.

There were now over a thousand people – mostly Chinese Canadians, but with a fair smattering of white faces – crowded on the sidewalks leading to the Chinese fortress. RCMP officers were milling all over the place, and one of them had told Susan there was no point in trying to get her car out of the underground garage. Shortly after she headed off, the Metropolitan Toronto Police had arrived with four horse vans, and a small mounted detachment was already patrolling St. George Street.

"Jamie, we could really do with your help. We're swamped down here."

It was Chris Bredin, the deputy managing editor, who was stuck on early Saturday-morning duty. His job was to get everything ready for the Sunday edition team, which didn't start coming in till after noon.

"What's happened, Chris?" Halpert asked, scratching under his arm. He hadn't slept better for weeks. For him, the sound of the drum – which had kept Susan up for most of the night – had been soothing.

"Everything's happened, Jamie. It's awful. The tanks have been pouring into that square, mowing down kids. It's a very confused picture, but it seems as if hundreds, maybe thousands, have been killed. It's just wild. Haven't you been watching CNN?"

"Nope. Just got up."

"On top of all that, there's a massive demonstration being planned against the Chinese embassy – "

"In Ottawa?"

"No, here."

"That's a consulate, Chris."

"Whatever." A note of impatience had crept into the deputy managing editor's voice. Halpert had really become a deskman, he thought. Nitpicking before he even breathed. "We're low in troops. Hanley can't manage the foreign desk till later this afternoon and the stuff's just streaming in. I've got to round up some hands to cover the demo and I can't get hold of Arch anywhere. Probably out on one of his benders."

"I'll be there in half an hour, Chris."

"Thanks, Jamie. I really appreciate it."

Sure he does, thought Halpert. Anything or anyone to save his bacon, even old Halpert. Pleased at the prospect of working, he was not, however, looking forward to editing the Beijing correspondent's handiwork. Most of his story, he figured, would be a self-justification for consistently downplaying the significance of the democracy activists and the rest will be an attack on the students' naiveté. The actual news will be irrelevant.

When Halpert got to his slot, Bredin came over. He was still bouncing off the ceiling.

"Jamie, I really appreciate this. We finally found Arch, and he said he'd come in, but I don't know how much help he's going to be. He sounded pretty hung over. We've got two people on the Toronto demo, but don't worry about them. I really need you to sort out the wires and *The New York Times* copy. I'd like a digest of what stories will hold up, what to expect, and a range of analysis pieces. If you can get that to me by noon, one at the latest, I'll light candles for you at the cathedral."

"What's the word from our man in Beijing, Chris? Has he sent anything yet? I better figure what he's up to so I can tell what we'll need to support it."

"Jamie, he's not in Beijing."

"What do you mean he's not in Beijing?"

"Just what I said. He started his leave yesterday. He's in London now. He will have just arrived."

"You've got to be kidding."

"What do you mean? Everyone knew he was going on leave."

"Well, we better get him back there as fast as we can."

"We're okay on that. I've already talked to Hilary. And besides, they've closed down Beijing airport till further notice, so he couldn't go back even if we wanted him to."

"What do you mean 'we're okay'? He's our man. How can he not be there? This business has been brewing for months. You don't go on leave in the middle of the biggest world story of the day."

"Hilary says the wire coverage will do fine. She says everyone has been watching CNN, and the last thing our readers need is a rehash of what they already know. She doesn't even think we need a local stringer for backup. Jamie, we have to help our readers understand how this happened and what lies ahead. I've got the Ottawa bureau standing by to get government reaction, and we'll have our own stuff out of Washington and London."

"Oh, that's just great. What about getting our little man who is not in Beijing to write one of his usual thumbsuckers anyway? It won't matter if it comes out of London. Now that I think about it, Hilary is perfectly right. It doesn't make much difference where he is."

"Scratch that idea, Jamie. Hilary says to leave him alone. He'll be tired after his long trip, and she doesn't want the Sunday edition to be late for any reason. She's got this big cost-cutting meeting planned on Monday, and I don't think she wants to be seen overspending the day before."

Halpert turned away in disgust. Something strange was happening to him. He could feel anger for the first time in ages. It wasn't anger at the events unfolding in Tiananmen Square in Beijing. It was anger at the non-events at the *Observer*. By the time Arch Crawley had arrived, he was in full flight, and Crawley sensed the transformation immediately.

"You're buzzing today, Jamie."

"This used to be a newspaper, Crawley. A goddamned newspaper. Look at us now."

He picked up a copy of the Saturday edition and threw it down contemptuously on the national desk. There was a one-column story on the events in China, above the fold, on the left-hand side. "STUDENTS WINDING DOWN CAMPAIGN," the headline read. It was the last dispatch of the *Observer*'s own man-on-the-spot. The rest of the top half of the page was devoted to one of Hilary Faire's favourite innovations, Focus Fanfare.

"We need short, snappy refreshments for the readers," she had written in one of her Delphic memos to the copy desk. "I want editors to forget all the old rules and concentrate on the rewards readers will pay us if we offer them intelligent, balanced analysis on the questions for which they never seem to be able to find the answers. We are the answer-givers, and 'The Thesis,' the deck which will now adorn each Focus Fanfare, not only heralds, in summary, our intentions, but — more importantly — draws the *Observer*'s reader into our careful package of balanced information. By so empowering people in this fashion, we not only generate reader gratitude and loyalty but also take our old newspaper into a new era, shorn of tired formulae and liberated from the arbitrariness of random events."

This to Arch Crawley and company!

∾

Crawley put a hand over the mouthpiece of his telephone.

"Mr. Halpert, sir," he said in mock deference.

Halpert had not been friendly during the past hour and a half. He was finally immersing himself in the news of the unfolding tragedy in China. The minutia of details, the disparate accounts from various wire services, the threads of story lines left fraying in despair, the human-interest angles, the clear struggle of real journalists trying to come to terms with a huge news story: all these things buoyed him even as the great evil overwhelmed and throttled the youth of China. None of this was the cause of nostalgia, curiously, nor the reappearance of old wounds. Instead, he found the immediacy a kind of balm. And no one anywhere in the world had yet thought to file an analysis piece.

"Sir," persisted Arch. "If I may be so bold as to interrupt your deepest thoughts, there's an hysterical gentleman on the line insisting that he speak to you and no one else but you. Do you want to take it, or shall I tell him we are connected to a different reality today? Sir."

"Knock it off, Crawley. What line's he on."

"Extension 5165. I'll put the dear fellow on hold."

Halpert took a deep breath and raised his eyes from the computer screen as he picked up his telephone.

"National desk."

"Mr. Halpert?"

"Yes. I'm Jamie Halpert. Who are you?"

"My name's Danson, Mr. Halpert. Michael Danson. You don't know me, Mr. Halpert, but I remember the articles you wrote on China really well. Especially the one when you went to the ancient pottery yards. It was very influential in my life."

Halpert couldn't believe he was having to listen to this.

"Look, Mr. Danson. I'm very busy right now and I don't really have much time to spare talking about old articles. Maybe if you called back in a few weeks."

"Please don't hang up, Mr. Halpert. I need your help very badly. You see I work at Finch's Fine Porcelains. Or at least I worked for them until yesterday afternoon. We were all fired. Just like that. Well, I mean we were all fired except for the manager. And the bookkeeper, too. I'm pretty sure she's okay even though she got notice like the rest of us. The orders came from headquarters."

Halpert looked across at Crawley and rolled his eyes. A nuisance call.

"Look, Mr. Danson. I'm sure this is a difficult time for you. It's a difficult time for a lot of other people in the world, too. Why – "

"No. You don't understand, Mr. Halpert. Something very wrong has been happening at Finch's. I don't mean it's wrong that I got fired. I'm a salesman. I'll find another job. But I've got some information, and I have been trying to get Mr. Cameron to understand it, but he's a very strange man, Mr. Halpert, and he frightens me almost as much as the situation I seem to be stuck in. I really think someone should do a story about it because it's just plain wrong what's going on."

Christ! An exposé. Didn't this fool know the *Observer* didn't approve

200

of exposés anymore. They offended too many people. Worse, an exposé on China when China is in turmoil.

"Cameron?" asked Halpert. "Do you mean Geoff Cameron of this newspaper?"

"Yes, sir. I contacted him about two weeks ago when I discovered a few things that were really bugging me. But Mr. Cameron is a bully and he's also a very ignorant man. I'm really worried that he doesn't understand enough and that he will destroy me without ever getting to the bottom of this trouble. And I mean trouble, Mr. Halpert. They locked us out yesterday afternoon, but I had a suspicion they forgot to change the locks on the back door, so I came back to the office at night and I was right. I got in. I have some documentation you should see, and also something which will interest you very much. Do you know anything about porcelain-ware, Mr. Halpert? I assumed that you did from that article."

"I do, as a matter of fact. Not a lot. But I know a little."

"Well, I have a small example of blue and white porcelain that you will want to see."

"So do a lot of people. So what?"

"Well, this piece was made during the tenth century. During the Sung dynasty. Do you understand what that means, Mr. Halpert?"

"I sure do. Where are you now?"

"I can't see you till later, Mr. Halpert. I'm not staying at my home right now. When they discover this piece is missing, there's going to be a lot of trouble, so I'm staying with a friend out of town. But I can meet you somewhere by four this afternoon."

"We can meet at the rooftop bar at the Park Plaza Hotel. Do you know where that is?"

"Of course I do. I work just . . . at least I used to work just a few blocks away. How will I know you?"

"I suspect it won't be too busy. Anyway, I'll be at the bar itself. I'm tall and my hair's growing grey."

"Well, I'm normal height and I have red hair."

"We're bound to recognize each other. See you at four. Wait, are you still there?"

The dial tone came through.

"Damn!" said Halpert.

"What's wrong, sir?" said Crawley. "Is someone blackmailing you over your torrid secret life?"

"No, Arch. I agreed to meet a guy at four, but of course I might still be stuck here. Oh well, I'll deal with that when I have to. Have you read this dispatch by Kristoff from the *Times*? It's superb. Really superb."

Crawley's eyes narrowed as Halpert was talking.

"Keep thy head down, Mr. Halpert. We are about to be graced with the presence of the she-wolf."

Hilary Faire came striding through the newsroom doors. She looked cool and smart in a turquoise linen pantsuit, and she seemed happy enough until she spotted Crawley and Halpert over on the national desk.

"What on earth are you two doing in here on the weekend?"

Halpert didn't look up. It was Crawley's job to talk to Hilary on the rare occasions she deigned to notice anyone's presence at the national desk.

"Uh, Chris called us both in to help out on the China story."

"The hell he did?"

"Ma'am?" said Crawley.

"Where the hell is he?"

"Do you mean Chris?"

"Yes, I damn well mean Chris bloody Bredin. There he is. Chris, could you come here? *Now*."

The deputy managing editor was back from the library where he'd been organizing the weekend staff to look up tidbits of information on China for Hilary's editorial page. In the Sunday edition, she had recently started a new "refreshment" for readers in the form of a column entitled "By the way. . . ." It was a potpourri of little facts and figures that was meant to provide "synergy" with the big stories of the day. Arch Crawley had won a chuckle or two by suggesting it be renamed "Hilary Ripley's Believe It Or Not." But that was then. Right now he was looking forward to the dust-up about to happen before his very eyes.

"Oh, Hilary. Good to see you. You're in early. I thought you said you weren't coming in till after two"

"Who the hell gave you permission to bring in deskmen on over-time? And weekend overtime, too!"

"Hilary," said Chris in as low a voice as he could manage, hoping somehow to diminish her volume, "this China story is very big. We were real shorthanded and I – "

"Chris!"

" – so I thought if we got some handle on all the, you know, uhhh, there's a huge demo being – "

"Chris!"

" – being planned right now in Toro – "

"Chris! *Excuse me!* I think the question was, 'Who gave you permission to bring in deskmen on overtime?' If you give me the answer to that, then I'll know where to go to get the situation corrected."

"I did it on my own authority, Hilary. I'm the duty editor on Saturday mornings."

"Excuse me, Chris. You don't have any authority to do any such thing. There's been a standing memo to all managers since last February explicitly banning any overtime for any reason whatsoever. Any reason whatsoever, Chris."

"Well, Hilary, I'm truly sorry, but . . . Hilary, why don't we go into your office to discuss this?"

"It doesn't need discussion, Chris. It needs correction."

Crawley stood up at his seat. He had a sheepish grin on his face. "Ma'am, I think I can solve this for you fast. Mr. Halpert and I will just vamoose. Right out of your life."

She didn't twitch a muscle in Arch's direction, but kept her laser vision directed at the abject deputy managing editor. Her voice was very calm, almost sensuous. "I'm not talking to you, Mr. Crawley. You're not the one who's paid to solve a problem like this. That's Christopher's job and I want to know what his solution is going to be."

Bredin turned to the two deskmen, but kept his head down so he didn't have to make eye contact.

"Well, guys, I guess that's sort of it. I mean, thanks a lot for coming in, ahhh, well, you know. I think it's okay now. You can just go and, ahhh, about the overtime, what was it? About a couple of hours? Ahhh, why don't you just come in a little late on Monday? I'll make sure you're covered. Okay? Okay, guys?"

"Sure, Chris. That's fine," said Halpert, who had already switched off his terminal and was locking his desk drawer. "Have a swell weekend."

As they were leaving, they could her voice, oozing with freighted concern for her young deputy. "I guess I have to blame myself, Chris. I'm the one who took a chance on you. They told me you didn't know how to listen, but I said we should give you a chance. I guess I was wrong, Chris. I'm terribly disappointed."

"Hilary, uhhh, you know when we talked earlier, there were, uhhh, so many things you wanted done. I guess I just wanted them done right – "

"And so you asked Crawley and Halpert to come in? Oh, Chris, that's almost worse than breaking the overtime ban. It's going to take me a little while to absorb the implications of all this. I am surrounded by fools. You aren't the only one."

She shook her head and bit her lower lip, just like Bette Davis did in *Little Foxes* before she administered a *coup de grâce*.

"It's all right, Chris. Pull yourself together. I'm here now. Let's get on with our work. I'm sure you've lots to do."

The two went in opposite directions. Hilary Faire headed towards her office, even happier than she was when she first arrived. *He's going to work out just fine*, she thought. *He may even make managing editor before the month is out.* Out of the corner of her eye, she spotted Geoff Cameron tapping away at his computer in a corner cubicle. *Christ, all the insects are here today.*

"Mr. Cameron," she bellowed across the newsroom. "Mr. Cameron."

He lifted his head from the screen and, somewhat dazed, peered over in the direction of the familiar voice.

"Dear Mr. Cameron. Why ever did you send me that foolish memo? I thought you wanted to continue working here. I think the only thing missing in it was a side trip to Rio."

Everyone in the newsroom had stopped working and was listening attentively. Geoffrey Cameron had got up from his desk and was slowly walking in Hilary Faire's direction.

"Hilary. You can't dismiss it just like that. I have to speak to you."

"Nothing's sinking in, is it? We are not going to speak about your memo. Not now. Not in the future. Not ever. Your memo doesn't exist. It wasn't even worth filing."

She made a sharp, adroit turn on the heel of one of her expensive leather pumps and disappeared into her office. Those closest to the door later swore they could hear her humming "Oh, What a Beautiful Morning."

❧

Crawley had invited Halpert to join him for lunch at the Royal York Grill, but he wanted to be free of any association with the *Observer*. The old numbness had returned, but not before he'd allowed himself to feel some minutes of heartache. He headed straight for the rooftop bar at the Park Plaza and started drinking.

By the time Michael Danson, red hair and all, arrived a few minutes after four, Halpert was more drunk than he had been since his youth. At the best of times, he was a cheap drunk, but this time two beers had only been a prelude to a lethal series of double bourbons. Before long, everything had become a complete mystery to him, including where he was and why he was there.

"Mr. Halpert?" said the man. His hair was sandy-red. He couldn't have been thirty yet, and he wore thin-rimmed glasses that gave his face a scholar's mien. His features were slight, and there was an obvious fastidiousness to him that, for reasons primarily rooted in the booze, immediately aroused Halpert's dislike.

"I suppose I am. Who are you?"

"It's Michael, sir. Michael Danson. You agreed to meet me."

"Michael Danson. That's a fine name. Michael Danson. Michael Danson. Now wherever did you get a name like that?"

"Mr. Halpert?"

"That's my name, but that wasn't the question. I asked you where on earth you managed to get a name like Michael Danson."

"I'm sorry. I don't really understand. Look, Mr. Halpert, could we sit down at one of the tables? There's something I want to show you and it'll be easier there."

"I like it here just fine."

"Mr. Halpert, I really need your help. As I told you on the phone, we all got fired by Finch's yesterday, including our bookkeeper, Mrs. Hamlyn. I was really surprised Mrs. Hamlyn got the sack because she was imported by Finch's from their head office in Singapore and she always seemed so independent from our business. I got really suspicious yesterday because she didn't seem to be upset at all at the dismissals. Now I know the reason why — "

"*The reason why!* Now, wouldn't that make a great little feature on the editorial page. The Reason Why."

"Mr. Halpert, I'm sorry. Is there some trouble? Maybe we should talk another time. This is very important to me. I've gone out on a real limb here."

"Noooo, Mr. Michael Danson. I'm all ears. I love your story."

"Okay, sir. So, as I was saying, Mrs. Hamlyn was playing a double game, as I discovered last night when I went through some files. I've got copies here with me. Finch's had one line of orthodox stock, which is what I and a saleslady sold. But there were certain customers who never bothered with this stock. I told some of this to Mr. Cameron, but he had a difficult time understanding the concept, and, besides, I didn't have any of the documentation then.

"These special customers were always taken into the manager's office, where there's a large vault. We never knew what was in there. It's a walk-in vault, which is just crazy because while we did well for a few years, the volume of sales hardly even justified a three-drawer filing cabinet.

"Anyway, when I got into the office last night, I could tell the manager had only left a short time before. The place was an absolute shambles. I think I told you they forgot to change the locks on the back door. There were papers all over Mrs. Hamlyn's desk and on the floor. It took me a while to figure out what was going on, but I'm sure I'm right. There was a private stock of porcelain, kept in the manager's vault. I found five references to items in some of the bookkeeper's papers. So far as we knew, the company had done about six hundred thousand dollars of business in 1988. That was between myself and my colleague. But I've got papers that show Finch's Toronto branch did over seventeen million dollars of business. So this doesn't figure, because I'm sure there hadn't been more than a half-dozen special customers who went to the manager's office."

Halpert was in a semi-doze. His glassy eyes were open, but he had trouble focusing on the red hair. *If this young man isn't careful, Hilary's going to make mincemeat out of him.*

"The manager must have been in a panic, because when I went to his office next, everything was in a mess there, too. And the vault door was open. My God, Mr. Halpert, what he has inside there is amazing. There's about fourteen — well, thirteen now — bowls and vases. He must want to move them out quickly, because some of it was already packed. It's all blue and white, you know, like Ming porcelain. Except it isn't Ming at all. The designs are all different in style. I've never seen anything like them, and I've sold a lot of Ming blue and white. And there's some documentation. The porcelain comes from China. Official China. And it's from an Imperial Sung tomb. I read a copy of a secret memo from Finch's to the manager. Mr. Halpert, do you know what that means? It's incredible stuff. It should be in museums, and it's being sold off around the world by Finch's, which obviously has some secret deal with the Chinese government. We do all our banking with the Bank of Montreal, but there's a special account in Prince Edward Trustco. I've got copies of some of the transfer payments and, and, Mr. Halpert? Are you still with me."

"All the way, all the way, all the way — "

"Look what I've brought, Mr. Halpert. It's extraordinary. I took it from the vault. They can't really report me to the police because it's not supposed to exist, but they aren't going to be happy. I'm going to need help and protection when they find this missing. They'll figure out it's me. They'll discover the back-door locks weren't changed and I was the only one who didn't hand in a key. I told them I'd left it at home by mistake and would bring it in Monday. So they'll know it's me for sure."

Halpert's gaze moved off the red hair over to the surface of the bar. A small bowl with a wide mouth, about two inches high, sat gleaming under the bright lights shining down from above the bar. The lip of the bowl was ringed in gold. Not gold leaf, but a strip of beaten gold that had somehow been attached to the blue and white porcelain. A single dragon, each paw displaying seven claws, surrounded two-thirds of the bowl.

The detail on the dragon was meticulous, and had Halpert been able to focus his eyes, he would have seen that nothing done since in Ming porcelain decoration had ever quite matched it. The artist's lines that comprised the dragon's body seemed to have infinite variations in texture and depth of colour. The field of white reflected the overhead lights, distorting its purity but in no other way marring the transcendent beauty.

"How nice," said Halpert, reaching out to touch the bowl. As he reached, he slumped abruptly forward and his arm shot out ahead of him, striking the small bowl and sending it winging over the back of the bar. The sound of shattering porcelain made the bartender jump.

With a line he had used so often it came to him automatically, he smiled over at his two customers: "Just a glass. No harm done."

The young man did nothing at first. Slowly, he looked at Halpert, whose head was lying on top of the bar. And then his tears started welling up. "My God, my God, Mr. Halpert – "

Something of this got through to Halpert, but the mental filter was dysfunctional. "It's okay, okay, okay, okay, okay. Chris, it's okay. I'm here now. Everything will be okay."

∾

He remembered nothing when Susan came for him less than an hour later. The terrified Danson had simply fled, and the bartender had gone through Halpert's wallet, where he found his *Observer* business card, and called the newspaper. The national desk called Susan at Paulsen's, where they contacted her in the limo over the two-way radio. Since the crowds around the consulate-general had now swelled to over ten thousand citizens chanting their outrage at the mute building, she still couldn't get their car. When the driver dropped her off at the Park Plaza and she finally beheld her sodden man, she realized there was no way to get him home. Taxis couldn't get through the police blockades, and besides, Halpert couldn't even stand up straight. She decided simply to take a room at the hotel for the night and let him sleep it through.

She was glad not to go back to the apartment. The man had called her again in the morning, before Halpert awakened. This time the instructions had been more specific.

$$\boxed{11}$$

She was there beside him, sitting on a chair, when he awoke. Most of the Sunday morning had gone. Halpert remembered nothing, or almost nothing. Eventually, he recalled going to the hotel, but the only time he thought of Michael Danson was simply to wonder why he had never turned up. Apart from the foul taste in his mouth and a crashing headache, what he felt most sharply was the impossibility of ever working for Hilary Faire again. Maybe he could get a job at *The Post*. God help him, even the *Mirror* seemed a better prospect than the *Observer*.

Halpert looked at Susan. Her face seemed newly wrought. Unadorned, with her hair hanging loose and still unbrushed, she looked sad and beautiful. From far, far away, a sense of real longing stirred him, but when he tried to sit up his head felt as if all of Niagara Falls was thundering down within it. He fell back onto the pillows, the memory of his desire bobbing around the surface of his libido like the *Maid of the Mist* darting in and out of the spume and fury of the Falls.

How could he ever have been so stupid? All she had ever done through the years of their marriage was minister uncomplainingly to him. If that passivity had irritated him, today the collected memories of her love and devotion both shamed and excited him. For a few moments, he suddenly felt an embracing lucidity he had never before experienced: *I am loved, and there is nothing more that I ever have to know.*

"I've got some coffee in a Thermos," Susan said. As she got up and went over to the bureau, he gazed at her in adoration. She was wearing a hotel terry-cloth robe that was too large, but she had pulled the sash tight around her narrow waist, and the contrast between her small frame and the bulky dressing gown made her seem that much more alluring.

"I think we should stay here another night, Jamie. The crowds will only be bigger outside the apartment."

He liked the idea. The hotel room was neutral territory, removed from all previous associations with anything. No China. No *Observer*. No past. No future. Just now. Just the minute and the hour ahead.

It was enough.

∽

After the headache had gone, after they had made the sweetest love he could remember, after he decided he had never been so hungry in his life, she told him. She trembled as she talked, and he could not hold her close enough or tight enough to calm her.

"Jamie, I need help," she began. "A man has called me twice. He's Chinese. From the consulate, I guess. He says I have to help him. He's a very quiet talker, but he says that I have to start going into the crowds outside the consulate and find out who the key leaders are and I have to start getting to know the Chinese community in Toronto better. And he says that my mother and my family are all well now, but he hopes they will stay well. He told me I can help my motherland and my family at the same time. Jamie, I'm very frightened."

Halpert held her tighter.

"I won't let them do this to you, Sui-san. They can't do that."

He thought for a moment. Then he kissed her on her forehead, loosened his arms from around her, and got out of the bed.

"I know who to call."

It took only two inquiries in Ottawa before he had Brigadier Henderson on the line. He had run across Henderson once since he had worked so hard to avoid him on the airplane flying out of Beijing. That was in Toronto four years earlier. Henderson had continued his smooth ascent up the Canadian Forces' bureaucratic ladder and was now chief liaison officer for the Forces with the Privy Council Office, the army's ambassador to the government.

That meeting four years earlier had been uncomfortable as Henderson probed Halpert's decline with studiously upbeat summaries of every failure in his life. Such as, "Well, the book deal may have fallen through, but at least you've got a good job." Or, "Those were exciting times in China, eh? I bet you'd give your eye teeth to get back there." Or, "No kids? Oh well, you're lucky. They all turn into teenagers anyway."

"Jamie, how are you? A voice from the past. What a surprise."

Halpert took a deep breath. Asking a favour of someone you loathe diminishes the soul. He was businesslike as he recounted Susan's dilemma, but Henderson immediately caught the note of concern in Halpert's unconvincing matter-of-fact voice.

"Jamie, give me an hour and I'll get back to you. This is pretty serious and I'm really glad you called me. I'm going to phone someone and get you the name of a top CSIS officer you can speak to, and they'll take over from there. Tell your wife she's completely safe. They've gone berserk over in China, but their tanks can't reach our shores. Give me your phone number."

Halpert explained that they had gone to the Park Plaza Hotel because of the crowds around the Chinese consulate-general and gave him the number of their room. After thanking Henderson and hanging up, he phoned down to the front desk and said that he and Mrs. Halpert would be staying for another night.

Then they made love and laid in bed until it was time for dinner.

And after dinner they made love again. In Beijing, a man stood in front of a tank and made it stop.

∽

The Toronto offices of the Canadian Security and Intelligence Service were located in a building beside the city's domed sports stadium ("largest retractable roof in the world") and the CN Tower ("tallest free-standing structure in the world"), just along the street from the Royal York Hotel (formerly the "biggest hotel in the Empire").

Halpert and Susan double-checked the number of the building with the note Halpert had made from his second conversation with Brigadier Henderson. It was Monday morning and they'd been told to be there by "ten hundred hours." On the fifth floor, they rang the bell beside the plain wooden door. High up in a corner of the hallway, a Japanese-made security camera had already fixed them with its zoom.

"Yes," said a voice from the doorway intercom.

"It's James Halpert."

"Yes, Mr. Halpert," said the voice. "We're expecting you. Please come in."

There was a buzzing noise and Halpert pushed the door open. Inside, a tiny reception area seemed crowded with two plain chairs and a coffee table. At the counter, behind a solid sheet of plate glass, the CSIS receptionist was solicitous to excess.

"Oh hello, Mr. Halpert. And Mrs. Halpert. I'll just let Officer Grudon know that you're here. I know he's very anxious to speak to you. Would you like me to get you some coffee or tea?"

Halpert turned to Susan. She shook her head. The minuscule reception room was already closing in on her and she felt like screaming and running out.

"I guess I'll have a coffee. My wife is fine. Black, please."

"Now just make yourselves comfortable. It'll hardly be a minute."

Before the coffee arrived, a side door opened. Out stepped a man about Halpert's age. His hair was cut short and he wore a navy-blue suit, white shirt, and a dark-maroon tie.

"Mr. and Mrs. Halpert?" he asked.

"Hi," said Halpert. "James Halpert. This is my wife, Susan."

"I'm Scott Grudon. I'm a CSIS officer, and I've been assigned to your case. Will you follow me, please?"

As they went into the interior offices, the receptionist came up to Halpert with a Styrofoam cup of black coffee and asked Susan if she was sure she didn't want some tea or a soft drink. Susan didn't even acknowledge the question. She was walking like an automaton.

"Now," said Grudon when they were all seated in his office, "I wonder if you could go over with me what you told Brigadier Henderson. I

212

should tell you before we start that whatever you say is treated confidentially within the service."

He turned to look directly at Susan. "Nothing you tell me will get back to the Chinese authorities. We have no relationship or arrangements with their security services — "

This struck Halpert as an extraordinary thing to say, until Grudon let the other shoe fall.

" — at least not yet."

A security officer with an edge. How un-Canadian.

After Halpert explained the reason for their presence at the CSIS branch as he understood it, Grudon turned to Susan. Halpert sat back in his seat.

"Mrs. Halpert, I take it this is not your first contact with the Chinese security apparatus."

"You mean in Canada?"

"I mean anywhere. I'm assuming you had contact with them in China before you came here."

Halpert leaned forward. He didn't like the tone of the question and was about to say something when Susan put her hand on his knee to stop him.

"I was called into a Public Security Bureau office when I was a student at Nanjing University. It was after my department leader had reported me because of my relationship with a foreign student. My family still had its black label — "

Grudon smiled thinly. "I know about black labels," he said. "Your family had a hard time during the Cultural Revolution?"

"Very hard. My father died and we never knew how. The black labels were being taken away from people, and ours didn't stop me from going to university, but we were still being watched."

"So. The PSB called you in about your relationship with a foreign student. What did they say? Did they tell you to end the relationship?"

"No, they didn't," continued Susan. "It wasn't a threatening meeting at all. They said China was changing, and that within certain circles, it was all right to maintain friendships with foreigners. But I was never to forget that all foreigners were ultimately enemies of the motherland.

The motherland had to protect itself always, and even the best-intentioned foreigner would exploit the country in the end."

"Were you asked to inform on this foreign friend."

"No. Not that time. Later I was. I was told to report to a PSB official at the university every two weeks and to bring a daily diary of what I did. So that's how it began. I had to turn up every . . ."

Halpert started to understand. He had truly fallen in love with his wife only the day before, and now the love seeped out of him. *The whole time Gordon was with Sui-san, she had been playing a double game.* The hand upon his knee felt like a vice. Yet he could not remove it. Nor could he make his leg move. He was immobilized, and with that immobilization, his hearing ended.

He took in nothing more of the present. Back came the memory of Gordon's bloodied head. Back came Susan's phony fears. Back came the face of Kwai Ta-ping. Back came Joan's words about betrayal over the phone at the Hong Kong Hilton. Back came all the frantic arrangements to get to Thailand and the visit to the Cambodian refugee camp where he had found Susan, lying in the corner of a fetid hut, hugging her knees in a kind of stupor. The hand on his knee got heavier and sharper.

"Mrs. Halpert, this has been very good of you. I don't think you have to worry too much. We already know that Chinese officials at consulates in Toronto and Vancouver, as well as some of their people at the embassy in Ottawa, have been busy over the past couple of days trying to control all the damage that has resulted from the massacre in Beijing. I suggest that you get an unlisted number so you will be spared any more phone calls. I'm going to give you my card, and you are to call me in case anyone approaches you on the street. I don't think this will happen, unless they've gone completely bonkers. They're not being very sophisticated at the moment because there's a lot of panic. They're making some very bad mistakes and we are monitoring everything. When the fuss dies down, they will come to their senses and start operating in a more normal way. Mr. Halpert, is there anything you want to say?"

Halpert managed to shake his head at the same time as he finally found he could shift his leg away from Susan's hand. She looked at him quickly, but he averted his eyes and did not see the tears streaming down her face.

"What you have done, Mrs. Halpert, is very important. We have a government in Canada that simply doesn't believe that the Chinese side behaves in this manner, so having testimony like this is very important. Now you call me if anything happens. *Anything*. Or if you have questions. Thank you very much for coming in."

As they were being escorted out by Grudon, Susan tried to take Halpert's hand. He didn't resist, but the hand she held remained limp and unresponsive, so she let it go and mumbled a small vocal sob in Chinese under her breath.

When they got out on the street, he looked at his watch. "I better go to the *Observer*," he said blankly. "There's a meeting."

"I don't want to be alone today, Jamie. Please stay with me."

He looked at her through a prism of pure hate.

"I want to know one thing. At what point after Gordon was killed did you tell them about Kwai?"

"I didn't tell them anything about Kwai," she said, looking totally perplexed. "Didn't you hear me in there? And I didn't tell them anything important about Gordon or his work. I just told them what I felt I had to tell them to be left alone. Jamie, I need you so much. Don't be this way."

"I have to go to the office," he said dully. "I'll see you later. You'll be okay. At least you're alive and not in prison."

"Oh, Jamie, don't do this. . . ."

But he'd already left her and was striding along Front Street.

∽

Everyone had assembled in the cafeteria by the time Halpert arrived for the noon meeting. He had stormed around the back streets of downtown Toronto for over two hours, trying to fit it all together.

The ten years since Gordon's death contracted into a minute as he regarded a world he had never fully imagined before, but a world that now made terrible sense. From here on there would be no more fiction, no more self-deception, no more delusion that honour and loyalty and patience can wage honest battle with duplicity and cowardice and aggression.

Gordon had found something the Chinese didn't want him to find, for whatever reason. Halpert himself had stumbled across part of the mystery at the Sung tombs, as Professor Johnson had indicated. So they killed Gordon. Wittingly, Susan had passed along everything to the PSB and her reward was flight to the West, once – presumably – she had also told them what they needed about Kwai Ta-ping. Now she wanted to be left alone, but that wasn't convenient. Her minders wanted to activate her again. *Jesus!*

He saw Arch Crawley beside Geoffrey Cameron, both standing up against the back wall of the cafeteria, beckoning him to come over. He pretended not to notice and took a chair on the sidelines. But there was no avoiding the two of them. When they saw Halpert take his seat, they inched their way through the crowd at the back and sat directly behind him. The first and second rows in front of the makeshift podium and lectern were empty, as if close proximity to the leadership of the newspaper would taint anyone so foolish as to sit there.

"Jamie, I have to talk to you," said Cameron. "You have to intervene for me with Hilary. She doesn't understand what a great story I've got."

Halpert was about to tell Cameron to get lost, but Arch did it for him, more kindly.

"Dum-de-dum-dum. And here comes the lovely Lady Luck herself."

Hilary Faire was first through the cafeteria door, then the publisher, and finally – Arch supplied the "Oh my God" – Chris Bredin. The publisher was all smiles, Hilary was all business, and Bredin kept his head down, looking neither to the left nor the right.

The publisher was the designated master of ceremonies. Hilary and Bredin sat in chairs immediately behind the lectern. Bredin managed to avoid eye contact with anyone, while the editor-in-chief crossed her legs and looked out on the assembled multitude with a tight smile.

"Thank you all for joining us this morning," said the publisher. He was a stout fellow, relatively new to his august post having been snared by headhunters from outside the industry. The *Observer*'s owners, terrified by the steep drop in advertising lineage, had decided they needed a supreme manager with proven cost-cutting skills from anywhere but the newspaper business. In his previous incarnation, the new publisher had made a name for himself in furniture and small appliances.

Eight years earlier, during a recession, he had hit the front pages of the *Observer*'s business section with his decisive and brutal firing of nearly half the workforce at the venerable firm of Dominion Appliances Ltd. The company had gone on to post record profits, but after a few years the board had become uncomfortable with his management style. He'd commissioned too many studies into consumer needs, and the hero of yesterday was indecisive and lax when the times dictated constant attention to the bottom line. He could still fire people beautifully, but he was otherwise useless.

None of this later reputation was revealed to the *Observer*'s board when it was hunting for a new CEO. They had gobbled the headhunter's recommendation whole, not realizing that the new publisher had been desperately jobbing his services for over a year to *anyone* who could come up with a six-figure salary.

"We come before you with only good news during a very difficult time," he began.

"Nice start," whispered Arch. "He's got my attention."

"After careful study, we have decided that our present staff levels in all departments are about right. Any more reductions might jeopardize the quality of the product we are known for."

The collective sigh of relief could be heard throughout the entire cafeteria. Hilary Faire didn't change the brittleness of her smile, but she cocked her head at a bit of an angle, indicating that she, too, was pleased at this news.

"But it doesn't mean that those of us who remain here can afford to sit around twiddling our thumbs. I realize there has been considerable dislocation in every department because of previous staff reductions over the past six months. And I have to tell you, we do not see any economic indicators which would suggest that the recession we have entered into will end quickly. Even though our readership remains stable, and I must salute our editor-in-chief for the remarkable job she has done to ensure this stability, our ad lineage continues to drop.

"Ladies and gentlemen, I don't have to tell you what that means. If ad revenues are falling and staff levels remain static, we will start sustaining heavy losses. So what do we do? Well, that's what we're here to tell you. . . ."

The publisher droned on for another five minutes with the usual catalogue of desperate measures newspapers employ at moments like this: Reduce the overall size of the newspaper, continue the overtime ban, raise the price of subscriptions, close down another foreign bureau, limit the use of taxis, et cetera. No one was really listening anymore. Their jobs were safe for the moment, and those who were not from the newsroom just wanted the meeting to end.

Those *from* the newsroom, however, wanted to know what Bredin was doing up beside Hilary Faire. Arch *really* wanted to know. After yesterday's drama, he wondered if Hilary would make Bredin pull down his pants in front of everyone while she took a switch to his rearside.

". . . and so I'd like to call upon our wonderful editor-in-chief to outline some of the new measures she is planning that will not only sustain reader interest but help us all to understand more clearly that what we are facing is not in any way a setback. It's a new challenge and a new opportunity. Hilary, if you please."

No one applauded. Hilary Faire rose slowly from her seat. She had been thinking about what a little worm the new publisher was, but at the same time how useful he had become as receiver-general for the pent-up frustrations of the staff. Though increasingly peevish when put under pressure, he was easy enough to manipulate, so she was perfectly content to play a deferential role – at least for the moment.

"I just want to start off by saying what a wonderful job our publisher has been doing. These are very difficult times economically, and having such a cool, competent helmsman makes us all feel more confident. Thank you, sir, on behalf of everyone."

There was a smattering of applause, just enough to prevent embarrassment. The new publisher was grinning like a jackass and made a little salute to Hilary.

"The publisher used two words I want us to think about very seriously. 'Challenge' was one and 'opportunity' was the other. There's a wonderful synergy between these two words, and I would like to see

218

them become our motto, especially in editorial, which is the department at the heart of this great newspaper. Our 'challenge' is to do better with less and our 'opportunity' is finally to take seriously our crucial mandate to remake this newspaper into a fit organ for the times and for the future."

"Here it comes," hissed Arch into Halpert's ear. Halpert hadn't been taking in anything except the general self-serving relief and cynicism. And into this noxious brew, he had thrown the memory of all his own querulousness over the past decade. The characters around him had become faceless blobs in a nightmare starring ghouls and monsters. Even Arch. Halpert howled on his heath, while Arch played the fool.

"I have become increasingly dissatisfied at the unresponsiveness of the stratified departments in editorial. Here we are, only a decade away from the end of the twentieth century, and our structures remain hitched to nineteenth-century thinking processes. This has to stop right now. It's as simple as that. As part of the new era at the *Observer*, I am very happy to announce the appointment of Chris Bredin as our new managing editor to replace Dick Thomson, who, as you know, is still on leave and dealing with his nervous breakdown. Chris has really earned his spurs in the newsroom over the past year and I have a great deal of confidence in him. . . ."

Arch could not sit still. He shifted restlessly in his seat, a wild and loopy smile all over his face. "This is incredible, fucking incredible," he kept whispering to no one in particular. Then he turned to Halpert. "Jamie! Jamie! Did yesterday happen? Was all that shit just foreplay? This is fucking incredible – "

"Over the next days and weeks, Chris will be meeting with everyone in editorial to outline the new strategies. I think you'll like them. They'll stretch your talents and give you a new professional lease on life. Thank you all very much. Now everyone back to their posts. We have a great newspaper to put out."

∾

Halpert came straight home from the meeting. He didn't stop to gossip with Arch. He didn't go back to the Park Plaza to get drunk. He came straight home, and when he walked through the door, Susan ran to him and put her arms around him.

He threw her off with such force that she stumbled. Then he went to the coat closet. She looked at him blankly, her rejected arms dangling uselessly at her sides.

"There's been a woman calling long distance for you every ten or fifteen minutes. She should be calling again in a minute."

"Who is it?"

"I don't know, she said – "

The phone rang and Halpert went for it gratefully. Anything to avoid his wife.

"Jamie? Jamie Halpert? Is that you finally?"

"Yes. Who's this, please?"

Halpert could tell she was calling from an airport or train terminal. There was a dim, echoing drone of public announcements in the background.

"It's Julie Potlow, Jamie. It's been a very long time, and this isn't the moment to get caught up. I'm at Heathrow waiting for a plane to Zurich, and I have something very important to discuss with you."

Julie Potlow! Halpert sat down in the low seat beside the telephone desk in his apartment. They had only had one other encounter after the flirtation on the airplane and that had been in Toronto a few years back when a new Chinese antique porcelain store had been officially opened. He and Susan were invited to the festivities, but he didn't know why until he saw Julie's face at the rear of the first-floor showroom.

It had been a dead encounter. Halpert could tell within seconds that she had judged him a loser. She could barely avoid talking down to him and ignored Susan altogether. He did not have trouble squaring the beguiling seatmate on the airplane out of Beijing with the new-wrought virago, and there was a bleak satisfaction in discovering that the winsome Julie Potlow was a well-groomed monster.

"Jamie, there's a little creep at your newspaper named Cameron. He's a reporter. Do you know him?"

"Yes, I know Geoff Cameron. How does he fit into your high life?"

"Spare me the sarcasm." The voice was hard. "If you have any regard for him, tell him to keep his nose away from Finch's. He won't like the consequences."

Halpert wanted to say a lot of things. "Is this a threat?" for example. Or, "Why the hell are you phoning me?" Even, "Fuck off." But he didn't. He didn't say anything. He couldn't summon up a single word. Susan was still standing dumbly in front of him, the tears pouring down her face. Slowly he took the receiver away from his ear and hung it up.

"Jamie. I want, I don't know, I – "

Halpert stood up and slapped her. Hard. Twice. He was so tall beside her, he actually had to lean over to hit her. The full force of his hand across her face sent her reeling back to the wall. Halpert barely felt a thing. Walking over to where she lay crumpled on the floor, he had trouble comprehending that something that had caused him so little physical effort had so completely felled her. He thought of saying something cruel to her, but couldn't form a sequential sentence, so said nothing. She had started moaning and rocking herself exactly the same way he remembered her on the sofa back in Beijing when he brought her the news of Gordon's death. *At least this time she isn't faking.*

She wasn't. Nor was she thinking of Halpert or of Gordon. She was far, far away. The voices had come back to her. She heard her father's closest colleagues and her own best friends screeching abuse at her. She felt their fists pounding on her back. She heard her father yelling impotently for them to leave her alone. It was happening again, all over again. This time, though, she wasn't so sure she'd survive.

When he was halfway out the front door, Halpert turned to her and found the words he wanted. "You're the reason Gordon is dead and you're the reason Kwai is in prison. I don't know how you can live with that."

Then he walked out of the apartment.

PART THREE

August 1994

$$\boxed{12}$$

Ace Ventura, "pet detective," was grimacing again. Halpert didn't have his earphones on, but from time to time the rubber face on the screen caught his eye and momentarily diverted his thoughts. Even in the comfort of one of Cathay Pacific's more than ample Club-class seats, he felt defensive, as if the silent, marauding Jim Carrey and his menacing leer would suddenly break his celluloid bounds and come lurching at him. All around he could hear high-pitched, convulsive laughter, childish laughter, and it added further to the total sense of unreality. What was he doing on this plane? Why had he agreed to go to Hong Kong? What good was it going to do? Where was he headed?

He had talked about these things with Father Bell at St. Aidan's Restways Retirement Village while he was struggling to make up his mind. Maybe the old priest was his best friend now, he wondered. Who knows what a friend is, least of all a best friend? Halpert certainly didn't anymore. After he and Susan had split up, after he had quit the *Observer*, after the unemployment insurance cheques had run out and he could no longer afford the apartment on St. George, he had thought of the old priest.

A telephone call to the parish secretary at St. Aidan's had got him the information that Father Bell took one service a month on Wednesday mornings. The secretary said that his next service was in less than a week. She offered a home phone number at the neighbouring seniors' home, but Halpert didn't want it. He decided he would just go to the early morning service and stay at the back of the church.

At the time, Halpert felt he was as close to the edge of the gutter as he cared to go, but he hadn't a clue where else to head. Something in the back of his mind reminded him that Christianity began as a religion of slaves and helots for whom Christ's promise of deferred hope held out some meagre solace in a world of unremitting cruelty and pain. And then there was his memory of Father Bell. In that memory, Halpert thought of the old priest as being as woebegone as he now felt himself, so off he went to St. Aidan's early the next Wednesday morning, with no expectations and a heart that was not so much contrite as shattered. Once inside the church, he realized his careful plan to hide away at the back behind all the other worshippers had a major flaw: there were no other worshippers. Halpert was the only one to turn up.

The moment he realized he was alone, he chastised himself for his sentimentality, but he was a broken man, and the edge of the gutter wasn't the only precipice on which Halpert felt himself teetering. Thoughts of suicide had also intruded into his diminished world over the past few weeks.

To avert such desperation, he had turned up at St. Aidan's, resolved only that he wasn't going to take Communion. He wasn't sure if Father Bell had even noticed him in the dark body of the church, and, on the whole, he preferred not to be seen. But when the old priest had finished his solitary ablutions and just before he left the altar, he peered out into the nave, shielding his eyes from the glare of the sanctuary floodlights with his hand.

"I know there's someone out there. There's a pot of coffee waiting. Won't you join me?"

Halpert was unshaven – two days' worth – and was wearing an open-necked tartan shirt and threadbare pair of dark-green corduroys. His hair had been cut very short, almost to the scalp. He was not a pretty sight.

"Mrs. Stoute usually comes to my service," the priest said after he tried to lift the coffee pot without success and asked Halpert to fill the two mugs. His hands shook now, he said. The result of "the palsy."

"She was a great friend of my late wife's. I'm a little worried she might be ill. I shall phone her when I get home."

He asked Halpert no questions. He made no pronouncements. If he remembered him from their brief previous encounter, he didn't let on. Instead, he chatted on about nothing in particular, and Halpert reciprocated with monosyllabic grunts. Halpert was agitated, he needed to speak but he did not know how to form the words – the final collapse, perhaps, of all he had trained himself to do professionally. When there was no more reason for lingering, and the priest himself was clearly ready to depart, Halpert tried to stand up but the effort turned out to be beyond his abilities.

"I don't understand anything," he finally blurted out at the unsurprised priest. He practically spat the words.

"Nor do any of the rest of us, my dear fellow. Not a single blessed thing."

He looked at Halpert carefully, and with concern.

"We know each other, don't we?"

Halpert nodded and looked down at his empty coffee mug. "It was Gordon Wrye," he said.

"Ah yes. Gordon Wrye. And you were writing a book."

Only then did it all come spilling out. Catatonic inarticulateness transformed into compulsive confession. Halpert's need to give an accounting was fierce. Some of it – the specific words and, often, the logic – was incoherent, but the old priest seemed to understand everything. When he was done, and he had withheld *nothing*, including hitting his wife, he looked at Father Bell with an almost satisfied air, as if to say, "Well, you may have heard some pathetic stories in your life, but I bet you haven't heard any as pathetic as mine."

The old priest looked down at the lap of his black cassock. For longer than a minute, Father Bell didn't say anything. He started scratching the back of his left hand. Another freckle had started growing and had darkened in colour. Every couple of months, the little cancers erupted – on the back of his hands, on his nose and high forehead, on his back. The dermatologist removed them, but the priest knew they were still his heralds, announcing the coming of the final confrontation.

"I have no special comfortable words for you," he said at last. "There aren't any to be had, really. The world was sent some solace once, but we killed it, so that was that. We have a tradition, a church-committee memory of the sacrifice, but it's not much. The institutional church trains its priests to offer redemption, but it seems to me a hollow thing. I must confess to you now, Mr. Halpert. These past three decades, I have never once been able to get beyond the betrayal of the crucified Christ. And I'm not talking about the betrayal by men. We are all born betrayers, every man, woman, and child. I'm talking about the betrayal of God. That's an awesome thing to contemplate."

"Not if you don't believe in God," said Halpert too quickly. He regretted saying it, not because it might hurt the old gentleman but because it was such an obvious thing to say.

"You're wrong! If there is no supremacy to existence, then all the betrayal can be dealt with. We would have the Godlike powers within us to legislate its end, or scientifically remake our race so that no one ever again had to shriek in pain and loneliness from a cross, whatever the cross. If *only* there was no God! Then this restlessness inside us could be satiated, we could reshape the peace our souls long for through our own devices. What I always found so daunting was not 'the peace of God which passeth all understanding' – that's a chimera. It's the wrath of God that passes my understanding. When you get old like me, these things just sit like a lump on your heart. We're beyond care, I suppose, but memory can still be a ferocious companion. My Christ is the Christ of the betrayed. He does not offer me solace, but he helps me understand and to accept. And in acceptance, there is the possibility of calm and the possibility of understanding the world. You need to find some calm, Mr. Halpert. I found it in prison, where I had been sent for something I didn't do. You can surely find some measure of calm without going to such an extreme. I had a son, you know. A sweet boy. He was taken from me. . . ."

Halpert saw that his own desperate need had robbed the old priest of whatever precarious share of calm he had managed to construct, for his eyes had filled with tears. In knowing that, in understanding the generosity of the priest's confession, in trying to find from somewhere within him some desperate words of comfort to fling at this old man's far deeper desperation, Halpert comprehended that he could muddle through somehow.

And it was a muddle. He got drunk again and stayed drunk at Arch's seedy apartment for two days. Even for Arch this was a bit much, and the great trogdolyte bestirred himself and found Halpert a room in a boarding house off Beverley Street. It was owned and operated by a Cantonese crone whose tantrums at alleged tenant malefactions punctuated Halpert's otherwise gloomy nights. A couple of weeks later, Arch dropped by to tell Halpert about an editing job at the monthly *Medical Messenger*.

"It's not much," he said, "but it's a place to go to, and you don't have to get your assignments from Chris fucking Bredin. You should hear him now when he's at the editorial management meetings with Madam. As soon as she opens her mouth about some new madness, he blurts out, 'Oh, Hilary, that's so brilliant. How do you keep coming up with these great ideas?' I take Gravol every day, but I still can't shake the nausea."

Despite himself, Halpert had smiled. Thereafter, once a month on the appointed Wednesdays, he returned to St. Aidan's. He never took the consecrated wine and bread, but he always waited to share a cup of coffee.

∽

"Do you want a last drink, sir?"

The flight attendant smiled at him as he tried to decide.

"We'll be landing at Kai-tak airport in under an hour and we're closing the bar after this call. Do you want another bourbon and soda?"

"How about just the soda," said Halpert. The 1994 Halpert. The fifty-three-year-old Halpert. The self-renamed James Halpert. The sensible James Halpert. The meticulous, slightly fuss-budget James Halpert. The editor-in-chief of the *Medical Messenger* James Halpert, a respected journal with a staff of four, which included himself, an assistant, a full-time copy editor (his former job), and a part-time art director. These days, even Arch Crawley found him a bit of a bore.

When Susan had called him from Hong Kong a month earlier and told him Kwai Ta-ping was out of labour-reform camp and was working

229

in the Shenzhen New Economic Zone with one of the joint-venture projects her boss's husband dreamed up, he did not at first know what to make of it.

Susan's phone call wasn't the problem. He had forgiven her by now. The old priest had taken him through the metaphysical rubric of absorbing pain, and he had reached a state of almost unctuous pride in his ability to comprehend the weaknesses of others, as well as his own capacity to absorb their sins. It was himself, he came to see, who had precipitated Kwai's betrayal. Susan may well have ratted on Gordon and this may well have led to his murder, but she was the victim of a diseased political system, not the disease itself.

If she sensed the stinging condescension of his forgiveness, Susan didn't let on. After Mrs. Li had taken pity on her and offered her the position of personal assistant, she had maintained a tenuous link with Halpert by phoning him each January during Chinese New Year, with a midyear follow-up call in July on his birthday. Since the call about Kwai Ta-ping had come three weeks before his fifty-third birthday, he thought at first she must have written down the date incorrectly in her diary.

"Jamie," she said, "I saw Kwai yesterday."

"Kwai who?" he'd asked. She had phoned him at the *Medical Messenger*, and he was deep inside a feature story on a new surgical procedure to correct spinal curvature in scoliosis patients.

"Kwai Ta-ping."

"Oh my God, you're kidding," he said, straightening up in his chair. The article had made him wonder if his own back was giving out. "How on earth did you run across him?"

"He's working in Shenzhen in a textbook publishing company. I was there yesterday with Mrs. Li."

She didn't tell him she had read an article in one of the Hong Kong Chinese-language dailies about his release from labour-reform camp and the attempts Western journalists had made to get him to talk about his experience, attempts he reportedly resisted with a wry, mostly toothless smile. Susan had used connections to get through to him and arranged for the work in Shenzhen, which required him to edit a range of middle-school geography textbooks. She had talked to him twice before she decided to phone Halpert, and even after she had rung him up she nearly put down the receiver before he answered.

"He wants to see you. I think you should come. I can make the arrangements if you want."

Something stuck in his craw. Who the hell was she to be organizing such a meeting?

"If I do decide to come, I'll make my own arrangements, thanks. Look, it was good of you to let me know. I'll get back to you. Still at the same number?"

"Yes, Jamie. Still at the same number. How are you?"

"So, I'll call. Got to go now. Thanks again."

Had he not trained himself over the past several years to package all his thoughts into tidy concepts, he might have recognized that his capacity for forgiveness had become parsimonious. The cramped world he had so carefully constructed for himself did not leave room for any emotional extravagance.

So he stewed about it and mulled it over. He talked to Father Bell and decided a half-dozen times not to go. But each time he resolved to maintain the calm in his life, the compulsion to reopen all the old wounds became stronger. And that was how it came to be that he and Ace Ventura were floating together high above the Pacific Ocean, both of them lost in a miasma of uncomprehended motivation.

∾

When Halpert had finally called Susan, all he said was, "I'm coming next week. I'll phone you when I get to Hong Kong. Thanks for the news about Kwai."

That was it, but it was enough for Susan. The man who had held her when she found out Gordon was dead, the man who arranged her escape from China, the man who rescued her from the refugee camp in Thailand, the man she made love to one night and who beat her the next, was coming back. If there was any motivation in her life beyond mere survival – and for a Chinese from China, surviving was a stronger instinct than copulating or even eating – it was to mitigate the notion that all life led to betrayal. She had no sense of Christian or Buddhist or

Confucian metaphysics to support her in this curious quest, just the brutal experience of its opposite. A contrary nature guided her. That, and a revulsion for Maoist materialism.

On most days, her philosophical mentor and sometimes sparring partner was Mrs. Li, who had scooped her up in Toronto five years ago and placed her under a protective wing.

"Men bad, bad, bad," Mrs. Li had said, after guessing what had happened to Susan. Mrs. Li accepted that men were a necessary evil in making babies, but she had a corollary. "Men say nice things, then do bad, bad, bad." She had paused for a moment, looked at Susan's bruise closely, and then took her hand. "Very bad, very bad."

Susan's life in Hong Kong had been busy from the first day, as Mrs. Li rose higher in prominence than ever before thanks to her husband's adroit new relationship with the neighbouring Communist government readying itself to take over the Crown colony.

The day Halpert telephoned to say he was coming, she had been involved for much of the morning in a heated and sometimes embarrassing confrontation with Government House. On behalf of her husband, Big Huang Dafu, Mrs. Li – via Susan – had turned down the sixth invitation in a row that year to dine with the governor at an official function. And this time, the governor, increasingly isolated from the encroaching power of the mainland, had decided that enough was enough.

He had ordered his chief aide to harry Big Huang, through his wife – and therefore via Susan – to come up with an acceptance. Since there was no possibility whatsoever of Big Huang going to Government House and jeopardizing in any way his increasingly extensive joint ventures with the Communist government, it was Susan who had to take the heat from the governor's office.

"I see no decent purpose served by this kind of studied insult to His Excellency," said the aide at one point, coming back for the third and increasingly bitter assault.

"It's not an insult. Mr. Huang and Mrs. Li have a previous engagement. It's a very simple matter, as I said. They are so sorry things have not worked out this year."

"Sorry! Don't talk rubbish. You people aren't sorry at all. Look, if you're so sorry, why don't you ever give us a date you know will work out and then we can plan around it."

"Well, I don't run Mr. Huang's office, as you know. I am Mrs. Li's personal assistant, and my job in this situation is simply to co-ordinate their two schedules. And there are contradictions in their schedules with your date, so once again I just have to say so sorry we can't accept the kind invitation of His Excellency the Governor."

"Look!" The aide exploded now. "How the devil are we going to get through the next years unless all sides co-operate. His Excellency is a reasonable man and is well prepared to make reasonable concessions. He does not intend to be held accountable for any consequences if this attitude persists. . . ."

She listened patiently, even sympathetically. They were two well-paid ciphers unable to respond differently than they were told. Susan understood that the aide was either taping his conversation with her or else was talking in the governor's office with the governor himself hovering over the aide's shoulder. Susan was alone during the conversation, but Big Huang's orders were inviolable.

"So I am very sorry once again to say there are contradictions in the diaries of Mr. Huang and Mrs. Li. I hope that the next time those contradictions will not be there."

The aide was silent for a moment. Then she heard the other voice in the background. "Oh, ring off. She can't change anything."

"Look," said the aide, hastily adopting a voice of plummy conciliation. "You and I should have a lunch some time. I'm making the assumption your diary doesn't have the same number of contradictions as your employers."

"I would like lunch with you. That would be very nice. Why don't I give you a call sometime?"

"Why don't we set it up right now? I've got my diary open on this week and the next."

"I'm so sorry. I don't have my diary with me. Why don't you let me give you a call some day?"

It was like a reversed conversation with Jamie, endlessly stretched out. Big Huang would never countenance an unseemly break in relations with the governor because you never could tell how the immediate future would work out. Right now, though, the governor was in the doghouse, and one of the key entrepreneurs of the newly emerging Hong Kong was not going to be seen sharing his meatless bones.

After she had dispensed with the governor's aide, she looked through Mrs. Li's bulging invitation file. Most would have to be regretted. On an average, she was now refusing close to two dozen invitations a week. It was understood that many cash-starved institutions, as well as the up-and-coming (or the down-and-going), wanted to use Mrs. Li as a means of getting a foothold into Big Huang's ever-expanding empire and influence.

Part of Susan's job was to know who could be rejected without consultation or remorse and who needed to be catered to or stroked. The invitation to the forthcoming opening of an exhibition of "new archaeological discoveries from the People's Republic of China," co-sponsored by the New China News Agency in Hong Kong and Finch's Importables PLC in partnership with Potlow Investments, was simply a matter of checking with Big Huang's appointment secretary to clear off anything in his calendar that might be a conflict. There was no question that he and Mrs. Li would attend.

She looked out her window at the great crescent of office skyscrapers along the rim of Hong Kong Island. Her office, an adjunct to Big Huang's executive suite high up in the new World Trade Centre on the Kowloon side, gave her one of the best views anywhere into the heart of the vertical megalopolis. As usual, she paid it little regard. Expansive views made her uneasy, and often enough she partially closed the blinds on a panorama others were prepared to pay a hundred thousand Hong Kong dollars per square foot to have.

Her only solid memory of total security was the walls of her father's courtyard house in Nanjing when she was a little girl. There was a small, octagonal stone pool with a fountain in the middle of the courtyard. The pipe leading to the fountain had corroded and ceased functioning, but at each of the eight corners of the stone pool were carved heads of guardian dragons, and she had a name for each one of them. They were her friends and would protect her from all harm.

In the end, the dragons had betrayed her, too, all eight of them. And so had the walls that were not stout enough to stop evil when it was on the march. Yet, paradoxically, she clung to her faith that secret, quiet places could somehow offer refuge and protection. Faith is a strange thing: impervious to rational analysis, but also sometimes quaint and remarkably modest in its objectives.

Susan once thought Halpert was a man who embodied four stout walls. Despite everything, she was not yet an apostate. She picked up a small pile of telephone messages and other scraps of paper, going through them carefully till she found what she was looking for. Then she dialled the number in Shenzhen.

It rang three times, and then she heard the little click that indicated an answering machine. She listened to Kwai Ta-ping's message in Cantonese, Mandarin, and English. The English version was distinctive: "Congratulations! You have reached my own office. I am not here, or maybe I am here. If you talk soon, I will hear what you're sayings. Goodbye."

"*Lao* Kwai," she said in Chinese. "Old Kwai, it's Sui-san. He's coming next week. Please be ready. I'll call again when I know more details."

∾

Halpert looked out across the harbour to the Kowloon side. The last time he had awakened in the Hong Kong Hilton and pulled back the curtains on this panorama was fifteen years ago, the morning of the day he had flown to Bangkok to find Susan. Immediately, he noticed the differences.

There were no junks *anywhere*. In 1979, the harbour was still so full of the feisty little wooden ships that they used to provide the definitive proof to busy tourists that they really were in the Far East: the high-backed stern and snubby bow, the bat's-wing sail, and the barefooted skipper, times a thousand, darting in and around giant ships in the world's busiest harbour was an extraordinary sight. Now it was gone, maybe forever.

Halpert also noticed that the actual harbour size had contracted and was still diminishing. Busy trucks and tractors were hauling the infill in an unending procession to claim back the sea. The Star Ferry Line was still operating, but surely Kowloon and Hong Kong Island would be joined within a few years and the ferries, too, would be no more. Kowloon's skyline had changed dramatically. About all he could recognize was the old Peninsula Hotel, if only the corner of it left unobscured by the vast new World Trade Centre and a dozen other eighties buildings.

He looked at his watch. It was nearly 10:30 a.m. He had slept for close to eleven hours, after registering at the hotel the night before and making a brief phone call to Susan.

"I'm here," he had said. "I'm not sure why, but I'm here. Have you any idea of how I am to go about trying to see Kwai? I haven't a visa to go into China, you know."

"Why don't you telephone him in Shenzhen tomorrow, after you've slept? I'll give you his office number. Then we can work out how to get you together. Here's the number."

He had patted the outside of his jacket to find a pen on the inside pocket. It wasn't there, so he started feeling around the telephone desk for a pencil. He was going to tell her that he had come to see Kwai Ta-ping and couldn't see any point to the two of them meeting, but he held back — not out of kindness, but for reasons of strategy. He might need to see her, after all. He took down Kwai Ta-ping's number and hung up with a terse "Call you tomorrow. Bye."

The hotel porter had turned on the television when he brought Halpert's bags up, and the set had been tuned to "The Welcome Channel" featured by all the better Hong Kong hotels. It provided a bit of history of the Crown colony, shopping tips (cameras), a hotel directory, some shopping tips (jewellery), directions on how to use the Star ferries and the island tram to the Peak, more shopping tips (recorders and calculators), exchange rates for most foreign currencies, specialty shopping tips (bespoke tailoring and custom-made shoes, all done in under twenty-four hours), the location of churches and temples as well as the times of various services, a shopping feature on Chinese arts and crafts (excluding porcelain), a propaganda segment detailing the joy people in Hong Kong feel as they contemplate the warm embrace of the motherland in 1997, part two of the shopping feature on Chinese arts and crafts (focusing on porcelain). . . .

Halpert had flicked channels and listened briefly to a local newscast.

". . . after this latest rebuke. Governor Patton said later that the continuing intransigence of the Beijing authorities in refusing to deal with his administration will only serve to further complicate the transfer of powers by 1997.

"In other news, the riot at the Kwongtai Vietnamese refugee camp last week has resulted in calls to speed up the repatriation of all the so-called Vietnamese boat people. The Kowloon Businessmen's Association joined with other organizations to demand that the government immediately . . ."

Halpert had just managed to turn the set off before he fell asleep. When he awoke, it was almost time to telephone Kwai Ta-ping.

∽

Pressing the buttons on the Hilton's telephone halfway through the number Susan had provided, Halpert suddenly remembered the sensation he had felt as he flew out of Beijing at the end of his posting. Once again, technology had become a grinning jester. Then it had been an airplane simply whisking him away from all the turmoil he had left behind, from all the sordid tricks a totalitarian government gets up to, from a civilization that had endured for longer than ninety-nine per cent of its history without any knowledge or need of airplanes.

And now he was dialling back into it, dialling a great survivor, dialling back into his guilt. As the phone rang through, he remembered – for the first time since Susan called him, amazingly enough – that Kwai spoke hardly any English and that his own limited command of Mandarin had long ago rusted away and was virtually non-existent.

There was a click. A voice said, "*Wei.*" Halpert could think of nothing to say, in any language. "*Wei!*" came the voice, louder the second time.

"*Duibuqi,*" said Halpert. "I'm sorry." Where did that word come from? He had no idea. "*Wo*, ahhh, *wo yao Kwai, Kwai, Kwai Ta-ping*, ahhh – "

"Yaahhh. Hai-pert! It's me. Kwai. It's A-okay. Speak real good English now. Sui-san tell me you are the callering me. I am so happy. How are you my very good friend?"

Halpert could still not find any words. His brain was not registering anything quickly enough. Finally, he took a deep breath.

"Kwai, I've been so worried about you. Are you okay? I feel so badly about everything. All your trouble."

"Kwai okay, Kwai okay. Real nice holiday in Northeast. Big joke. Food not so good. Lots of English teachers."

"Your English is great, Kwai. What did they do to you? I can't tell you how sorry I am for everything."

"Why Hai-pert sorry?"

"I'm the reason you ended up in prison. You know that and I know that. When I asked you to help Sui-san, I might as well have taken you personally to the Public Security Bureau."

"Don't understand, Hai-pert. Public Security Bureau real big boys. Hai-pert help not needed."

"I know, I know. I just mean that by forcing you to help Sui-san, I caused your terrible trouble."

"Sui-san no trouble, Hai-pert. She best friend. Sui-san get me far away Beijing. Real fast. Get job for Kwai in Shenzhen. Always help me. Sui-san my angle."

"Your what?"

"My angle. You know, from the god?"

"Oh. Angel. Yah, she's an angel all right. Well, it's the least she owes you, Kwai. She put you in prison. Maybe it's right that she looks after you now."

"You crazyman, Hai-pert. Sui-san not put Kwai in prison. PSB put Kwai in prison. Remember day you give Sui-san to Kwai? At New China Bookstore?"

"I sure do. I couldn't – "

"I see Sui-san one minute only. Maybe not one minute. I give Sui-san to friend, friend give Sui-san to next friend, and PSB never know how she go goodbye China. Sui-san no trouble."

"But Sui-san told the police every – "

"*Bu bu bu bu*, Hai-pert. No Sui-san. Sui-san not make any trouble.

PSB want one hundred young people. Deng Xiaoping very angry. Make big noise. Scare all little mice. Kwai one in one hundred. Big campaign. No help Sui-san, still trouble. No help Sui-san, still Kwai go to North-east. Hai-pert understand?"

"Not really. Kwai, do you know who killed Gordon?"

"Hai-pert, good friend of China. Very busy now. Telephone not good. Tomorrow come Shenzhen. We talk."

"I can't, Kwai. I don't have a visa. It may take a few days."

"No problem. Call Sui-san. Tomorrow we talk."

Call Sui-san? This is madness. She put him in prison, she's his angel, I'm in cloud-cuckoo-land. What to do?

~

Halpert was still suffering from acute disbelief when the tourist bus approached the border area between Hong Kong and China. He had called Susan after talking to Kwai Ta-ping to see how he could go about getting a quick visa. Her answer astonished him.

"Just go down to your lobby and book the one-day Shenzhen Cultural Trip. They'll ask for your passport and that's all there is to it. I think the bus leaves around 7 a.m. After you get across the border, it will stop at the Lucky Ninety-Seven Hotel. Kwai will be there and you can leave the tour bus for the day. You'll have to be back at the same hotel by 6 p.m. to rejoin the bus and cross back into Hong Kong."

At the border, the bus came to a noisy stop and the Hong Kong guide made a brief announcement: "This is where I say goodbye to you folks. Take all your belongings. You have to walk to that building just ahead and go through Chinese border security and customs, but it's just a formality. Your Chinese Travel Service guide will meet you on the other side to escort you on the rest of your tour. Have fun!"

Halpert figuratively rubbed his eyes in amazement. He remembered the disorienting passage across the very same spot nineteen years before when he had travelled up to Beijing to begin his posting. The border crossing took him into the tiny Chinese fishing village of Shenzhen, population approximately twenty thousand on a busy day.

In those days, it had taken three hours to process his papers, and he

239

remembered the customs hall where returning Hong Kong residents were put through a terrible ordeal. Guards barked ferociously at them, all their belongings were hurled about by customs officers, and the assumption was that everyone in Hong Kong was a spy intent on undermining the purity of the Communist regime.

As Halpert went effortlessly through the 1994 border formalities and walked out into the brilliant early morning August sunshine, Shenzhen lay before him in the near distance, a vast panoply of high-rises spread out as far as the eye could see. Population now? Who knew? Maybe ten million, maybe twenty. All built-up in under a decade and a half. Here was where Big Huang's joint ventures were humming with the cheapest labour the world has known this side of slavery. This was the vision that transformed Reaganites and Thatcherites into orthodox left-wing Dengists. Here, at the anus-end of the Communist motherland, was global capitalism's greatest hope. A contradiction? Only to plodding sentimentalists or romantic ideo-logues. For all the rest, you could walk through the valley of the shadow of Shenzhen and fear no evil. The improved bottom line would comfort you, while productivity and profits overflowed your performance graphs. Truly, the Shenzhen New Economic Zone is a land of great opportunity and you can make short-term investments there almost forever.

But before Halpert could board the China-side tourist bus, there was a little echo of olden times.

"Hello, everyone," said the China Travel Service guide. "My name is Chuck, Chuck Chen, and I am your guide. Please to welcome you to the People's Republic of China and Shenzhen New Economic Zone. We are seeing many beautiful and wonderful sights today, but first I think you appreciate the opportunity to visit a real Chinese store — "

There was a hint of a groan from a few of the forty disparate souls picked up that morning from various Hong Kong hotels.

"Oh, please, foreign friends, don't worry. All the China stores you visit today are very happy to take your money in any currency. Hong Kong dollars are good. American dollars very good. Any of the foreign monies are very good."

"What about the Chinese monies?" asked Halpert somewhat maliciously since he'd already guessed the answer.

"Ah. The foreign friend asks about the Chinese currency. I'm so sorry. Because of China currency laws, you cannot use ordinary Chinese monies. But to make you happy, China has special foreigners' China money and if you want to use these Chinese monies, you are very happy to. So first, the good foreign friends, shall we go to this special store we make just for you right here at trip's starting in beautiful Shenzhen? Our store is called the 'Glad Reunion Store' because we Chinese people are so happy to welcome back our Hong Kong compatriots so soon."

Halpert thought he would just stay outside till everyone returned, but then curiosity got the better of him.

He never got beyond the first department, the "Glorious China" department. Transfixed — awestruck, even — Halpert surveyed the serried ranks of Han dynasty warriors, of Sui dynasty funereal figures, of Tang dynasty horses, of ladies of fashion from the Sung dynasty, of blue and white Ming dynasty vases, all a uniform ten inches in height, all priced at thirty-two Hong Kong dollars regardless of object and regardless of dynasty, all formed from durable plastic, and all made in Shenzhen. There were thousands of them, lined up on six ascending counter shelves behind which a smiling sales representative of the Glad Reunion Store swelled with pride at her proffered wares.

"You buy some ancient Chinese potteries?" she asked Halpert. "Look, this nice horse. Tang dynasty horse. The foreign tourists very much like the Tang horses. Maybe you have little boy who is liking a Chinese horse?"

"No little boy," he said. But she picked up a horse anyway and held it out to him. Like a fool, he took it. The plastic replica had been made in a two-sided mould, and the join had been crudely melded so that there was a rough rim of plastic around the entire animal, including its tail and modestly redesigned genitalia.

Halpert looked up at the salesclerk. There was a dizzy smile of stupefaction on his face.

"Very nice horse," she said. "Everything plastic. Good plastic."

"No more clay?" he asked, almost in a whisper.

"The clay potteries so dirty," she said. "Plastic potteries much better. Clay potteries in other store, but very expensive. This better. Not break so much. Clay potteries very, very dirty."

Almost reverently, he put the Tang horse back in its spot and brushed the store dust off the palms of his hand.

$$\sim$$

Kwai Ta-ping was waiting for him in the lobby of Lucky Ninety-Seven Hotel. Halpert wasn't quite sure what was going to happen, but before he even had a chance to say anything, Kwai was already talking to the China Travel Service guide. After a minute or so, he handed the guide an envelope, the contents of which were quickly inspected, bringing out a smile on the guide's face, and the two shook hands.

Halpert had recognized Kwai immediately. He didn't look haggard or nearly as old as he expected. But when Kwai laughed with the guide, Halpert saw that many of his teeth, upper and lower, were gone. Finally, as the tour guide summoned his charges — minus Halpert — and headed back to the waiting bus, they embraced each other. First a handshake and then Kwai hugged him and gave him a kiss on the side of his cheek. Back in Canada or in the United States, Halpert would have stiffened at such an emotionally effusive display, but here and with this man he went limp. Being held tight in his arms, however briefly, finally made Kwai tangible. All the years of guilt and worry seemed vanished. All the questions could wait.

They went to the hotel's coffee shop and ordered some Chinese tea and sweet buns.

"Your teeth, Kwai?" Halpert asked as he noticed him tearing off little pieces of bun and consuming them with a strange sucking noise. "What happened?"

"Not nice camp bosses," he said, his eyes winking as they widened. "One day very big trouble. Kwai get too angry. I try, try, try not be angry because too much trouble. But camp bosses very cruel to old friend, very, very cruel. Old man big Communist Party cadre from

Anwei. He really love Communist Party, and Anwei so poor, you know. Anwei people eat the grass sometimes and many die each year from no food. And this guy, he's real good guy. He have the love of the good Communist Party very strong in his heart and when he was the big cadre in Anwei he make trouble for the bad Communists who cheat the people. So. So sorry. Go Northeast labour-reform camp. Bad Communists more powerful. One day, Kwai not know why, they start hitting old man and this makes very big angry. Big fight. Kwai not successful. Teeth say bye-bye."

He laughed an outrageous laugh, and Halpert was able to see more clearly the stumps of broken teeth. For the first time, he also noticed the lattice work of scars on the left side of his face. And there was something he didn't see. Under Kwai's unkempt frizzy hair — which was always cut very short when he knew him in Beijing and now looked peculiar on a Chinese face — part of his left ear was missing.

"Are there dentists in Shenzhen who can help you with your teeth?"

"No problem," said Kwai. "Sui-san all the time want Kwai go to dentist. Maybe go. Maybe not. No problem."

They both looked down into their cups of tea and silence enfolded them. Once or twice Kwai started to say something, then stopped. At least for the moment, Halpert had no questions to ask. There were dozens he'd meant to ask, but none seemed immediately pertinent. It was enough just to sit there quietly with his friend.

Not so for Kwai Ta-ping. His agitation mounted at each failed attempt to say something. Finally, he sat back in his seat and focused on a far window in the coffee shop.

"Hai-pert, my good friend," he said. Halpert loved the way he said his name, part Chinese and part English, all to avoid the "l."

"Hai-pert. I have some news. Maybe strange news. Maybe make Hai-pert strange."

"Are you going to tell me you want to marry my ex-wife?" Halpert smiled. He was ready for almost anything, and he found Kwai's new diffidence endearing.

"Not marry, Hai-pert. Strange news. Gordon not dead. Gordon in Shenzhen."

"I'm sorry?"

"Gordon not dead, Hai-pert. Gordon big, big, big boss in Shenzhen. He – "

"*Kwai!*" Halpert shouted his name to try and stop him. There was madness in the air and he had to help his friend, to slap his face with a shout, without hurting him, without being a labour-reform camp boss, without being Susan's scourge.

But the toothless hero persisted, and now he was looking directly into Halpert's eyes.

"Is true, Hai-pert. Maybe just few days after Kwai come Shenzhen. Every person talk about very strong boss in Shenzhen called Zhong Bai. Means 'White Chinaman.' Kwai just crazy all this time. Maybe one week after camp, Sui-san get me. Two days later in Shenzhen. Crazy, crazy, crazy. Kwai not worry about Zhong Bai. Then one day, Kwai go to hotel – not this hotel, other hotel – and many, many people in main hall. So. Very interesting, so many people. Kwai ask, 'What happens?' and girl says, 'Zhong Bai is here.' So Kwai look and look. See Gordon. Gordon is Zhong Bai."

"Kwai, you're crazy. I saw Gordon dead. I touched him. Dead. Gordon is dead. Maybe this man looks like Gordon, but Gordon is dead. I saw him."

"Dead man not Gordon, Hai-pert. Zhong Bai is Gordon. Kwai not crazy. Maybe make Hai-pert crazy."

"Did you talk to this Zhong Bai?"

"Kwai not talk. Zhong Bai big boss in Shenzhen. Many Chinese police always with Zhong Bai."

"Well, then it's someone who looks like Gordon. Kwai, I don't think you ever met Gordon. How do you even know what he looks like?"

"No, Hai-pert. Zhong Bai is Gordon. Gordon not dead. Sure Kwai meet Gordon. In Beijing. Maybe three, four times. Gordon friend of friend. You remember? Kwai so happy, so sorry. Not know what."

The silence returned, but this time it shrieked at Halpert, ripping out all his underpinning, lacerating anything he had ever understood, shaking his foundation more violently than anything he had ever before experienced.

It was Kwai, again, who broke the silence.

"We go Zhong Bai office building. Maybe Zhong Bai come. We wait. Kwai wait with Hai-pert."

And they went. And waited. For just under two hours.

∾

In the taxi, Kwai gave instructions that Halpert wouldn't have understood even if he had spoken flawless Mandarin. His mind was trying to balance improbability with conspiracy, and improbability – which offered a few seconds relief in the rolling cycle of his heated thoughts – was losing out to conspiracy. *If Gordon was alive, Sui-san must know about it. Sui-san must always have known about it. Maybe Kwai was part of it, too. And Hilary Faire.*

The taxi careened wildly down a main housing thoroughfare in Shenzhen. Halpert noticed nothing, but anyone else would have seen that the gleaming new apartment towers glimpsed from a distance were rotting from top to bottom when viewed close up. Badly mixed concrete was crumbling at main entrances, and many of the glass windows were boarded up with garishly contrasting materials: blue cardboard over one window, parts of wooden packing crates on others, plastic sheeting elsewhere. There were no sidewalks, and rubble was strewn everywhere.

Once past this domestic Armageddon, the taxi turned right and they came to the Shenzhen commercial and business district. In the haze of the sweltering noontime sun, they pulled up in front of a thirty-five-storey office building seemingly carved out of white marble. There was a guard post outside the building compound's walls, and the taxi let the two men off just a few feet away. Kwai pulled out some Chinese currency, but the driver started shouting at him.

"Hai-pert, so sorry," said Kwai. "This is New China. Comrade Driver wants foreign currency. So sorry."

Halpert reached into his pants pocket and threw a hundred-dollar Hong Kong bill the driver's way. Not bad for a seven-minute drive.

"More, more," said the driver in flawless English.

"Fucking Jesus," muttered Halpert, who nevertheless reached down into his pocket again. He tossed another hundred-dollar bill at the driver. "That's it," he said definitively. The driver took the money without acknowledging it or the source.

A security guard came swaggering over. The arrival of a taxi was an ordinary event for him, something that happened dozens of times a day, seven days a week: a foreign businessman and his Chinese interpreter. He'd seen them all. Kwai said something that seemed to work and they were waved into the compound, but not before Halpert had noticed the sign beside the guard post. Underneath a long string of Chinese characters, it read: Han Investments Company Limited, International Headquarters, Shenzhen, China.

The lobby was large and cool. The air-conditioning came as a relief to both men. Kwai motioned to Halpert at a cluster of chairs to the left of the elevators.

"We wait," said Kwai. "Maybe Zhong Bai come."

Many other people came and went throughout the next two hours. Halpert had arrived at the beginning of the lunch hour, and whatever went on inside Han Investment Company Limited, it was clear that it employed the sleekest young Chinese professionals Halpert had ever seen inside the People's Republic. Just like in Hong Kong, everyone seemed outfitted in designer clothes – Armani-style suits for men, Ports International for women.

Kwai and Halpert hardly spoke a word. Sometimes one of them would get up for a stretch and a short walk, but it was usually Kwai. For the most part, Halpert stayed glued to his seat, keeping his eyes trained on anyone who moved about.

Shortly after 2 p.m., six young men and two women emerged from an elevator and walked briskly to the revolving doors at the main entrance. At almost the same time, a vast Mercedes-Benz limousine came through the compound entrance and drove slowly up the paved ramp to the front of the building. Two other smaller Mercedes followed, and men in sunglasses got out quickly and ran to the limousine. One of the men who had been in the elevator went to the rear door of the obese vehicle and opened it.

As soon as Halpert saw him, he knew Kwai was right. It was Gordon. He was dressed in a carefully tailored Mao suit of cream-coloured silk and linen. Turning around to look back in the car, he pointed his right-hand index finger to one of his retainers and then, with an abrupt motion, pointed it next at the interior of the car. One of the two women came quickly forward and removed two attaché cases.

Zhong Bai moved ahead of everyone, pushed through the revolving door, and started walking briskly towards the elevator bank as various aides tried to catch up with him.

"*Gordon! Gordon Wrye!*"

Halpert shouted the words as loudly and distinctly as he could. Everyone else in the large lobby came to a standstill and turned around to see who was making the commotion. Only Zhong Bai kept walking, but he slowed his pace and then he, too, stopped. He stayed on his spot for five or six seconds and finally turned in Halpert's direction.

"Jamie. What a surprise."

Halpert went lurching towards him. Zhong Bai's security people tried to block his way until their boss indicated it was all right.

Although Halpert had instantly recognized him as Gordon Wrye, now that their noses were only a couple of feet apart, he found it extraordinary how Chinese Gordon looked. The Mao suit – the only one Halpert had seen on anyone since crossing the border that morning – was undoubtedly part of it. And the severe haircut. But there was also a Chinese air about him. Maybe even a Chinese smell.

"Well, I suppose this was bound to happen one day. How are you, Jamie? You look old."

"What the fuck is happening, Gordon? I touched your dead body in Beijing. I saw your clothes and your ring. What in God's name is going on?"

"What you saw was what you were supposed to see. Gordon Wrye is dead. Why don't we leave it at that?"

"The hell we'll leave it like that! I don't know where the fuck to begin."

"Don't then. Let's just say goodbye and leave it as an exquisite mystery."

"There are people, Gordon. People who have suffered because of you. Does Sui-san know you are alive?"

"Who?"

"Sui-san. You know the student you left behind in Beijing. Is she in this with you?"

"Oh, my goodness. Little Sui-san. I haven't thought of her for a very long time. Is she yours now, Jamie? Nice lay, as I recall. Very generous."

Halpert's head was exploding. He did not know really if he wanted answers to the past or explanations about the present. Kwai had shrunk back to the rear of the lobby and was far from Halpert's view.

"Goddammit, Gordon, we have to talk. I want to know what this is all about, and I want to know now."

"I'm terribly sorry. I have meetings I'm already late for and I don't see what purpose would be served by going over the past."

"I'll expose you in every newspaper in the world."

"Really? Do you think anyone will believe you? I mean it's a pretty far-fetched story."

"They damn well will believe it. Now that I know you exist. . . . Who the hell was that dead man, Gordon? Who had to die in your place for whatever this fraudulent life is that you wanted to live?"

"Haven't a clue. Probably someone from a Caucasian national minority. But you are being melodramatic. He wasn't killed for my sake, Jamie. He was either already dead or executed, I don't really know. I wasn't hanging around, as you know. But it was all done rather well. We do these things quite professionally."

"Look. I know you're alive now and that means there is a trail leading from that dead man all the way to here in Shenzhen. And I'll follow it and I'll expose you."

Zhong Bai looked at his watch and signalled to one of his aides, who left the periphery of the nearby group and went towards the elevators.

"That's a joke. First of all, it supposes that your research skills have improved since the days we knew each other. I suspect that's a big 'if.' And anyway, what if you write your story? What do you figure these days, Jamie? First day on the front page if you make it lurid enough, then a couple of follow-ups. Three-day wonder, Jamie? Four days at most. No one's story is worth more than a week anymore. Now look, fascinating as this little encounter has been, I think we should just go our separate ways and get on with our lives."

"People have suffered because of what you've done. A boy committed suicide back in Toronto. Does that concern you?"

"What are you talking about? I don't kill people. I don't need to.
Who are you talking about?"

"Father Bell. The old priest you accused of sodomizing you. His son
committed suicide."

"Good God. Have you been living my life for me, Jamie? First
you're screwing my old flame. Are you buggering my old headmaster,
too?"

"You son of a bitch. He never did anything to you and you sent him
to prison."

"You don't understand anything, do you? You never did. That old
priest wanted to screw me. He'd pant every time I came near him, but
his stupid religion fucked him up like all religions fuck everyone up. All
I did was give him a chance to embrace his guilty soul. What happened
to him . . . well, it's what he wanted to happen. No wonder you've
become pals. Kindred spirits. It's pathetic."

"Goddammit, Gordon. You're going to be held accountable if it's
the last thing I do on this earth."

"You still don't get it, do you? Gordon Wrye is dead. We finished
him off fifteen years ago. He had served his use. These days, we do more
than sell porcelain trinkets. Don't you realize what is happening in this
country now, Jamie? The world is changing fast, and we are reshaping
it. It is our destiny to lead. That destiny is the fulfilment of our history.
It is not that we are invincible. We are simply inevitable."

"Who the fuck is this 'we,' Gordon?"

Zhong Bai looked at his watch again and smiled at Halpert.

"Now this is really getting boring. If you don't understand that, you
won't ever understand anything. I'm not your minder anymore. You
have to figure this one out on your own."

Two aides were holding open an elevator, and Zhong Bai turned
away from Halpert and walked directly into it. As the doors were
closing, he turned around to look out. And then he was gone.

Halpert stood motionless in his spot. As Zhong Bai's flunkies started
dispersing themselves, Kwai came running over. "Hai-pert! Hai-pert!
Everything okay? You okay?" But Halpert wasn't listening. He was

back in Beijing again, back in the Australian diplomat's apartment. Once again he was overwhelmed with despair and concern and desperate to get going. He put both his hands on Kwai Ta-ping's shoulders.

"Sui-san," he said softly. "Sui-san."

∾

Two days later, the hundreds of well-dressed people waiting to get through the receiving line at the Shaoling Centre moved amiably, but slowly, through their appointed paces. The amiability was encouraged by a host of waiters who served small delicacies and short drinks to them while they stood in line. As the glittering people approached the reception's hosts, other waiters were in attendance to take back glasses and announce names.

Along the waiting route, the exhibition sponsors – the New China News Agency in Hong Kong and Finch's Importables PLC in partnership with Potlow Investments – had set up beautifully reproduced colour photographs of some of the key recent discoveries by Chinese archaeologists. The major excitement was the first public showing outside mainland China of an important hoard of porcelains taken from an early Sung dynasty emperor's tomb.

The photographs showed vibrantly coloured earthenware figures, their glazes seemingly as fresh as when they first emerged from their kilns. They were all typical examples of Sung pottery. Even the figures of domestic animals – pigs and chickens, oxen and ducks, which were the delightful novelty of the exhibition because no one had ever seen anything quite like them before – were done in styles associated closely to Sung-era techniques. The exhibition provided stunning new corroboration to the well-established history of technological development in pottery-making.

At the main entrance to the Shaoling Centre, Susan and Halpert were waiting outside. She had bought him a new dinner jacket for the occasion, made in Brooks Brothers style by busy fingers at Savile Row Tailors of Hong Kong. Halpert seemed much younger than when he was last seen in public, and Susan looked beautiful.

A huge white Mercedes-Benz limousine inched forward behind a red Mercedes, which had followed two black Mercedes and five Infinitis of various hues. Big Huang and Mrs. Li got out, and Susan immediately greeted them.

"We are going to a different reception line," Susan said.

"Good, good," said Mrs. Li. "Who we say hello to?"

They walked away from the long line-up and towards a discreet door about fifty yards away.

"There's Dr. Potlow, of course," said Susan, "and Mr. Finch-Noyes from London. I told you the minister of culture cancelled at the last minute. Apparently, he's got political trouble in Beijing. Anyway, the deputy minister is here. His name is Ng. And his assistant, Mr. Wang. I met them a half-hour ago. They seem very nice. Quite easy to talk to. He says he's very much looking forward to meeting you."

"Yo, yo, yo," said Mrs. Li as she neared the private entrance for very special guests. "Everyone want see wife of Big Huang. Pickle before duck."

Two uniformed attendants of the Shaoling Centre stood on guard outside the special entrance. As Big Huang and his wife approached, one of them pulled open the door.

"Where your husband?" asked Mrs. Li abruptly, stopping dead in her tracks. Big Huang looked at his watch and huffed a little.

"Right behind us. Jamie, this is Mrs. Li."

"Good, good, good," she said, beaming approval. Then, with the look of a conspirator, she leaned forward and whispered into Halpert's ear. "You get baby quick. Many, many boy babies in China. You get girl baby. Girl babies best. Do it."

Halpert smiled. He could make sense of nothing that had happened during the past seventy-two hours, but Mrs. Li had a point. Doing was better than trying to make sense of nothing. Doing was better than brooding. Doing, he realized, was everything.

ACKNOWLEDGEMENTS

At the top of a considerable list of debts are those owed to Chinese friends, most of whose names cannot be printed but which are nevertheless engraved on my heart. I especially remember Ren Wanding and Wei Jingsheng, whose lives have been such shining lights to the world and whose persecution has been the shame of the People's Republic of China.

Robert Fulford and Douglas Coupland read the first draft of this novel and offered crucial advice. I am immensely grateful to both of them. At McClelland & Stewart, Dinah Forbes was an ideal editor, posing constructive questions and providing excellent suggestions on structure and characterization, and Heather Sangster was a meticulous style and copy editor. Also at M&S, the support of Douglas Gibson, Publisher, and Avie Bennett, Chairman, was hugely appreciated.

Special thanks are due to my affable agent, Bruce Westwood; to the invaluable and uncomplaining Anna Luengo, Assistant in the Master's Office at Massey College; and to my loyal, sharp-eyed stepmother, Mary Fraser, who once again did me the great favour of proofing the galleys.

My three daughters – Jessie, Kate, and Clara – showed great forbearance during the writing of this book, much of which was done during their summer holidays in Georgian Bay. My wonderful sister, Barrie Chavel, was her habitual source of enthusiasm and encouragement.

The happiest debt, however, is owed to my wife, Elizabeth MacCallum. It has been a constantly accruing debt through nearly a quarter-century of compounded courage and constancy, shared tribulation, laughter, and deep love: *Tecum vivere amem, tecum obeam libens.*

Massey College
Toronto
April 1996